BLOODBATH

Clay Taggart rode in front of the other members of the band, a soldier's cap pulled low over his brow. It had been his idea to don the uniforms of slain troopers. He counted on the ruse fooling the Mexicans long enough to get into their camp, and he was right.

Slowing so that Delgadito and Cuchillo Negro could draw even with him, he said softly in their tongue, "I will take the smaller woman. Which one of you wants the other one?"

Delgadito and the rest took action, and their fierce war whoops were like the yipping of a frenzied pack of wolves.

BLOOD TREACHERY

"Now then, White Hair," Palacio said. "To what do I owe the pleasure of your visit?"

"Desperation," Colonel Reynolds said. "I want to stop the White Apache once and for all."

"We share the same dream," Palacio said, his countenance clouding. "But we have tried many times and he is still alive."

"I have a new idea," Reynolds said. "And I want to make one of your people very rich."

Palacio had to bite his lip to keep from howling for sheer joy. "Never fear, White Hair. The renegades are as good as dead."

Other *White Apache* Doubles:
HANGMAN'S KNOT/WARPATH
WARRIOR BORN/QUICK KILLER

PB

McMasters, Jake

Bloodbath
Blood Treachery

DEMCO

To Judy, Joshua, and Shane.

A LEISURE BOOK®

June 1997

Published by

Dorchester Publishing Co., Inc.
276 Fifth Avenue
New York, NY 10001

BLOODBATH

Chapter One

The blazing sun scorched the dry earth of Sonora, Mexico.

Maria Gonzalez stared bleakly out the window of the carriage in which she rode. She was tired of the heat and dust. Most of all, she was upset because she was sweating so much.

Maria Gonzalez did not like to sweat. At the family hacienda she had servants who kept her cool every hour of every day. They bathed her when she was hot. They fanned her when she was the least bit uncomfortably warm. They brought her cool drinks when she was thirsty. The hacienda was heaven compared to the miserable carriage ride.

It bothered Maria that her father had decided to visit his brother at Janos. The family made the trip at least once a year, and it was a nightmare journey that Maria dreaded. The long hours on the dusty road, the constant jolting, the oppressive heat—all combined to make her utterly miserable. Small wonder that on these long journeys Maria missed the thousand and one little things her servants did for her throughout the day.

Maria Gonzalez never did anything for herself if she could have it done by others. She had been reared from infancy in the lap of luxury. Since she was old enough to walk, servants had waited on her every need and whim. They dressed her. They cooked her food and served it to her. They made her bed. They cleaned her room. They even saddled her horse when she wanted to go for an evening ride.

Yet here she was, many miles from the hacienda, without a single servant. On these trips she had to do everything for herself. Maria hated that. As one of the wealthiest senoritas in all of Mexico, she hated having to do menial work that was beneath her dignity. Why should she bathe herself? Why should she comb her own hair? Why should she have to fold her own clothes at night? It was an insult to her dignity.

The carraige suddenly hit a bump, throwing Maria into the air. She smoothed her dress, glared at the ribbon of road ahead, and then fixed her glare on her mother.

"Do not look at me like that, young lady," Theresa Gonzalez said stiffly. "I am not to blame for your suffering. If you must be mad at someone, be mad at your father."

"You let him bring me," Maria snapped. "I have every right to be as mad at you as I am at him."

"Why must we go through this every time we journey to Janos?" Theresa asked. "I should think that by now you would be used to this."

"I hate going and you know it," Maria said. "No matter how many times we make this trip I will never get used to it."

Theresa Gonzalez sniffed. "It saddens me that I have raised a daughter who can be so ungrateful. Your father loves you dearly. I would go so far as to say he spoils you. Yet once a year, when he asks you to make this little sacrifice, you always have one of your temper tantrums."

Maria opened her mouth to respond, but thought better of doing so. She might have said something that would have angered her mother. Then the stay at Janos would have been even worse. Her mother would have refused to speak to her. She would have been left alone with no one to talk to. Her father always forbade her to talk to the soldiers. Without her mother to talk to, she had no one.

Maria lowered her veil against the dust and stared out the window again. She had never been so depressed. She had to learn a way to prevent her father from forcing her to make these awful trips. After all, she was eighteen, a grown woman in her eyes and the eyes of many young men who came to court her.

At that exact moment, another pair of eyes were on Maria Gonzalez. Hidden behind a low bush so close to the road that he could have thrown a stone and hit the carriage was a Chiricahua Apache named Fiero. His bronzed body was covered with dirt that he had thrown over himself as camouflage. His face was pressed so close to the bush that they seemed to meld, which was exactly the impression Fiero wanted to give.

He had seen the carriage coming from a long way off. A plume of dust raised by its wheels and the hooves of the horses made the carriage easy to spot.

As Fiero watched the carriage go on by, his mind made note of several important facts. There were two men on top of the carriage—one driving and another armed with a rifle. Behind the carriage rode six men all well armed. In front of the carriage rode eight more men. And in front of them rode a tall bearded man who not only carried a rifle across his thighs, but also had three pistols strapped around his waist.

Fiero glanced again at the young woman he had caught a glimpse of. She was quite attractive for a *Nakai-yes*, not that Fiero had much interest in women. They were weaker than men, more emotional than men, and less skillful at war. Above all else, Fiero lived for war.

Fiero waited as motionless as a statue until the carriage and its escort were out of sight. Then he rose, and without bothering to brush himself clean, he turned and headed to the north at a trot that could eat up miles at a stretch. In his right hand he held a Winchester. On his right hip rode a big knife. His only clothing was a breechcloth. A red headband held his long black hair in place.

For half an hour Fiero ran. The hot sun beat without mercy on his broad back, but had no effect on him. His feet, covered by knee-high moccasins, slapped the hard ground in a steady cadence.

Presently Fiero came to rolling foothills. He

climbed swiftly using a deer trail. When he came to an arroyo he squated, cupped his hands to his mouth, and imitated the call of a red hawk. Moments later the strident cry was answered from deep within the arroyo.

Fiero descended the steep slope as nimbly as would a mountain sheep. At the bottom, where decades of erosion had worn a wide path, he ran fluidly, avoiding brush and boulders.

Not a Mexican alive knew that a small spring was located under a rock overhang where the arroyo merged with a hill. Here there were a few small trees, enough grass to graze a small number of horses for a week or so, and shade from the blistering heat.

As Fiero neared the spring he saw four fellow Apaches waiting for him. Or at least they looked like fellow Apaches, although in truth only three of them were.

Seated to the right of the spring was Delgadito. Formerly a warrior of repute, his standing in the Chiricahua tribe had fallen when he let his band be wiped out by savage scalphunters. For the longest while Delgadito had schemed to regain his lost esteem. But of late, he had not given the matter much thought. He had been content to roam far and wide raiding in Sonora, in Chihuahua, and along the border between Mexico and the United States. It pleased Delgadito immensely to bring suffering to those who had brought so much suffering to his people. It gave him a good feeling inside when he made the people of Sonora pay for having hired the scalphunters that had wiped out his band. It pleased him when he burned the wagons of white traders and tortured the traders in return for the stealing of Apache lands by the white government.

Near Delgadito sat Chuchillo Negro. His name was Spanish for Black Knife. Amoung the Chiricahuas his skill with a knife was legendary. He could slit a man's throat in the blink of an eye. He was so quick that when he stabbed, his hands seemed to become invisible. Unlike Fiero, Chuchillo Negro did not kill for the sake of killing. Like Delgadito, he killed because he considered himself at war with both the whites and the *Nakai-yes* and he would continue on the warpath so long as blood pumped in his veins.

Kneeling at the water's edge was the youngest member of the band. His name was Ponce. His reason for killing was different from all the rest. Above all else Ponce wanted to be a great warrior. He aspired to become a leader of his tribe, a fighter whose fame would spread far and wide. Ponce had joined Delgadito's band to raid, kill, and plunder.

Most of Ponce's people were on a reservation, living in squalid poverty. It tore at the young warrior's insides to see them reduced to such a low state, and he hoped that one day he would lead them in an uprising to regain their ancient lands.

The fourth man at the spring was the one who was not an Apache. No one would have known it from his appearance. His hair was long and dark, like an Apache's. His skin had been burnt brown by the sun, like an Apache's. He wore a breechcloth, a headband, and moccasins, like an Apache. The one trait that marked him as a white man were his lake-blue eyes. And even they had a flinty aspect seldom seen in the eyes of whites.

This man had two names. In the white world he was known as Clay Taggart, a rancher who had gone bad. The Apaches knew him as Lickoyee-shis-inday.

Few whites knew it, but the Apaches had another name for themselves. They were the *Shis-Inday* in their own eyes—the men of the woods. So when Delgadito had named Clay Lickoyee-shis-inday, he had forever branded Taggart the white man of the woods.

For several months, the White Apache had roamed with his red brothers, going on raids deep into Mexico and attacking travelers north of the border. On this particular day, before Fiero arrived, Taggart had been gazing thoughtfully into the spring.

Clay Taggart marveled at the reflection that stared back at him. It amazed him that he was looking at the same man who only a year ago had been a typical Arizona rancher. If pressed, Clay would have been the first to admit that in his heart and soul he felt more Apache than white.

There had been a time when such thoughts would have troubled Taggart greatly. After all, for many years, he had considered Apaches the bane of the territory. That attitude was not uncommon—most whites hated the tribe. Whites wanted to see the Chiricahuas and other Apache branches wiped off the face of the earth. For Clay to have taken up with his lifelong enemies was a step so profound that even to this day he was sometimes bothered by it, but not for long.

Clay Taggart owed the Apaches a lot. He owed Degadito for saving his life. He owed the others for siding with him against his enemies. And above all else, Clay wanted vengeance on those who had wronged him.

Who could blame him? A wealthy rancher by the name of Miles Gillett had stolen Clay's land right out from under him. And worse, Gillett had stolen the woman whom Clay had loved.

Gillett had tried to have Clay killed. Had it not been for Delgadito's band, Clay would have been the guest of honor at a necktie social. Delgadito had saved Clay, taken him into his wickiup, and allowed his woman to nurse Clay back to health. Clay Taggart owed Delgadito a lot, and he was a man who believed in paying his debts.

In recent months, because of the many raids Clay had led, he had become the most wanted man in the territory. A 5,000 dollar bounty had been placed on his head, dead or alive, although it was no secret that most lawmen would have prefered the latter. Every sheriff and marshal north of the border and every law officer south of the border was on the lookout for him. Plus the U.S. Army was under standing orders to bring him in at all costs.

None of that concerned the White Apache overly much. So far he had eluded or slain all those who had been sent after him. Thanks to Delgadito and the others, his skills were so finely honed that only a true Apache could have hoped to have gotten close enough for a shot. And he was supremely confident that he could have eluded any who tried.

On this day, hearing Fiero mention the carriage and the young woman inside, the White Apache was reminded of an idea that had come to him some time ago. He stared at each of the warriors in turn and then focused on Delgadito. "I say we capture this woman and take her with us."

Delgadito did not let his secret delight show. Lickoyee-shis-inday had shown no interest in women since being betrayed by the one he had loved. It was wonderful, though, Delgadito thought, that Taggart had finally seen the truth, which had sprouted from a seed of suggestion Delgadito had sown many days ago. But he had a part to play, so he said merely, "Why?"

"This one would be the first," White Apache said. "She and others like her are the key to our future."

"I do not follow the path of your words."

White Apache saw that he had everyone's attention and he stood. He chose his next words carefully, pronouncing them as best he was able. Since being saved by the band, he had toiled long and hard to learn their tongue. His effort had made him one of a handful of whites who spoke the Apache language fluently.

"I have been thinking, my brothers, about our situation," Clay said. "About how best we can pay the white-eyes back for the wrongs they have done us. We five have killed many or our enemies, taken much plunder, and punished those who have abused the Chiricahuas. But the five of us can only do so much. If our band were bigger, just think of how much more we could do. We would be able to go on twice as many raids, steal twice as many horses, kill twice as many of our enemies. The whites would tremble in fear."

Fiero snorted. "The Americans already fear us. In the settlements they talk of us in whispers.

They are afraid we will spring at them from out of nowhere if they say our names too loudly."

"What you say is true," Taggart said "but only to a point. The whites know there are only five of us. So while they fear us, they do not fear us as much as they would if there were ten or fifteen or even twenty of us." He gestured at each of them. "My kind have a saying: In numbers there is strength. What we need are more warriors."

Delgadito shifted and studied Taggart a few moments. "We know this as well as you, Lickoyee-shis-inday. We too would like to have more warriors join us. But no others are willing to leave the reservation because of what the soldiers would do to their families if they were caught." He folded his brawny arms. "I do not see how this one woman will draw them to us."

The White Apache squatted. "When you broke out of the reservation many moons ago, Delgadito, you had the right idea. You knew that for a band to survive, it must include women and children. Without their families, most warriors drift back to the reservation in time, no matter how opposed they are to the whites and the *Nakai-yes*. You were smart enough to take along the wives and children of all those who sided with you, insuring your band would stay intact and the warriors would never give up."

"I do not think that I was so smart. All the wives and children died." The reminder disturbed Delgadito greatly. Yes, once he had thought that he'd done the right thing, but he had changed his mind after the scalphunters had virtually wiped out his band. War was for warriors, Fiero often said, and Delgadito had come to think the firebrand was right. Women and children had to stay on the reservation where they were safe.

Clay Taggart went on. "If we are to see this band grow, we must show the warriors on the reservation that we are strong enough to withstand the whites and the Mexicans at every turn. We must build their confidence in us. And there is no better way to do that than to have women and children of our own. Once the reservation warriors see that we have families, they will feel free to bring their own and join us."

Fiero saw that his companions were moved by the idea, and he quickly spoke against it. "Women and children are not so easy to come by. They do not sprout from the soil like plants."

"True," Clay said, "but there are plenty out there for the taking—like this woman you saw. Each of us will steal a wife and a child or two, and in no time we will be a true band of Apaches. Your brothers on the reservation will no longer see us as isolated warriors fighting a lost cause."

It was Cuchillo Negro who spoke next. "Your words ring true, Lickoyee-shis-inday. But they are not practical. You were with us when Blue Cap and his men wiped out our families and friends. You saw the slaughter. How can you ask us to risk the same thing all over again?"

"Look at it this way," Clay answered. "You are at war with the white-eyes who took your land from you and forced all of your people onto the reservation. To win your war, you must take risks." He paused. "I happen to be at war with those who stole my land out from under me and tried to stretch my neck. And I would risk anything, *do* anything, to see they get what is coming to them." He paused again. "How about all of you? How badly do you want to see the white-eyes pay?"

Clay did not wait for an answer. He knew that if he did, a few of them might elect to argue the point. When dealing with Apaches, he had learned it was better to seize the bull by the horns, as it were. Rising, he strode off down the arroyo, saying over a shoulder, "I will go to see if this woman is worth taking. Any who wants to come can."

Rare hesitation gripped the warriors. Fiero was the first to follow in the White Apache's steps, but not because he wanted to waste time stealing women. He simply couldn't resist a chance to spill more blood, and there promised to be plenty spilled if Lickoyee-shis-inday tried to wrest the senorita from her protectors.

Ponce was the next to stand. In order for him to earn the reputation of a great war chief, he must never shirk a chance to go into battle. The thought of stealing women mattered little to him. Not very long ago he had lost the woman he wanted as his wife to an army scout sent to kill the band, and he had not yet recovered from her loss.

Cuchillo Negro and Delgadito stood together and walked from the spring side by side. Cuchillo Negro glanced at the former leader and let the corners of his mouth prick upward.

"He plays right into your hands, does he not?"

"Into our hands, you mean."

"I am not the one who craves to be a leader again. I am not the one who needs to build up a large band to see his fondest wish come true."

"Do you hold it against me?"

Bloodbath

"No," Cuchillo Negro said. "What is good for you is good for all our people, and what is good for us is good for Lickoyee-shis-inday. The more of us there are, the easier it will be for him to take his revenge on those who wronged him."

"I still do not understand why you like him so."

Cuchillo Negro stared at the rippling muscles on the white man's back. "I am proud to call him my friend. He has put his life in danger many times to save ours. What more need he do to prove his worth to you?"

"He is white. Never forget that."

"His skin was white once. Deep inside, I suspect, he has always been Apache and just not known it."

Further talk was brought to an end by Clay Taggart, who broke into a trot, forcing the rest to do the same to keep up. Clay intended to reach a certain spot bordering the road to Janos before the carriage passed by, which meant they must hurry.

The White Apache felt the warmth of the sun on his shoulders and the dry wind caress his face. The land around him gave off shimmering waves of heat. Once he would have withered in that burning inferno like a pampered houseplant suddenly thrust outdoors. Now he savored the sensation.

Clay Taggart knew he was a man reborn. The Apache way of life had forged his body into a vibrant whipcord of power and speed. He was three times the man he had been before he'd joined Delgadito, and he reveled in the change.

The time passed swiftly. From atop the last of

the foothills the White Apache spied the pale track of the road. He made for a cluster of boulders adjacent to it. Once there, he checked both ways before stepping to the middle of the rutted track to see if the carriage had already gone by. To his annoyance, it had, not more than half an hour before, judging by a pile of fresh horse droppings.

"We are too late," he said.

When Fiero grunted and pointed northward, the White Apache looked. His eyes were not anywhere near as sharp as Fiero's but they were sharp enough to spot the distant riders coming toward them—riders who wore the uniforms of Mexican soldiers.

Chapter Two

Capt. Vincente Filisola had always had a weakness for the ladies. Ever since the age of seven, when he accidentally caught sight of a cousin taking a bath, he had been keenly fascinated by the female form.

Being the dashing man that Filisola was, he had more than his fair share of conquests to boast of—which he never did since he was a perfect gentleman. But he often thought about them. Even when on duty, in the midst of the desert, Filisola would let his mind drift, savoring each delicious memory.

Of late, though, the poor captain had few such conquests to reminisce about. Being posted to the frontier had turned out to be a calamity for a very simple reason: there were too few women to satisfy his constant craving.

In Mexico City it had been different. Filisola could have dated a different senorita every night.

Janos was another story altogether. A small, pathetic town that probably would have dried up and blown away if not for the garrison there, it could boast of few attractive prospects. Most of the women were plump matrons, as appealing to the captain as roast pork, which he detested. The score or so of unmarried women were either desperate spinsters or untouched maidens kept under lock and key by wisely protective fathers.

It was so distressing a situation that Capt. Filisola had taken to running up quite a tab at the cantina he frequented. The alcohol helped to drown his sorrow at the cruel fate that had befallen him. His tour at Janos had become one of abject despair.

And then Filisola saw her. Not half an hour earlier the captain had been surprised to come upon a carriage under armed escort. He had reined up as the party approached, slapped some of the dust from his uniform, and put on his most officious air.

The man leading the party had an air that was more commanding than the captain's. He drew rein and, without bothering to introduce himself, asked, "How is the road between here and the post?"

Capt. Filisola had half a mind to tell the rude stranger that he could ride on and find out for himself. But he held his tongue. Having to deal with temperamental superior officers on a regular basis had bred a certain degree of tact in him, which served him in good stead.

"We saw no sign of savages, senor," he answered. "I would advise you to proceed with caution anyway. There have been reports

Bloodbath

of Apache raids near Hermosillo."

The bearded man adjusted his sombrero. "How well I know the dangers," he said, half to himself. "We make this trip once a year. I am Martin Gonzalez, by the way."

"Gonzalez?" Filisola repeated. "Are you any relation to Col. Jose Gonzalez, the officer in charge at Janos?"

"He is my brother."

Vicente Filisola inwardly thanked the Madonna that he had not given his tongue free rein. Stiffening, he gave a little bow and introduced himself, adding, "I would be remiss in my duty if I did not put my men and myself completely at your service. If you want, we will go with you the rest of the way to guarantee your safe passage."

Filisola had an ulterior motive. He despised long patrols. If Martin Gonzalez agreed, he could cut this one short and return to Janos. In two days he would be in the cantina drowning his sorrows again. At least it was cool there.

Just then a figure appeared in the carriage window. The captain's pulse quickened as a veil was lifted to reveal a beautiful young woman, the likes of whom he had not seen since leaving Mexico City six months earlier. His breath caught in his throat. Something on Filisola's face made Martin Gonzalez turn.

"Ah. This is my daughter Maria, Captain."

"I am honored, senorita," Filisola said with all the dignity he could muster.

Maria grinned, showing teeth as white as pearls. "My, my. You must be new to the post. I know I would remember if I had met so dashing an officer on my last visit."

21

Martin Gonzalez lifted his reins. "I am sorry to cut this short, but we have many more miles to cover before sunset. Since we will be at Janos for a week or two, perhaps you will do us the honor of coming to supper one evening? That is, if your duties will permit it."

Maria's smile widened. "Oh, please do. I starve for polite conversation when I am there."

"I would be honored," Filisola said, bowing again. When Filisola straightened up, Gonzalez was already in motion. He doffed his cap to the daughter, who gave him the sort of inviting look that brought gooseflesh to his skin.

Only when the Gonzalez party had dwindled to the size of ants did Filisola ride on. So euphoric was he over the chance encounter that he had gone a quarter of a mile before he realized with a start that he would be unable to see Maria again. He was under orders to patrol far to the south and west of Hermosillo, a task that would take him the better part of three weeks. By the time he returned to Janos, Maria Gonzalez would be gone.

That thought put the captain in a foul mood. After so much time he had finally met someone who ignited his passion, yet he would be unable to have the pleasure of her company! Sometimes life could be so unfair it hurt.

Caught up in his inner turmoil, the young officer failed to pay much attention to his surroundings or to give any thought to the Apaches reputed to be in the region. He spied a large cluster of boulders bordering the road, but he did not give them a second thought.

All he could think of was Maria Gonzalez.

Bloodbath

Hidden among those boulders, the White Apache firmed his grip on his Winchester and allowed himself a grim smile. Few of the weary soldiers showed any interest in their surroundings, an often fatal mistake in the wilderness. Even the officer had his eyes on the road. They were riding right into the ambush.

White Apache glanced to the right, where Fiero was concealed, and then to the left, where Cuchillo Negro had gone to ground. Neither were visible. Nor were Delgadito or Ponce, who were across the road. The soldiers would never know what had hit them.

Clay placed his cheek flat on the ground and listened to the approaching drum of hoofbeats. Soon he heard the creak of saddles, the rattle of accoutrements and the nicker of horses. A soldier coughed.

It was up to Clay to give the signal. He waited until he judged that fully half of the patrol had gone past his position; then he surged to his knees and uttered a piercing Apache war whoop. At the same time he jammed the rifle stock to his shoulder and fired at the nearest trooper. In that instant, all hell broke loose.

Delgadito, Cuchillo Negro, Fiero, and Ponce also popped up and cut loose, their rifles decimating the patrol in the span of seconds. Men and horses went down, some of the men cursing and screaming, some of the animals squealing in agony.

The first soldier Clay shot had the side of his head blown off. Clay pivoted, aimed at a second Mexican, and sent a slug into the man's chest. As

23

he took aim at a third, another throaty war whoop rose above the general din and Fiero hurtled from out among the boulders, a glistening knife in his right hand.

Like a diving bird of prey, Fiero swooped down onto a mounted soldier, landing astride the horse behind his quarry. The soldier tried to bring his carbine into play. Fiero merely gripped the man's hair, yanked the head back, and slit the man's throat with a neat, swift stroke.

Ponce had also charged into the fray, shooting his rifle as fast as targets presented themselves.

The patrol broke and scattered, few of the soldiers having the nerve to stand and fight. But there was one exception.

Clay had risen for a better shot at a fleeing trooper when out of the corner of one eye he glimpsed the young officer. The man had courage. A pistol in hand, the brash captain was bearing down on Ponce, who was too busy shooting to notice. Clay spun, took a hasty bead, and stroked the trigger.

At the blast, the officer jerked backward, but somehow was able to cling to his saddle horn. Doubled over, swaying badly, the man hauled on the reins, cutting to the right to swing wide of the boulders. In moments his mount was in full flight off across the desert.

The White Apache aimed deliberately. He was on the verge of firing when a bullet spanged off the boulder in front of him. It sent rock slivers into his cheek. Whirling, he discovered a wounded soldier in the middle of the road reloading to fire again. Clay cored the man's head from front to back.

Bloodbath

Suddenly the gunfire died out. Eleven soldiers lay dead or dying in the dust. Five horses were down, five more milled about in confusion. The eleventh had raced off in a panic.

Fiero, with feral glee, was dispatching the wounded. Ponce stood ready, covering him. Only Delgadito and Cuchillo Negro remembered Clay's instructions and dashed out to claim the loose mounts.

The White Apache ran to a fine sorrel and grasped its bridle. The horse shied at his unfamiliar scent. It tried to pull free but Clay hung on and spoke softly to soothe the animal's fears. After it quieted down, he looped the reins around a dry bush.

A gravely wounded soldier, no more than 18 years old by the looks of him, had been propped against a boulder. Fiero had ripped off the trooper's shirt and was carving off thin strips of flesh. Delgadito and Cuchillo Negro had caught three horses. Ponce, seeing them, nabbed a fourth.

Clay reached Fiero as the warrior lowered his knife to inflict more suffering. The hapless soldier, too weak to cry out, could only watch with dazed eyes as the bloody blade bit into his skin.

"We have no time for this," White Apache said. "I told you what was most important and you did not listen."

The firebrand looked up, his hand poised on the knife. "You forget yourself, Lickoyee-shis-inday. White-eyes and *Nakai-yes* take orders from others, but never Apaches. We are free to do as we want, when we want. We only do as our leaders say when it suits us."

There had been a time when Clay would have

25

flown off the handle at such a reply. The band had, after all, picked him as leader over his strong objections, so it was only fair that the warriors do as he wanted. But Apaches were notoriously independent. Every man was his own master. No warrior did anything he did not want to do. For Clay to criticize the Apache way would only sour Fiero against him, and he needed the fiery troublemaker as much as he needed the others.

"For the plan to work," Clay said, "we must all do our part. Am I to take it that you do not want to join us this time?"

"I never said that," Fiero snapped. With a sharp flick of his thick wrist he drove the razor-sharp blade into the young soldier's heart. The man gurgled once and perished. "I will help you even though I think it foolish to burden ourselves with women and children."

Delgadito came over, carrying a shirt he had stripped from a slain soldier. "I hope you know what you are doing," he said in heavily accented English. He liked to speak the strange, birdlike language as often as he could just to keep in practice. After having labored so hard to learn it while teaching Taggart the Apache tongue, he did not care to let his newfound ability go to waste.

Clay gave the warrior a friendly clap on the shoulder. "You and me both, pard," he said. "If I don't, they're liable to put windows in our skulls before we get off a shot."

Capt. Filisola became aware of low voices and of fingers probing his temple. Thinking he had fallen into the clutches of the dreaded Apaches, he automatically grabbed the hand and sat bolt upright. The abrupt movement lanced his skull with pain. Pinwheeling points of light danced before his eyes. It was several moments before his vision cleared and he saw that he held Sgt. Amat.

"Can you stand, captain? Or would you like help?"

Filisola realized eight other troopers stood around him. "I can manage." He blinked a few times, girded his legs, and rose unsteadily. There was a nasty gash on his temple and he had lost a lot of blood, but he would live. "Did those red devils get all the rest?"

"I don't know. I have not been back to check." Sgt. Amat gestured at the barren expanse of desert. "I have been busy rounding up this bunch. If I had not spotted your horse, we would never have found you."

The bay stood nearby, caked with sweat. Filisola turned and was surprised to find the road no longer in sight. "How far did it carry me?" he asked.

"About two miles," Amat said. "I would guess you have been unconscious for an hour and a half."

"That long?" Filisola said, appalled. In that amount of time the Apaches could have done as they pleased with any of his men they took alive. "Mount up. Pronto. We must go see."

"Yes, Captain."

Their reluctance was obvious, and Filisola couldn't blame them. For more years than anyone could remember, Apaches had been raiding the states of Sonora and Chihuahua, striking at will. Countless men had been massacred, women and children carried away, whole districts laid to waste. Small wonder, then, that most who lived in northern Mexico regarded Apaches as demons incarnate rather than mere mortals.

Filisola didn't share that belief, thanks to an incident that had taken place six years earlier. He had been a lieutenant then, assigned to the staff of a general. The general had been making the rounds of remote outposts when the column stopped for the night at an isolated spring.

Filisola had been asleep during the night when a sentry sounded an alarm. Leaping to his feet, Filisola had dashed toward the horse string, where a tremendous commotion had been taking place. In the dark he had nearly bumped into another running figure. He had assumed it was a fellow soldier until a stray gleam from the flickering fire revealed a young Apache who had been caught in the act of trying to steal a few horses.

They had set eyes on one another at the same instant. Filisola had his pistol in hand. The stripling had a knife, nothing more. In sheer reflex Filisola had fired, and his slug had ripped through the Apache's stomach, dropping the warrior where he stood. It was then, as Filisola watched blood spurt from the lethal wound and saw the acute pain reflected on the warrior's face, that he had realized Apaches were flesh-and-blood creatures like himself, not inhuman monsters.

The memory comforted Filisola as he trotted toward the road. He wished he had some way of imparting the knowledge to those under him since it was apparent they would bolt if set upon again.

Bloodbath

Moments later Amat called out and jabbed a finger at the sky. Filisola titled his head and placed a hand across his eyebrows to shield his eyes from the harsh glare. The stark silhouettes of ungainly big birds flew in circles on the horizon.

"Already!" Filisola barked in disgust.

"The buzzards must eat when they can," Amat said.

Jabbing his mount in the flanks, Filisola brought his horse to a gallop. The soldiers did the same, riding in a short column of twos, their carbines at the ready.

The captain slowed down when the boulders were less than 500 yards off. He divided his small command in half and sent the sergeant to the left while he went to the right. Boulders hid the grisly tableau until he came to the edge of the road.

Vultures were everywhere—on the bodies of the men, on the few dead horses, and on the boulders. The birds were waiting to feed. The rank odor of blood hung heavy in the hot air, as did another foul odor that made Filisola want to retch. He held the urge in check and dismounted.

"Mother of God!" one of the troopers said.

So much blood had been spilled that a sticky layer caked the road. A number of the slain had been mutilated. A few had had their throats slit wide. One soldier had been gutted, then strangled to death with his own intestines. Even one of the mounts had been carved up, which was not unusual. It was widely known that Apaches ate horseflesh.

Filisola held his breath and advanced. A vulture hissed at him, but gave way when Filisola took another stride. With its huge wings flapping loudly, the bird slowly climbed into the air and soared off. Others did likewise. A few refused to budge even though Filisola shouted at them and waved his arms.

One particular vulture saw fit to peck out the eyeball of a dead trooper. It paused to glare at the officer, the eyeball dangling from its beak by a thread. Racked by revulsion, Filisola shot the bird dead. At the sound of the gunshot the rest flew off. Filisola looked up to see over 20 circling high overhead, biding their time.

"Bastards," he growled under his breath.

Sgt. Amat came from the other direction. Halting, he covered his nose and mouth. "All the men are now accounted for, Captain."

"Yes," Filisola said sadly. He knew that his superior, Col. Gonzales, would be furious with him. It wouldn't surprise him if the colonel called a board of inquiry to determine if he had been negligent.

"Strange, is it not, sir?" the sergeant said.

"What is?" Filisola asked absently.

"Apaches usually don't bother to take clothes. Why do you suppose they did this time?"

Only then did it occur to Filisola that a number of the bodies lacked shirts and pants. And some, he was puzzled to note, had been stripped of their boots.

A half-breed had once revealed to Filisola that Apaches had a deep dread of the dead. The half-breed had claimed that after a raid, Apaches went through a purification ceremony. Furthermore, Apaches were reputed to burn any article that touched a dead person in the belief that the article would bring nothing but bad medicine. Why then, the officer wondered, had this band made an exception to the general rule?

"Should we bury them?" Amat inquired.

"Need you ask?"

"No, sir." Amat pivoted and issued commands. A burial detail was hastily formed and the men set to work digging.

Filisola moved to a small boulder and sat down. He had a decision to make. Should he continue on his patrol or report the clash to the colonel? With so few men he stood little chance of catching the band. He might as well go back, he reflected.

There was another factor Filisola had to consider. If the band responsible for the Hermosillo raids had been the same one that sprang the ambush, it was safe to assume they were heading in the same direction as the Gonzalez family, which put the family in great peril. It was his responsibility to warn them.

The officer decided to head back just as soon as the last corpse was laid to rest. He idly scanned the grisly unfortunates. Six of them were without shirts, five without pants, five without boots. His gaze roved and he spied a torn shirt across the road. That made the numbers even. Five complete uniforms had been taken.

"Why only five?" he mused aloud. Had there only been five Apaches? It had seemed as if there were many more.

Seconds later the sergeant hurried up. "Captain, five horses are still unaccounted for. They must have run off. Say the word, and I will take a private and go hunt for them."

"Five horses?" Filisola said, troubled by the

news although he could not say why. Apaches stole horses all the time. So what if they had stolen some now? But then he thought of the five uniforms.

"Yes," Amat said. "What would you have us do?"

Instead of responding, Filisola rose and walked to the north. He was not much of a tracker but he tried to read the prints anyway. Between the boulders it was impossible. There were too many jumbled together. Past the boulders he came on a spot at the side of the road where he found moccasin prints, bare footprints, and boot tracks. It took him a minute to appreciate the significance.

"Dear God," Filisola said.

"Captain?" Amat said. "I do not understand? What is the matter?"

Filisola had to be sure. He ran a dozen yards farther. The tracks made by the five horses were easy to make out, all bearing to the northeast. The ravishing image of Maria Gonzalez filled his mind, and he shuddered as if cold. "Forget the graves. We must mount and ride."

"But we owe it to those who were slain to give them a decent burial," Amat objected.

"Our first duty is to the living, not the dead," Capt. Filisola said. "Now get the men on their horses, or you will be the one who will explain to our colonel why we did not arrive in time to save his brother from the Apaches."

Sgt. Amat glanced at the ground, then at the winding road. The color drained from his face and he spun on a heel. Snarling orders, he had the men on their mounts in record time.

To Capt. Vicente Filisola, it wasn't fast enough.

Chapter Three

Adobe Wells had been aptly named. It was located on the road that led from Hermosillo to Janos. The village was a day-and-a-half ride from the border between the states of Sonora and Chihuahua. An old well was the chief attraction. Nearby were the ruins of an adobe house. Countless weary travelers had stopped there over the years. This night, it was the Gonzalez party.

The cool of the evening brought refreshing relief to Maria Gonzalez. She donned her silk wrap and went for a short stroll to stretch her legs. The pair of vigilant vaqueros her father had told to tag along stayed a discreet distance behind to afford her privacy.

Maria made a slow circuit of the ruins, often turning her face into the invigorating breeze. She would have given anything for a long soak in a tub or to have a servant fan her while she sipped a cold drink. It was unthinkable that such luxuries were to be denied her until she returned to the hacienda.

Maria toyed with the idea of having a vaquero fan her, but did not because she knew her father would not approve. She walked toward the well, pausing when the distant wail of a lonely coyote rent the tranquil desert. She felt sympathy for that coyote, which she imagined to be all alone in the middle of nowhere, just as she was. Then she heard another wail and another, and she knew the coyote was with others of its kind.

The thought reminded Maria of the handsome captain. How sad, she mused, that she was denied the pleasure of his company. His gracious manner had marked him as a true gentleman, just the sort of man whose company she preferred. She craved a few hours of witty talk and merry laughter almost as much as she did a bath.

There were footsteps behind her. Maria turned and inwardly steeled herself. The look on her mother's face warned her that she was in trouble again. She put on a bold front, saying sweetly, "Have you come for a drink, mother?"

"I have come to talk, daughter," Theresa Gonzalez said sternly. "Your father is very upset with you and wants me to set you straight."

"What have I done this time?" Maria said, thinking that her father's anger must have something to do with her complaints about the trip and the barbaric conditions she was forced to endure.

"I think you know. Your father says that you were brazenly flirting with that young officer this afternoon."

"Nonsense. All I did was exchange pleasantries," Maria said, genuinely surprised. "Where did father ever get such a crazy notion? How could I have flirted when I was seated in the carriage?"

"Do not play the offended innocent with me," Theresa said. "I did my share of flirting before I wed your father. I know that all a woman has to do is bat her eyes a certain way and it is the same as exposing herself."

"Mother!" Maria said, shocked as much by the admission as the crude comparison.

"Don't look at me like that. Do you think I am a saint? All young women flaunt their charms. It is the bait with which we hook the fish of our dreams." Despite herself, Maria broke into gay laughter. "Even so, I was being no more than polite to Capt. Filisola. As a general rule I do not flirt with a man unless I have known him at least five minutes."

Now it was the mother's turn to laugh. "I was the same at your age." She clasped her hands to her bosom. "Oh, Maria, how I envy you. Savor this time. These years are some of the most wonderful you will ever know."

"Married life will be wonderful too."

"Oh, it will be, but in a different way. Once a woman takes a man into her life, everything changes. She has new responsibilities, new burdens. Nothing is ever the same again."

That last comment was uttered almost wistfully, prompting Maria to ask, "Do you regret marrying father?"

"Certainly not. As men go, he is better than most. He doesn't beat me or drink to excess. And he works hard, that man, so very hard. Sometimes I think his work will be the death of him. It is all

I can do to get him to take time off once a year for this trip."

Insight made Maria gasp. "So that is why you refuse to put a stop to these nightmare journeys?"

"Stop them? Child, I encourage them. As you will no doubt learn, men are stubborn creatures. Their pride makes them believe they are invincible. Your father knows he must take time off, but he never would if not for me." Theresa gave a wise smile. "Women must always use their wiles when dealing with men. Managing a husband is a lot like managing an oversize ten year old."

Maria politely placed a hand over her mouth to stifle an unladylike snort. It was rare that her mother talked so frankly with her, and she enjoyed it immensely. "Tell me more," she said.

Theresa hooked her arm around her daughter's and strolled back toward the fire. "Another time, perhaps. Supper is almost ready."

One of the vaqueros had made the meal—a tangy rabbit stew flavored by the roots of a plant the vaquero had picked along the route.

Maria ate hers slowly, glad the vaquero was along so she did not have to soil her hands cooking. It had never failed to amaze her how self-sufficient the vaqueros were. They prepared their own food when they were away from the ranch, mended their own clothes when necessary, and took care of their own horses. All the little things that servants did for her, they did themselves. Secretly, she pitied them and frequently gave thanks that she had not been born poor.

Suddenly a burly vaquero with a jagged scar on his right cheek hastened out of the darkness

Bloodbath

to her father's side. "Pardon, sir. Riders come."

Martin Gonzalez rose, his brow furrowed. "Who could it be at this hour, Pedro? Fellow travelers perhaps?"

"Maybe," Pedro said. He had worked for the Gonzalez family for over 20 years and was as loyal to the brand as any Texas cowpuncher would have been. "But to be safe, perhaps you should take the senora and the senorita and go in among the ruins."

"You would have us hide, Pedro?" Martin responded. "What would my men think of me if they saw me act like a coward?"

"They know that you have your family to think of," Pedro said, refusing to be cowed. All that mattered to him was the safety of those he worked for.

The other vaqueros had gathered around, some with rifles, others with their hands resting on their pistols. All of them heard the beat of hooves, the creak of leather, and the clank of gear, such as a cavalry patrol might make.

"It must be the officer we met today," Martin Gonzalez said and glanced sharply at his daughter. "I wonder what prompted him to turn back to Janos."

"Don't look at me," Maria said, a trifle indignant. "All I did was pass the time of the day with the man."

Many of the vaqueros had started to relax. A few had turned to go about their business.

Martin cupped his hands to his mouth. "Is that you, Capt. Filisola?" he called.

"Yes," came the muted reply.

"There. You see?" Martin said to Pedro. "As I

thought, we have nothing to worry about. Put on another pot of coffee for our guests. They have been on the trail all day and will be grateful for our hospitality."

Maria set down her bowl and stood. She needed several minutes to freshen herself so she would look her best for the dashing captain. Without saying a word to her parents, she slipped off toward the ruins, grinning at the thought of the pleasant interlude she was about to have.

But she was wrong.

The White Apache rode in front of the other members of the band, a soldier's cap pulled low over his brow. It had been his idea to don the uniforms of slain troopers. He counted on the ruse fooling the Mexicans long enough to get in close to their camp, and in this he was proven right.

Clay answered the hail, his hand over his mouth to muffle his voice. He saw vaqueros clustered near the fire. There were also two women present, not one. Slowing so that Delgadito and Cuchillo Negro could draw even with him, he said softly in their tongue, "I will take the smaller woman. Which one of you wants the other one?"

"Not me," Cuchillo Negro said. "Look at her. She has many winters behind her, and old *Nakai-yes* make poor wives. They do not hold up well."

"We should just take the young one," Delgadito advised. "Later we can find more like her."

"Very well," Clay said, pulling ahead. "At my signal." His Winchester was balanced across his thighs. He gripped it and slowly pulled back the hammer so the click would not be loud.

The younger woman had risen and was moving toward the ruins. A bearded man was giving directions to a swarthy vaquero.

Martin Gonzalez saw several silhouettes materialize in the gloom. The foremost rider wore a trooper's cap, he could tell. Martin took a step to greet the newcomers when it occurred to him that the hat was the kind worn by privates, not the shorter version worn by officers. It was strange, he thought, that a private would be out in front of the patrol. By tradition, officers usually assumed the lead.

Clay noticed the bearded man staring hard at him. He suspected the man was suspicious, and not wanting to lose the element of surprise, he let out with a bloodcurdling screech at the same instant he opened fire, levering off four shots so swiftly that two vaqueros were down and another wounded before the remainder awakened to their peril.

Delgadito and the rest took that action as their cue to cut loose, fanning out as they did. Their fierce war whoops were like the yipping of a frenzied pack of wolves.

To say the vaqueros were taken unawares would be an understatement. Pedro was the first of the stunned group to overcome the daze that gripped him. Frantically, he clawed at his pistol. Others did likewise, but Taggart and the Apaches ducked low and weaved, proving difficult targets to hit.

Theresa Gonzalez screamed, a hand to her throat. She was too terrified by the sight of one of the riders bearing down on her to move.

Vaguely she realized her husband had sprung to her aid and felt his arm encircle her waist. As she fell to the ground, she twisted and saw the Indian veer aside.

Maria Gonzalez was terrified. Her feet were rooted to the ground. A thick cloud of choking gunsmoke clogged the air, and bullets whizzed by her to the left and right. As a rider bore down on her, she glimpsed his raven shock of black hair and felt raw fear knife through her insides. It galvanized her into racing for the ruins.

All of her life Maria had heard stories about Apaches—awful tales of the atrocities they committed, of the many women and children who had been abducted. Her own cousin, a sweet girl of 16, had been taken several years ago. Eventually the girl's father had been able to bargain for her release. The whole family had turned out to welcome her and been shocked beyond measure when it became apparent the girl's mind was gone.

The mere thought of suffering the same horrid fate was enough to make Maria dizzy with fear. She gritted her teeth and willed her legs to pump. Directly ahead appeared a low adobe wall. She was confident she would be safe once she hid behind it.

The drum of hooves grew louder and louder, becoming thunder in her ears. Maria was almost to the ruins when she glanced over her left shoulder and saw the rider right behind her. "No!" she cried, darting to the left to escape.

The White Apache anticipated such a move. He leaned far out, his left arm held low, and caught the fleeing female about her slim waist.

Bloodbath

Pulling upward with all his might, he swung her up in front of him. She seemed to weigh next to nothing.

"No!" Maria wailed. "Father! Mother! Help me!" She kicked and tried to hit her captor, but it was as if she struck solid rock.

Over by the fire, Martin and Theresa Gonzalez heard the terrified shriek of their offspring. Both forgot their own safety and rushed to her rescue, Martin with a pistol in each hand. They spotted a horse bearing two figures and knew it had to be an Apache making off into the night with their pride and joy.

"Save our child!" Theresa screamed.

Martin tried. He aimed carefully, but had to hold his fire when the mount swerved just as he was about to squeeze the trigger. In the dark he couldn't be sure if he would hit the warrior or Maria.

"Shoot! Shoot!" Theresa said.

Again Martin took aim, but by this time the figures were shrouded by the night. "I can't!" he replied. "I might kill her by accident!"

Racked by despair, the desperate parents watched the Apache vanish into the desert. Martin whirled. Of the 17 men he had brought along, eight were down. "Anyone who can, follow me!" he roared. "Those bastards have stolen my daughter!"

Martin sprinted toward the horse string, only to discover the horses were gone. Drawing up short, he glared at the empty space where the animals had been. "This can't be!" he raged.

From out of murk rushed Pedro, blood trickling from a cleft cheek, where he had been nicked by

41

a slug. "Two of those devils drove the horses off! Do not worry, sir. We will find them and save Maria."

Martin could only nod dumbly as several vaqueros dashed into the darkness to retrieve the animals. He knew how fast Apaches could travel. By the time the horses were rounded up, the band would be many miles away. The odds of rescuing Maria were slender, at best.

Clenching his fists in impotent fury, Martin threw back his head to rail at the wind, then changed his mind. He must be strong, if only for his wife's sake. Theresa was a kind, sensitive soul and the very best of wives, but she did not handle a crisis well. He recalled how once, when a relative of theirs had been kidnapped by Apaches, she had stayed in their room for days, weeping constantly. If she believed Maria was lost to them forever, there was no telling what she might do.

Martin Gonzalez turned to go comfort his wife. He wished that he'd had the good sense to ask that young captain to accompany them to the fort. His brother would have understood.

Pausing, Martin listened, hoping to hear the sound of the Apache mounts in the distance. All he heard, though, were the shouts of his vaqueros and the sighing of the wind.

Oh, Maria! he thought. My poor baby!

Maria Gonzalez ceased to struggle after a while. The Apache was too strong for her. And she did not care to make him mad. Apaches were masters at torture.

Many years ago Maria had seen the body of a lone traveler waylaid by Mescalero Apaches; they had gouged out his eyes, cut off his nose and ears, removed his tongue, and whittled him down until he was more bone than flesh. She would never forget that sight as long as she lived.

Behind her, the White Apache was pleased by the fact the captive no longer fought back. He had expected her to tear into him tooth and nail or to go into hysterics. Her composure impressed him. He assumed she must have great courage, which would serve her well in the days and weeks to come.

What Taggart had not expected, however, was the strange sensation that came over him at being so close to a woman after having been denied female companionship for so long. The soft feel of her body against his, the perfumed scent of her luxurious hair, and the earthy scent of her skin were enough to arouse stirrings in him the likes of which he had not felt since he had lost the woman he loved to Miles Gillett.

It disturbed Clay Taggart that he should feel this way. Of late he had taken inordinate pride in the degree of self-control he now had over his mind and body. He flattered himself that he sometimes exercised the same masterful discipline as the Chiricahuas. But clearly that was not the case.

Taggart shifted in the saddle to give the woman a little more room. He checked and verified that all five warriors trailed him. There was no sign of pursuit yet. It wouldn't be long before the woman's kin and the vaqueros came after them.

Long into the night Taggart and his band pressed on. They rode their horses to near exhaustion, stopping only when a pink band framed the eastern skyline.

In the foothills of the Sierra Madre Mountains, Taggart finally stopped. He slid off and, without thinking, offered his hand to the woman, who alighted as if stepping barefoot onto crushed glass.

Maria studied her captor, trying her best to conceal her fright. She noted his hard, cruel features, and the rippling muscles of his arms and stomach. He was studying her in turn. Maria looked into his eyes and was amazed to see they were blue.

Taggart could not help but notice the woman's reaction. It wasn't hard to guess the cause. "Yes, I am white," he announced in imperfect Spanish. "Your people know me as the White Apache."

The name rekindled Maria's fear. Every resident of the states of Sonora and Chihuahua had heard of the renegade known as the White Apache. He had burned many ranches and slain scores of helpless victims. It was claimed he was the worst murderer on the frontier, even worse than the Apaches with whom he rode. And she was in his clutches!

"Do you speak English?" Clay asked, still speaking Spanish.

"Yes," Maria responded in English. "A little, anyway."

In the increasing light Maria saw the rest of the band clearly for the first time. They were all full-blooded Apaches, and there was not a glimmer of compassion in the eyes of a single one. In fact, one of them glowered at her as if he wanted to wring her neck.

"Good," Clay said. "I don't get to hear it used

all that much anymore, so I'd be obliged if you'd speak English as much as possible."

There was no malice in the man's voice. Maria wondered if perhaps the rumors about him were false, if perhaps she could prevail on him to let her go. "What do you plan to do with me?"

"You can't guess?" Clay rejoined, grabbing her wrist and leading her to a flat rock, where he gestured for her to take a seat.

Maria almost refused out of sheer spite. But the Apaches were watching, and there was no predicting how they would take it if she gave them any trouble. "Please, senor," she said, easing down. "Can we talk?"

"About what?" Clay said in the act of turning.

"Me, what you are doing, and how you can become a very rich man."

"Don't tell me. You come from a rich family, and you figure your pa will be glad to fork over a king's ransom to get you back safe and sound?"

"Exactly."

"Save your breath," Clay said. "The Apaches have no use for money."

"What about you? My father will pay you in gold, not pesos—so much gold that you will need a wagon to transport it. Just think of how wealthy you would be."

"I've got news for you, lady," Clay said, and his next words surprised him as much as they dismayed her. "I don't care about being rich. There was a time, another lifetime ago, when I did. I'd have given anything to be like that hombre Midas and have so much money I couldn't count it all." Clay sighed. "Now there's only one thing

I give a damn about, and it sure as hell isn't being rich."

"What is it?" Maria probed, unwilling to accept that any American did not love money as much as life itself. Her limited experience with gringos had taught her they were all·devoted to gold.

"Revenge," Clay rasped.

The fleeting hatred that contorted his features convinced Maria Gonzalez. For a few seconds she swore that she saw red-hot flames in the depths of his eyes. Or was it a trick sparked by the rising sun? she wondered, as he faced his savage companions.

Rather abruptly a horse uttered a wavering whinny that ended in a strangled grunt. Maria jerked around and saw the animal thrashing feebly on the ground, its throat slit from ear to ear. The Apache who had glowered at her was the one who slew the hapless mount, and when he lifted his head from the sickening deed, he gazed straight at her and grinned wickedly. Maria shuddered and nearly bolted.

Taggart drew his knife and moved to help butcher the horse. "We must eat and be on our way before the sun clears the horizon," he stated.

"Why are you in such a hurry?" Fiero taunted. "The *Nakai-yes* will never catch up to us. And even if they did, they will run off like scared rabbits when we turn on them."

"It is not wise to be too confident," Taggart said. "Look at what happened with the scalphunters."

He glanced at the woman, who sat slumped over, as forlorn as could be. Taggart hoped Fiero was right. Most of the time when Apaches took captives there was no pursuit at all. But something, whether intuition or a premonition, warned him that this time it would be different. This time they might have bitten off more than they could chew.

Chapter Four

Capt. Vicente Filisola felt some of the tension drain out of him when he spied a pinpoint of light over a mile away. It was the glow from a campfire at Adobe Wells. He took it as a good sign. The Apaches hadn't wiped out the Gonzalez party, as he had feared they would.

Filisola slowed from a gallop to a trot. He had pushed the patrol mercilessly for hours and all the animals could use some rest. Not to mention the men. As for Filisola, what he wanted most was the company of the charming senorita. He envisioned the two of them seated by that campfire, warmed by hot coffee and the flames of the inner passion he hoped to stoke within her.

When Adobe Wells was only a quarter of a mile off, Filisola noticed a lot of commotion. Figures kept moving back and forth in front of the fire, which struck him as peculiar. At that time of night the Gonzalez family and their vaqueros should have been resting after their hard day of travel.

Presently Filisola heard a shout and saw men swinging toward him with rifles and pistols raised. Standing in the stirrups, he hailed the camp. "Senor Gonzalez, it is Capt. Filisola. Do not shoot. My men and I are coming in."

To Filisola's amazement, none of the men lowered their weapons. Not until he came within the circle of light cast by the crackling flames did they finally relax. Right away he saw that something was dreadfully wrong. Senora Gonzalez was in tears, her shoulders shaking with sobs.

Martin Gonzalez had never been so glad to see anyone in all his life as he was to see the young officer and the soldiers. Their arrival was a godsend, he reflected, as he hurried forward and took the captain's hand in his. "You could not have come at a better time!"

Only then did Filisola spy the bodies lying beyond the fire and see several men wearing makeshift bandages. He also realized the senorita was missing. "I am too late," he said sadly, his insides becoming like ice.

"You knew we would be attacked?" Martin asked.

The captain explained about the ambush and the missing uniforms and horses.

"I see," Martin said, then went on to detail the attack on the camp and the abduction of his daughter.

"We must go after her immediately," Filisola declared. He turned to remount.

"Wait," Martin said, placing a hand on the other's arm. "We must not be impetuous, my young friend."

"How can you say that when it is your own flesh and blood those devils have taken?"

"Believe me, fear for her safety is tearing me up inside," Martin said softly so his wife would not overhear. "But it would do Maria no good for us to rush blindly off into the night. We must wait for daylight. One of my vaqueros is a skilled tracker. Once he is on a trail, not even Apaches can shake him." Martin glanced at the white lather caking the officer's mount. "Besides, your horses are on the verge of collapse. They need rest."

There was no denying that Gonzalez was right, but Filisola could hardly bear the thought of the sweet senorita in the clutches of the terrors of Mexico. His only consolation was that in all likelihood the Apaches would not kill her unless she gave them trouble. "Very well," he said reluctantly. "We will do as you request."

"At first light we will head out," Martin said. "I will send the wounded on to Janos in the carriage with my wife. She will inform my brother. And knowing how much Jose cares for his niece, it is safe to say that he will do all in his power to help us."

Vicente brightened a little. His superior, Col. Jose Gonzalez, had fought in many Indian campaigns. There was no better officer in the entire army. Unlike many commanders who were sent to frontier posts as punishment, Jose Gonzalez had requested to be sent to the hellhole called Janos because he thrived on hardship and combat.

"Yes, he will," Filisola agreed. "I wouldn't be surprised if he calls out the entire garrison. Apaches might be demons, but five of them are no match for that many troopers."

For the first time in hours, both men smiled.

When faced with having to decide between the lesser of two evils, most people pick the one that will do them the least amount of harm.

Maria Gonzalez was no exception. She considered all five of her captors to be vile killers, but of the bunch of them, the American known as the White Apache was the one she feared the least. So far he had treated her roughly but courteously, which was better treatment than she would receive at the hands of the full-blooded warriors who dogged her heels. She made it a point to do her best to keep up with him and to stay close to him when they stopped, which wasn't often enough to suit her.

They had been on the go for five hours. Maria was on the verge of exhaustion. She was coated with sweat from head to toe, and her own body odor disgusted her. Her legs plodded mechanically onward mile after grueling mile, moving more out of dumb instinct than intelligent design.

Maria was not accustomed to traveling so far afoot. On the hacienda when she had to cover any great distance, she always rode or had servants transport her in a carriage. Now her legs and feet pulsed with torment with every stride she took, and she knew it was only a matter of time before they would give out on her.

The sun blazed down on the barren landscape like a golden inferno. Maria's hat had fallen off and none of her captors had bothered to replace it. Her shawl was gone too, which was a blessing since it had only made her hotter.

Maria longed for a drink or to lie down and sleep the day away. The Apaches, however, forged ever deeper into the Sierra Madre Mountains, running tirelessly. They showed no signs of being the least bit tired or thirsty or hungry. Maria mused that the stories about the red devils must be true: they were inhuman, endowed with powers no one else could hope to match. She glanced back at them, wondering what they thought of her and whether they would slay her before the day was done.

Had Maria been able to read their thoughts, she would have found the warriors held mixed feelings about her. Delgadito and Cuchillo Negro were both impressed by her stamina. It was unusual for *Nakai-yes* females to hold up well on long journeys, at least until they were properly broken in. While neither had ever taken a Mexican wife, both contemplated the merits of doing so. Neither were attracted to the captive by her looks. In their estimation she was too scrawny, more like a bird than a person, and her face was too pinched, her hair too short. They preferred a sturdy, competent, attractive Apache woman.

Fiero never gave the captive's charms a stray thought. She was a woman, and women were beneath notice in his opinion. They were put on earth for two things and two things alone: to bear children and to tend a man's wickiup. Nothing else about them was important. The only thing about this one that mattered was the foolishness of stealing her. It was a waste of their time, he figured. She would make a terrible wife.

The youngest Chiricahua, Ponce, likewise did

not give the captive much attention. It seemed in part from having lost the Apache woman he had loved. He was in no frame of mind to regard another woman with more than idle interest. As far as the captive was concerned, he had been reared to view the *Nakai-yes* with contempt. They were easy to kill, easy to plunder. Their men were as timid as rabbits, their women as useless as an extra foot. The captive was typical and did not merit any attention.

Ponce did agree that building the band up again was an excellent idea, but not with weaklings. He would have preferred going to the Chiricahua Reservation to find Apache women.

These, then, were the thoughts of the warriors regarding the woman they had abducted. Maria Gonzalez had only their inscrutable expressions to go by, and a lifetime of believing Apaches were the most bloodthirsty butchers on the face of the planet tainted her outlook. She would gaze into their dark, impassive eyes and read her death in them when they were not even thinking about her.

It was toward noon that matters came to a head. The band was making for a high pass that would see them through to the east side of the mountains. From there they would head northward into the Arizona Territory.

For the last mile or so it had been apparent to Clay that the woman was having a difficult time keeping up. He maintained a steady pace anyway in the belief that the sooner she became used to doing things the Apache way the better it would be for her.

Then, as they scaled the crest of a steep ridge,

Clay heard a low groan and a thud. He turned to find her on her side, breathing raggedly. "On your feet," he said.

"I can't," Maria puffed. An acute pain lanced her side, and her legs were leaden weight she could barely raise an inch off the earth. "Please. Let me rest a bit. Just a short while, I beg you."

The Apaches formed a semicircle around her.

"I knew she could not keep up," Fiero said scornfully. "We might as well slit her throat and leave her for the vultures and coyotes to eat."

"I agree. She will make a poor wife," Ponce said. "She is not worth the bother."

Clay planted his feet firmly at her side. "We have gone to all this trouble to bring her this far. I say we should take her the rest of the way."

Fiero motioned angrily. "She will just slow us down. She is weak, like all her kind."

"I was weak when you first found me," Clay pointed out. "If we give her a chance, she might surprise us."

Delgadito grunted. "Just so the surprise is not a knife in the back. A warrior I knew was slain in that very manner. He thought that he had tamed the woman he had stolen, but she tricked him to lower his guard and stabbed him one night while he slept."

"What happened to her?" Clay asked.

"She tried to run off but we tracked her down and brought her back. The man she stabbed cut off the fingers of her right hand so she could not use it to stab him again. He also cut her hamstring so she could not run off again. After that she was a perfect wife."

Maria listened intently although she could not

comprehend a word they said. She imagined they were discussing ways to kill her and once more appealed to the one man she felt might help her. "Please," she said. "All I need is a little time to catch my breath. Or perhaps you would consent to carry me for a while?"

"Carry you?" Clay scoffed. "Apaches never carry women or children, not even when they are sick. Stand up and keep going."

"I can't, I tell you," Maria insisted. "My legs gave out. And small wonder. I haven't done this much walking at one time in my entire life."

Fiero did not like the tone the woman used. Before Clay Taggart could stop him, he took a short step and kicked the captive in the ribs, snarling, "Get off the ground, woman, or suffer the consequences."

It annoyed Clay that Fiero saw fit to abuse the woman when he had been the one who had stolen her. "I took her, so by *Shis-Inday* custom she is mine to do with as I see fit. And I plan to keep her."

"Who are you to lecture me about our customs?" Fiero responded testily. "You are the white-eye here. I am Chiricahua."

Cuchillo Negro saw the firebrand's face harden and intervened to avert possible bloodshed. Fiero was not one to tolerate real or imagined slights and might well challenge Clay to ritual combat. "It is true that he is not of our blood, but we have accepted him as one of us. He has the right to live by our ways if he so chooses. That makes the woman his."

Fiero moved off and scanned the slopes above. There were times, such as now, when he keenly regretted ever having joined Delgadito's band. They wasted too much time on silly matters like stealing useless women when they should devote all their energy to killing their enemies.

Clay nodded at Cuchillo Negro. "Thank you," he said sincerely. Several times the laconic Apache had come to his aid in disputes involving Fiero and others, and he had yet to learn why.

"She is your woman," Cuchillo Negro said. "You must see to it that she does not slow us down."

"Yes," Delgadito said. "If she is not strong enough to hold her own, you must treat her as you would a horse that has gone lame."

"I will make her keep up," Clay said. The warriors continued on. Clay sank onto a knee and bent over the woman. "What's your name, ma'am?"

"Maria Gonzalez."

"Well, Miss Gonzalez, if you aim to go on living, you'd better light a shuck after my pards as best you're able, or you'll never live to see the night."

Maria couldn't decide if he was threatening her or warning her. Struggling to sit up, she brushed hair from her face and adopted the sort of expression that never failed to elicit the pity of any male she met. "Have a heart, senor. I have been trying my best. I just can't go on."

"Fine," Clay said and started to pull his Bowie knife.

The sight of the gleaming blade brought Maria to her feet, her heart leaping into her throat. Half expecting to be gutted, she recoiled a step.

"I don't want to have to go through this again," Clay said, shoving the Bowie back into its beaded leather sheath. He was glad he had scared her into obeying, because as much as he would hate to admit it to his Chiricahua friends, he had no desire to see any harm befall her.

Maria dutifully fell into step behind him. One of the Apaches, the warrior who scowled a lot, was sneering at her in blatant ridicule. She ignored him and concentrated on moving her tired limbs. After a while the sharp pain subsided and was replaced by a constant dull ache. To take her mind off her discomfort, she cleared her throat and said, "Do you mind if we talk?"

Clay was all set to tell her no. But the truth was that he had not talked with women in so long that he had nearly forgotten how pleasant their company could be. "Usually Apaches don't like to chatter when they're on the go, but I suppose I can make an exception in your case. What do you want to chew the cud about?"

"You," Maria said, for lack of anything else. "What is your real name?"

"Lickoyee-shis-inday."

"No, not your Apache name. I mean the name you had before you took up with them."

"Taggart. My handle was Clay Taggart."

"Was? Do you no longer consider yourself a white man?" Maria asked. She had a method to her questions. Long ago she had learned the basic lesson of dealing with the opposite sex that all women learned sooner or later, namely that men like nothing more than to talk about themselves, and that once they unburdened themselves to a woman, they regarded their confidante fondly. If she could gain his trust, she reasoned, she might be able to entice him into helping her escape.

"To be honest," Clay said, "less and less every day. The longer I'm with the Chiricahuas, the more I feel like one of them. They're the only friends I've got in the world."

Maria's interest perked up. If the gringo was that starved for friendship, she would have no problem wrapping him around her little finger. "Perhaps after a time you will regard me as your friend."

Clay had his back to her or she would have seen his grin. It amused him that so young a woman would try so obvious a ploy. "Maybe," he said.

"You mentioned before that there is only one thing you care about: revenge," Maria said, picking her words with care. "Revenge against whom."

"A sidewinder named Gillett. The son of a bitch stole my land and nearly had me doing a strangulation jig. I owe him, ma'am, owe him big. And I aim to collect."

"How did you get involved with these Apaches?"

"They saved me from Gillett. Twice over. When all my so-called white friends had turned their backs on me, the Apaches pulled my bacon out of the fire."

The revelation complicated things. Maria had assumed Taggart was just another amoral killer, just another of the deadly breed that infested northern Mexico and the southwestern part of the United States like fleas on a dog. But the man had a reason for his actions, and his loyalty to the Apaches would make gaining his help a much harder task. "I see," she said, stalling while she worked out how best to proceed.

From above them came the cry of a hunting

hawk. Clay glanced up at Fiero, who was pointing to the south. From their elevation a tiny cloud of dust was visible, drawing slowly nearer to the foothills.

Maria saw the dust also. "My father!" she exclaimed, clasping her hands in joy.

"If it is," Clay said, "you'd be smart to pray he doesn't get too close. My friends might take it into their heads to make sure he never finds you."

Raw terror coursed through Maria's veins. Should anything happen to her father, she was doomed. Her mother would never be able to track her down or know how to go about making an exchange. "You said that you would not accept money to ransom me. Is there nothing at all you would take? Horses? Guns? Trade goods?"

"All I want is you."

The slopes were steeper the higher they climbed. They passed the tree line and the Apaches had to avail themselves of what little cover was to be found. Maria marveled at their skill in gliding across the rugged terrain like disembodied spirits. They showed an uncanny knack for blending into the background. And the man once known as Clay Taggart was every bit their equal. She was right behind him, yet she never heard his sole scuff the ground. He seemed to have a way of setting his feet down that absorbed any noise he made.

The band crossed a gully, scaled a rock-strewn slope, and approached a towering cleft in a jagged spire of a peak crowned by an eagle's nest.

Maria was fast becoming winded. She labored for every breath and had to compel her legs to move through sheer willpower. Several times she stopped, but went on right away when Clay glared at her. She was so tired that she could barely hold her chin up. Head bobbing, she stumbled in her captor's wake. For seconds on end her eyes would close. Consequently she had no idea that Taggart had stopped until she bumped into him.

They were at the cleft. To the right shimmered a small pool of water. The Apaches were on their knees, sipping from cupped hands.

Uttering a cry of delight, Maria dashed to the spring and threw herself onto her stomach. She gulped greedily. Never had water tasted so delicious. Suddenly a hand fell on her shoulder.

"Not so fast, ma'am," Taggart said. "You'll wind up with a powerful bellyache if you don't take it easy."

Maria nodded, but could not resist drinking more. She finally sat up and looked down at herself. Her dress, which had been layered with dust and dirt, was soaked to the waist. She was a mess. Yet she didn't mind.

"We will rest a few minutes," Clay said.

"For my sake?" Maria asked, hoping he had convinced the Apaches on her behalf.

"No. My friends and I can go for long spells without water, but that doesn't mean we'll look a gift horse in the mouth. We're in no rush, ma'am. Your father is hours behind us. By morning I reckon we'll lose him for good."

Maria had to resist an insane notion to bolt down the slope. "You do not know my father like I do," she said. "He will never give up, not while he lives."

"I doubt he'll follow us all the way into Arizona," Clay said. "And once we reach our hideout in the

Bloodbath

Chiricahua Mountains, no one will ever find us."

The prospect was too depressing to ponder. Maria splashed water on her face, then tried to smooth and clean her dress. It was hopeless.

The man known as the White Apache was reminded of the woman he had once cherished more than life itself. Lilly had been a stickler for her appearance too. He shut his mind to the memory.

Near the pool towered a boulder the size of a cabin. Maria jabbed a thumb at it and made bold to ask, "Will you excuse me for a few minutes, Senor Taggart?"

"What for?" Clay said and felt like an jackass for asking when she blushed. "Oh, sure, go ahead. Just don't try to run off. You wouldn't get far."

"I won't," Maria said. She walked around the boulder and heeded nature's call. As she straightened, a piercing shriek echoed off the peak, and the next thing she knew, something sliced into her unprotected back.

Chapter Five

The sun had not yet cleared the horizon when Martin Gonzalez and Capt. Vicente Filisola set out to rescue Martin's daughter. They waited just long enough to see the carriage off with an escort of two troopers. Theresa Gonzalez waved, her cheeks streaked by tears that she thought would never end.

Martin started the day brimming with confidence. His vaquero, Pedro, was an exceptional tracker and would eventually run the Apaches down. There were only five of the savages, and between the soldiers and his own men, he had 16 guns to rely on. It was more than enough to get the job done.

Only one thing marred Martin's outlook. He did not like to dwell on the fate worse than death that might have already befallen his darling little Maria. Apaches stole pretty young women for only one reason. He could only hope the devils

Bloodbath

would not violate her while they were fleeing back to their stronghold in the north.

Capt. Filisola shared the father's fears, but he did not voice them. He was, after all, a gentleman. In his mind's eye he kept seeing Maria, kept recalling the veiled invitation in her eyes, the promise of the fine time they might have together. It bothered him a bit that he should find himself caring so deeply for a senorita he hardly knew. In all his many conquests of the fairer half of the species, he had seldom dwelled on one woman for so long.

The officer and the father rode at the head of the column. At Filisola's suggestion, Martin had directed his vaqueros to ride in twos, as the soldiers did. Far in front of the main group rode Pedro and Sgt. Amat. The sergeant had some experience tracking but nowhere near as much as the somber vaquero.

Until the middle of the afternoon the trail was easy to follow. The Apaches had stuck to open country, and they had made good time, given that they had not had the benefit of a moon.

The sun was high in the sky when Pedro, squinting ahead at the rolling foothills that bordered the high Sierra Madres, spotted a number of dark shapes. "Damn," he spat.

"What is wrong?" Sgt. Amat asked. A career soldier, he had tangled with Apaches many times before and knew to always expect the unexpected. It would not have surprised him if the red demons sprang another ambush. He was as highly strung as piano wire, one hand resting on the carbine across his thighs.

"They are on foot now," Pedro said. "It will be

much harder from here on."

Amat rounded up the four horses while Pedro rode higher into the hills, a cocked pistol in his right hand. He came on the charred embers of a fire and beside it the carcass of a horse the Apaches had roasted. Here he waited, studying the various tracks, until his employer and the others caught up with him.

"Well?" Martin asked bluntly.

Pedro gestured toward the stark peaks that speared toward the azure sky. "They went that way, sir. Up. Your daughter is still with them and has not been harmed. At least, she does not limp or show any other sign of being hurt."

"Thank the Lord," Martin said. He nodded at the slope beyond. "Go on. But always stay in sight. If you see anything suspicious, and I mean anything, you are to stop until we catch up."

Pedro hesitated. "There is one more thing, sir. It might be important. It might not."

"What?" Martin asked impatiently.

"These tracks. I have examined them most carefully. Four are the tracks of Apaches, of that there is no doubt. But the fifth man, he is different."

"Different how?"

"He walks like an Apache but he is not an Apache."

"I do not understand," Martin said. Coming from anyone else, he would have dismissed the remark as utter nonsense, but Pedro had worked for him more than 15 years and he had learned to rely on the man's judgment.

Pedro shifted from foot to foot and stared at a print in the earth by the fire. "I know this will sound crazy, sir, but I would swear by the Virgin that the fifth man is not Apache at all. If I had to guess, I would say he is white."

"You must be mistaken," Martin said.

Capt. Filisola had been an alert listener. "Perhaps not, Senor Gonzalez," he said, his fear for Maria's safety mounting dramatically. "Have you not heard of the White Apache?"

Excited murmurs broke out among the soldiers and vaqueros. All of them were aware of the latest scourge to plague their people. All of them knew his reputation. They were no longer hunting just five Apaches, which was enough of a perilous challenge in itself. They were after a man reputed to be a living terror, a man who took delight in slaughtering innocents. A few of them crossed themselves and others uttered silent prayers for deliverance. It never occurred to any of them that the grisly stories they had heard might have been mere tall tales, the sort that spread through cantinas like wildfire.

Martin Gonzalez had heard some of the same reports, and he blanched on hearing the name. "The White Apache," he said in an awed tone. "Dear God, my poor Maria."

"We will save her," Filisola declared, wishing he felt as confident as he sounded.

Pedro cleared his throat. "It is my guess, sir, that they will cross the Sierras and then head for the border. Once they are across, they know they are safe."

"They think they will be," Martin said, "but they are wrong. If they go across the border, so will I."

"We will catch them long before they reach it,"

Filisola remarked. "They made a mistake when they abandoned their horses."

The tracker was not so sure. "Apaches can go farther on foot in one day than a man can on horseback," he reminded the officer. "And they will stick to the roughest terrain to throw us off."

Martin motioned upward. "Enough talk. We are wasting precious time. Start tracking, Pedro. We will be right behind you."

"Yes, sir."

The rescuers climbed on, a solemn air about them, while high above an eagle shrieked.

Taggart heard that same shriek, then a low cry and the sound of a scuffle. Pushing erect, he dashed around the boulder the captive had gone behind and discovered her on her knees, swatting futilely at a large eagle that had dug its curved talons into her shoulders and was pecking at her head.

Taggart sprang to her defense, swinging his rifle. The eagle ducked, screeched at him, and tried to rip open his arm. He pivoted out of harm's way. Dodging to the right, he drove the stock at the bird's side but its flailing wing deflected the blow. Meanwhile its huge talons dug deeper into Maria's back. She cried out again and fell to her hands and knees.

Clay stepped back and took aim. As if an uncanny instinct warned it that it was about to be shot, the eagle vented a high-pitched screech and flapped into the air. Once clear of the boulder, it tucked its wings and dived. It was a blur as it streaked out over the base of the mountain and then spiraled back toward the nest high overhead.

Once Clay was assured the eagle was not going to attack again, he sank down beside the captive. She was on her knees, her arms pressed to her chest. She shook uncontrollably. Blood streamed from the nasty wounds the predatory bird had inflicted.

"Why?" Maria asked through clenched teeth. "Why did it come after me?"

"I have no idea," Clay said, leaning over so he could inspect the wounds. The sun flashed off a shiny object in her hair. Gingerly, he removed a silver barrette and held it where she could see it. "My guess would be this was to blame. I think it was female. Maybe it figured you were a threat to its nest or young'uns."

"I love birds," Maria said lamely. "I would never harm one." She was in such agony that she could hardly think straight. Looking up, she saw the four Apaches observing her with stony expressions.

"We'll need to patch you up," Clay said, putting an arm around her waist to help her stand. Changing to the Apache tongue, he said, "She is badly hurt. We must make a fire so I can tend her wounds."

Fiero snorted. "She has a couple of scratches. They are not worth bothering about."

"That eagle dug its talons in deep," Clay said. "We'd do the same for you if it had gone after you instead."

"I would laugh at such wounds," Fiero said. "Apaches are not weaklings who go all to pieces when they suffer small cuts."

"There is no wood here for a fire anyway," Delgadito said. "We must move on."

"You go ahead. I'll catch up," Clay said. Without waiting to see if they would do as he wanted, he scooped Maria Gonzalez into his arms. She stiffened and made as if to strike him, but evidently thought better of the idea and let herself be carried to the pool.

Clay deposited her gently, drew the Bowie, and reached for the hem of her dress.

"What are you doing?" Maria asked anxiously.

"We need bandages, and I doubt you'd want me to use my breechcloth."

For the first time since Maria had met him, Clay smiled. She couldn't help but return the smile until she realized what she was doing and adopted a more primly proper look. "Do what you must," she said softly.

It did not take long for Clay to cut off a three-inch-wide strip and soak it in the water. Since he knew she was not about to permit him to apply the bandage under her dress, he did so on the outside, wrapping it around her body and tying it under her right arm. It made a poor compress and hardly stanched the flow of blood, but it was the best he could do at the moment.

"Let's go," Clay said, offering his hand as he rose.

Maria balked, but just for a few moments. She accepted his help and stood. Her legs nearly buckled, catching her by surprise, and she would have fallen had her captor not caught her.

"I'll carry you, ma'am."

"No, I can manage," Maria assured him. She

felt the heat of his body against hers and abruptly became aware of the raw, animal power radiating from the man. That power was like a physical force, and it spawned disturbing sensations deep within her. She pushed back and shuffled toward the far end of the pass, glad for the cool breeze that buffeted the rocky defile.

For his part, Clay was trying to control similar feelings kindled by their brief contact. It had been so long since a woman's warm breath had fanned his face that hers set his blood afire. He would have liked to have jumped into the pool and stayed there until he cooled down. It angered him that he was acting like a randy schoolboy, yet there was nothing he could do about it.

The Apaches were hundreds of yards away, moving in single file as was their custom. In the lead walked Delgadito, a rare smirk creasing his lips. He was pleased beyond measure that Clay wanted to build up the band again. It had been Delgadito's plan to do so all along. And once the band was big enough to suit him, he would wrest leadership from Clay, at the point of a knife if he had to, and reclaim his rightful position as a leader of the Chiricahuas.

The dull crack of a shod hoof on rock brought Delgadito up short. Immediately he flattened against the stone wall of the pass, listening. The sound had come from the east side of the mountain.

Delgadito glanced around. His companions had also stopped, and they were staring at him, ready to follow his lead just as they had done in the days before the scalphunters wiped out the old band.

"Fiero," Delgadito whispered.

The most bloodthirsty Chiricahua who had ever lived padded forward to the end of the pass and halted in the shadow of a rock monolith. From his vantage point he could see the many slopes below and to either side. Less than 200 yards off, winding up a serpentine animal trail, were six Mexicans. The incline was so steep that they were walking their mounts.

All six wore sombreros and grungy clothes. All six had bandoleers crisscrossing their chests, and each wore two guns, tied down for fast draws. They had the haggard aspect of men who had traveled for many days, and the last one in line kept looking over his shoulder as if to spot pursuers.

Fiero pegged them as ruthless scavengers who preyed on anyone and everyone, much as Apaches did, but who did so for the most base of motives: greed. Apaches could never understand why some whites and Mexicans killed for dollars and pesos when there were so many grander reasons, like revenge and warring on one's enemies.

If there were an official Apache creed, it was to steal without being caught and to kill without being slain. Those were the precepts by which every Chiricahua lived, and none did so more fervently than Fiero. The moment he set eyes on the bandits, his agile brain was working out a way to kill them without being killed in order to steal their horses and possessions.

Whirling, Fiero raced to his friends and reported what he had seen, adding, "They will reach the pass soon. If we are to act, it must be now."

Bloodbath

"But what about *Lickoyee-shis-inday?*" Cuchillo Negro asked. "He must be warned."

"We do not have the time," Fiero said.

Behind them, Clay wondered why the four Apaches suddenly sprinted for the mouth of the pass. Were they leaving him behind on purpose? He would not put it past Fiero or Ponce, but he rated Delgadito a close friend and doubted that Cuchillo Negro would desert him under any circumstances.

"Where are they going, senor?" Maria asked.

"Beats me," Clay said. "Maybe they're tired of my company."

Maria was quick to exploit the opening. "If they care so little for you, why do you stay with them?"

"I told you before. They're my pards."

"Perhaps it is time you found new pards," Maria said. "What have they done for you but get you into trouble with the law? Or do you like being a wanted man on both sides of the border? Do you like being hated more than the Apaches themselves?"

"You keep missing the point, little lady. They'll do to ride the river with."

"What does that mean?"

"That I've thrown in with them, come what may. If I can help them take back the land stolen by my government, I will. After all they've done for me, I owe them that much."

"So you are saying you have a debt of honor?"

"Something like that, I reckon," Clay said.

The warriors had disappeared out the end of the pass, and he picked up the pace to learn why. Maria was dragging her heels, so he snatched her wrist and hauled her along, heedless of the pained look she adopted.

"What is the matter with you? You are hurting me."

"Tough molasses," Clay said. He was tired of her trying to turn him against the Chiricahuas, and figured it was about time she learned who the leader of the band was.

Clay was 20 feet from the opening when he heard the nicker of a horse. Instantly he dropped low, his senses primed like a mountain lion's, his mind empty of all save the matter at hand. In an instant, he had changed his mental attitude from that of a gruff rancher to that of a wary Apache. His posture, his movements, and his whole attitude were more Indian than white. He had became as much like a Chiricahua as the Chiricahuas themselves.

Clay crept closer to the sunlight. There was no sign of the warriors. He could tell that a number of horses were nearing the pass. Flattening, he let go of Maria and snaked to the edge of the shelf. He did not know what to expect but he was surprised to see six bandits a score of yards away. At the front was a giant bearded man who had a belly the size of a washtub.

Clay turned to take Maria into hiding, but as he twisted to the right, she sped past him on the left. Her slender arms overhead, her hair flying, she shouted at the top of her lungs in Spanish, "Help me! Help me! For the love of God! I have been stolen by Apaches! They are all around you!"

The bandits were riveted in place for several seconds, too startled to do more than gape. The one in the lead came to life quickest, clawing out his pistols and growling orders to those behind him.

Clay rose to try to stop Maria before she reached the bandits. But the leader saw him and opened fire, banging off shot after shot. Clay had to drop down again as slugs chipped at the shelf.

A war whoop wavered on the wind. A rifle blasted. Pistols cracked in cadence in reply, mingled with lusty curses and the frantic neighing of mounts.

Clay rose high enough to see the battle raging below. About 15 feet down, the Chiricahuas had hidden among boulders on either side of the animal trail. They would have ambushed the unsuspecting bandits had Maria Gonzalez not ruined everything. She was past the boulders, streaking for the bandits, some of whom were trying to climb on their animals while others blasted at the warriors.

Extending his Winchester, Clay fixed the front bead on the chest of the bandit leader. As his finger curled around the trigger, the leader's horse, trying to flee, yanked the man off balance. His shot missed.

Another bandit had a boot in a stirrup and was rising into the saddle when a slug slammed into his spine between the shoulder blades. He stiffened, clutched at his back, and toppled. The riderless horse, spooked, fled down the trail, colliding with other animals.

Cuchillo Negro broke from cover, going after the woman. A hail of gunfire drove him to ground.

Realizing he must act or lose Maria, Clay

launched himself into a roll that sent him over the rim and down the slope toward the boulders. He leaped to his feet before he stopped rolling and gained shelter as one of the bandits peppered his vicinity.

When Clay popped up to fire, he saw the leader in the saddle and Maria clambering up behind the man. Again he aimed, and again he was thwarted when the leader wheeled the horse and galloped madly down the slope, barreling past another bandit who was trying to climb on a frightened animal that wouldn't stand still.

Clay jumped up and tried to settle his sights on the leader's head, but Maria's was too close. He might hit her by mistake.

The last of the bandits had managed to mount. Hugging his saddle, he fled, firing blindly over a shoulder.

Rather than waste ammunition, the warriors stopped firing and came into the open.

Clay started down the trail. The horse of the slain bandit had been unable to run off because its reins were looped around the dead man's wrist and he wanted to get to it before it pulled free.

"Where are you going, *Lickoyee-shis-inday?*" Delgadito asked.

"After her," Clay answered without slowing.

"Wait," Cuchillo Negro said.

Against his better judgment, Clay paused. "What is it? I must hurry if I am to catch them."

"Why bother?" Cuchillo Negro said. "There are five of them and only one of you. They will be expecting someone to come after them."

"Does my brother imply I cannot handle five *Nakai-yes?*" Clay said.

74

Bloodbath

"These are not ordinary Mexicans. They are killers, mad wolves who attack in packs. Let them have the woman. We can always find another to replace her."

"I want this one," Clay said and raced on. "Head north. If all goes well I will meet you at Caliente Springs. Wait for me as long as you can."

He heard Delgadito call his name, but did not stop. The bandit's horse shied and tried to pull away from him until he had the reins in hand and spoke to it softly. At length it permitted him to fork leather.

Dust raised by the fleeing bandits still hung in the air. Clay wound down the trail into scrub pines. Here the wily outlaws had veered into the trees, bearing to the southeast. He glued himself to their tracks and presently glimpsed them about half a mile ahead of him, riding hell bent for leather.

Since Clay did not want them to spot him, he moved into thicker timber and slowed. There was no need to ride his horse into the ground. He could not wrest Maria from them until they stopped.

Clay had not thought to count the riders he saw. He did so when he reached a clearing and glimpsed them a second time. It puzzled him to spy only four where there should be five. He did not know what to make of the missing man. Then he came to the barren slope of a gulch the bandits had crossed, and he descended. Too late he spotted the glint of sunlight off metal. The next second a rifle boomed.

Chapter Six

Col. Jose Gonzalez was widely known as one of the bravest officers in all of Mexico. Those who knew him personally were also aware that he was one of the most vain.

On this particular day, the colonel stood in front of the full-length mirror that adorned the inner panel of the closet door in his office at the presidio of Janos. He had on a new uniform, which had arrived the previous day from Mexico City, and he was admiring the neatly pressed shirt with its many shiny buttons and the decorations he had won for his valorous service to his country.

The colonel overlooked the fact that his hairline had receded to a point above his small ears and that his stocky frame was more like that of a hardworking farmer's than the ideal of slim military perfection. In his mind he was flawless, as grand a warrior who ever lived.

Bloodbath

A commotion erupted outside. Col. Gonzalez heard a shout, then more yells followed by the drumming of hooves. Donning his hat, he sucked in his gut, clasped his hands behind his wide back, and stalked out to learn the cause of the uproar.

A number of junior officers and dozens of soldiers were clustered around someone near the hitching post. The moment Col. Gonzalez appeared in the doorway, one of those officers, Capt. Mora, snapped to attention and bellowed loud enough to be heard in town, "Commander!" Instantly the assembled soldiers fell in line.

Col. Gonzalez moved among them to the center of the cluster. Two exhausted horses were there, both lathered with enough sweat to drown an ox. Legs quivering, blowing noisily through their nostrils, they appeared ready to keel over at any second.

The soldier who had ridden them in was in scarcely better shape. His uniform was drenched, his face slick. His skin was red from the heat and he was having a hard time keeping his eyes open. The private was doing his utmost to stand at attention, even though his legs quaked worse than those of the two animals.

One of the abilities that made Gonzalez such an outstanding officer was his phenomenal memory. It was rumored that he never forgot a face or a name, and he often amazed casual acquaintances he had not seen in years by remembering the least little detail about them.

On this occasion Col. Gonzalez sorted through the file of his uncanny memory until he found the face of the soldier in front of him. "Pvt. Batres. You were sent out on patrol with Capt. Filisola, were you not? Explain yourself."

The private hiked his shoulders a hair higher and went to speak, but could not. He coughed a few times, then croaked, "I am sorry, Colonel. I have ridden over seventy miles to get here to report—" His voice broke, and he coughed more violently.

Col. Gonzalez glanced at Capt. Mora and snapped his fingers. In moments a canteen was produced. The colonel himself gave it to the private.

"Swallow small mouthfuls."

Batres did so although it was plain to all assembled that he wanted to gulp the canteen dry. He lowered it after a few sips and gratefully handed it back. "Thank you, sir. I could not have gone much longer without water."

"Your report, Private."

"Yes." Batres snapped to attention again. "I regret to inform you that our patrol was ambushed by Apaches."

The colonel took the news in stride. Apache attacks were common occurrences, and he had steeled himself to losing over a dozen men a year, on average, to the devils'. "Are you the only survivor?"

"No, sir," Batres went on hastily. "Only half the patrol was slain. The captain then led us on a forced ride to Adobe Wells—"

"Why would he go there?" Col. Gonzalez asked. "He should have gone on to Hermosillo and sent a dispatch to me."

"Capt. Filisola was worried about your brother and his family," Batres said.

Fear gripped Gonzalez. His brother was due to

arrive any day for his annual visit. "What about them?" he demanded urgently.

"We had passed them shortly before the attack. Capt. Filisola figured out that the Apaches were going after them, dressed in uniforms the savages took from our dead. He was very concerned for your brother's safety."

"You've already made that clear. Get to the point. What happened?"

"We reached Adobe Wells too late. The Apaches had already struck. Several of your brother's vaqueros were killed, and—" Private Batres hesitated, afraid to be the bearer of bad tidings.

"Out with it, man!"

"The Apaches took your niece, Colonel."

There was a collective intake of breath by the gathered troopers. Every man there knew what it meant to live under the constant nightmare of Apache raids. Every man there sympathized with their commanding officer. Furthermore, many of them had seen Maria Gonzalez. She was one of the few women permitted on the post and a vision of loveliness many secretly adored.

Batres went on in the stunned silence. "Capt. Filisola and your brother went after the Apaches. Pvt. Iberry and I were sent to escort the carriage bringing Senora Gonzalez. A wheel broke soon after we left the captain. Since there were enough men to protect the senora, I came on ahead with two horses, riding them in turns to make the trip without stopping. I thought you should know what had happened as soon as possible."

The soldiers turned their attention to their commanding officer. It was common knowledge that the colonel was a stickler for following orders.

Any man in violation was subject to the strictest possible punishment. But it was also common knowledge that the colonel appreciated initiative and rewarded those who showed loyalty above and beyond the call of duty. They waited to see which would be the case in this instance.

Col. Gonzalez had his surging emotions under control. He fixed his iron stare on the private and asked, "So Capt. Filisola did not order you to ride on ahead by yourself?"

Batres gulped. "No, sir. My orders were to stay with the carriage. But when it broke down, I thought—"

Gonzalez held up his right hand, silencing the man. "Nevertheless, you did not obey your superior. And you know that failure to follow orders must always be punished."

"Yes, sir," Batres said, crestfallen.

"As your punishment, I confine you to bed rest for three days—"

"Bed rest?" the private asked in astonishment.

"You are suffering from heatstroke, so you are not to leave your bed except for meals. I will have the doctor attend to you to make sure your recovery is swift, Sergeant."

It took a moment for the colonel's last word to register. "You called me a sergeant, Colonel. I have not even made corporal yet."

"As commander I can promote who I like when I like," Col. Gonzalez said stiffly. "As of this moment, you jump two grades to sergeant. I expect to see your uniform reflect your new rank the next time I see you."

"Yes, sir!" Batres responded, and there wasn't

a man present who didn't envy him.

"Furthermore, after I return, you are assigned to my personal staff. Report to me in person."

"Yes, sir."

"Now get to the infirmary, then to bed."

The private snapped a salute and turned about. He took only three steps when his legs gave out. Several soldiers cushioned his fall and carted him off.

Col. Gonzalez stomped onto the porch fronting the headquarters building and pivoted. "You heard him. The Apaches have abducted the sweetest senorita who ever lived. Are we going to let them get away with it?"

"No, sir!" roared from 40 mouths.

"Capt. Mora," Gonzalez snapped. "Assign fifty men to guard the presidio. Have one hundred and fifty mounted and ready to depart within half an hour. Full field rations and forty extra rounds of ammunition are to be given each man. Understood?"

"Yes, sir."

The colonel marched into his office and sat down to compose a dispatch to his superiors explaining his actions and requesting that 50 soldiers be sent from Hermosillo to reinforce the Janos garrison until his return. He noticed that his hand shook slightly as he wrote, and he honestly couldn't tell if it was because of his outrage over the kidnapping of his niece or the heady thrill he always felt before going into combat against his lifelong enemies.

Either way, the Apaches responsible were going to pay for their atrocity in blood.

*   *   *

In the second that elapsed between the moment Clay saw the glint of sunlight and the rifle of the concealed bandit blasted, he threw himself from the saddle, diving to the right into high weeds that choked the side of the gulch. He hit on his shoulder and rolled a few yards to make it harder for the bushwhacker to pinpoint his position.

Two more slugs sheared into the vegetation but wide of where Clay lay on his belly. Rising onto his knees, he watched his mount race in panic down the gully. Without that horse his chances of overtaking the bandits were slim. He took off after it, weaving as he ran, keeping brush and trees between himself and the rifleman.

Shots cracked on the opposite rim. Twigs and branches were splintered by slugs. One nicked Clay's shin. He halted behind a pine to return fire, levering off five shots in swift succession. The gunfire from the other side ceased.

Clay ran on. The horse had disappeared around a bend in the gully. He hoped it would slow down soon or stop. But when he reached the bend, the spooked animal was hundreds of yards away with its mane flying and tail high.

"Damn!" Clay said. Crouching, he zigzagged to the far slope and up to the top. He was surprised that the bandit did not try to pick him off.

The clatter of hooves on stone told Clay why. The bandit was fleeing too. Clay streaked toward the sound, over a knoll and across a narrow flat to a rocky spine 60 feet long. He leaped onto the smooth incline, braced his heels, and scrambled to the top.

Just in time. The bandit was relying on the

Bloodbath

spine to cover his flight and was moving along it with his body bent low over his saddle horn so he could not be seen from the gully.

Clay set down his Winchester, coiled his legs, waited until the rider came underneath him, and pounced. He wanted the man alive so he could force him to reveal the destination of the gang.

The bandit spotted Clay's shadow and jerked around, but he was too late. Clay's left shoulder rammed into the rider's side, spilling them both onto the ground. Clay regained his feet sooner and lashed out with a fist. The bandit handily jumped aside and went for one of the pistols decorating his waist.

Shifting, Clay slid in close and clamped a hand on the outlaw's wrist so the man couldn't bring the pistol into play. For hectic moments they danced in circles, each struggling for possession of the revolver. Clay forked a foot behind the man's leg and shoved, upending him. Clay landed on top, gouging his knees into the other's stomach.

A boot walloped Clay. He landed on his right shoulder next to the bandit, who redoubled his attempt to use the pistol. Clay had to strain to hold the barrel at bay. In their rolling and thrashing they smashed into the rocky spine. Clay, distracted for a heartbeat, felt a knee drive into his groin. Weakness and fleeting nausea came over him.

The bandit shoved free and jumped to his feet. Sneering in triumph, he pointed the pistol and thumbed back the hammer.

Clay snapped his left foot into the man's knee. A loud crack sounded a fraction of a second before the pistol went off. The slug thudded into the dirt inches from Clay's ear. Flipping to the left, he heard the gun thunder again but fortunately the wobbly bandit missed.

Abruptly reversing direction, Clay plowed into the bandit's legs. The Mexican staggered backward into the rock wall and cursed as his fractured knee buckled and he toppled forward, directly onto Clay.

In an instant, Clay swept both knees to his chest so that the bandit fell against the soles of his feet. Then with a heave, he hurled the man back against the spine with such force that the bandit slumped to the ground.

Clay rose. The man's pistol had fallen. He promptly picked it up. Drawing back his other hand, he gave the bandit a ringing slap across the cheek. The man started, blinked, and went motionless with fear.

"Where are the others going?" Clay asked in Spanish. To spur an answer, he cocked the pistol and pressed the end of the barrel against the tip of the man's nose.

"I don't know," the bandit said.

"Liar."

"I swear!" the man cried. "We were on our way to Hermosillo when your band attacked us. Now my amigos are running for their lives, and I have no idea where they are headed."

"I want the truth."

"That is the truth. By all that is holy, you must believe me."

"I don't," Clay said, straightening up. He smiled at the man, then shot him through the right shoulder.

Bloodbath

The shriek of torment the bandit let out with must have carried for half a mile. The man arched his spine and writhed about for a minute like a stricken wildcat, his teeth clenched, beads of sweat lining his brow.

"I would not lie again, if I were you," Clay said. "It is not hard to figure out what happened. Every outlaw gang has a leader, and yours is that big hombre with the gut. He wanted you to delay anyone who was on your trail. And he would have told you where to meet your amigos later." Clay paused and leaned down so the pistol was trained on the bandit's chest. "Where?"

The bandit licked his spittle-flecked lips, his gaze riveted on the six-shooter. "Honest to God, I do not want to die. I would tell you if we had set up a rendezvous. But there was no time. We were in too much of a hurry."

Clay lowered the pistol. There was a chance the man was actually telling the truth. He would have to do the job the hard way, by tracking the bandits. Turning, he stared at the man's horse, which had halted about 50 feet away to graze. Out of the corner of his eye, he watched the bandit. He knew what the man would do before the man did it. So when the outlaw slipped a hand onto the other pistol, he was ready.

In a smooth, fluid spin, Clay swung around and fanned the hammer twice. It was a trick few men mastered because of the tendency of a heavy-caliber pistol to kick when fired, but with practice, a skilled gunman could fan accurately at short ranges. And Clay Taggart was very skillful. Both slugs ripped into the bandit's heart, dead center. The man died without uttering another sound.

"Idiot," Clay said as he squatted to strip off the twin gunbelts the man wore. After strapping them around his waist, he loaded both pistols and slipped the bandit's bandoleers over his own chest. He retrieved the Winchester before hurrying to the sorrel, which gave him a wary scrutiny, but did not run off.

Forking leather, Clay pulled out the bandit's rifle, a Henry in excellent condition. He decided to keep it and shoved it back into the boot. Clucking the sorrel into a trot, he placed his Winchester across his legs.

A man could never have enough guns.

Martin Gonzalez felt his mouth go dry from apprehension. He looked at Pedro and asked, "You are sure of this?"

"Yes, sir," the tracker answered, motioning at the tracks behind the huge boulder. "Your daughter came behind here by herself. Then something happened. I do not know what. But she bled badly and was carried off by the White Apache."

Capt. Filisola frowned. "The ruthless butcher must have stabbed her."

Pedro cocked his head. "I do not think so, Captain. All his tracks are on top of the blood. From what I can tell, he came running, as if to help her. Then he carried her back. The four Apaches came over, but stood back, doing nothing."

"Why was she bleeding?" Martin asked, clenching his fists in frustration. "What could have happened?"

Bloodbath

"The tracks do not tell me," Pedro said. "I am sorry, sir."

Martin led the way to the spring, where the rest of the men were watering the horses. A vaquero offered him a canteen and he took it and drank without being aware that he was doing so. All he could think of was his beloved Maria.

"How soon before we catch them?" Capt. Filisola asked the tracker.

"I cannot say. Perhaps tomorrow sometime if they stop for the night."

"Tomorrow!" Filisola said. "It might as well be next week. We must push even harder if we are to save the senorita. Can you track by torchlight? It would permit us to travel on through the night."

"It is very hard to do," Pedro said. "I might lose the trail, and I would not like to risk that."

Sgt. Amat, standing nearby, overheard and said, "If I may be so bold, sir, we must also think of the horses. They are very tired. Pressing on until morning would exhaust them. Then how will we catch the savages?"

"We will go on foot, if need be," Filisola said crisply. He disliked having his judgment questioned.

Martin removed his sombrero and mopped a hand across his forehead. "No, we won't. It is my daughter they took, and I say that we will make camp once it is too dark for Pedro to track. We all need a good night's rest."

Filisola disagreed strongly, but made no objection. Martin was a civilian and as such Filisola had the right, under Mexican law, to require the rancher to do as he wished. But Martin was also the colonel's brother, and the colonel would not take kindly to having his brother treated like a common peon.

The rescue party rode on through the pass. They were almost to the east opening when three gunshots shattered the stillness; they were the signal that Pedro had found something of interest.

Martin spurred his horse into the sunlight. The tracker and the sergeant were scouring a game trail below. Near them was a body partially hidden by small boulders. Fearing the worst, Martin galloped to the spot and could not hide his relief when he discovered it was a dead stranger, not Maria.

"What now?" Capt. Filisola asked. Dismounting, he turned the body over and examined the fleshy features. "I know this man. His name is Sesma. He is a bandit who rode with that pig, Vargas."

"Vargas and his men fought the Apaches, then fled," Pedro said.

"That sounds like Vargas," Filisola said. "He is a coward who is all too willing to kill innocents, but he runs if his own life is in danger. Col. Gonzalez claims that Vargas is the very worst of his breed— a filthy cockroach who has murdered many men, women, and children. It is too bad the Apaches did not do us a favor and wipe his gang out."

Martin saw his vaquero's features become downcast. "What is the matter, Pedro?"

"I have bad news to relay, sir."

Martin did not know what could possibly be worse than having his daughter in the clutches of vile Apaches. "Out with it."

Pedro hunkered down and touched a single

slim footprint at the side of the trail. "I think Maria was taken by this Vargas and his men."

The revelation shocked everyone into silence. Martin climbed down and inspected the track for himself. He saw where the ground near it had been chewed up by hoofprints when a horse turned to flee. "Can it really be?"

"I am afraid so. She ran to the bandits. You can see her tracks there. And this horse, when it rode off, was carrying double. See how deep the tracks are, compared to the others?"

"Dear God," Capt. Filisola said. Apaches were bad enough, but at least they would keep Maria alive to become the wife of one of their warriors. Bandits were another story entirely. Vargas killed women as readily as most men killed insects. He had also tortured and raped many of them. Maria was much worse off now than she had been before.

"Maybe she did not know these men were bandits," Pedro said. "Maybe she thought they were her only hope of escaping the Apaches."

Martin Gonzalez bowed his head in abject despair. "My poor, poor Maria! Where have the bandits taken her? What will they do to her?"

There was no answer, other than a chill gust of wind that moaned down off the mountain.

Chapter Seven

It had seemed like a good idea at the time.

When Maria Gonzalez had seen the six men approaching the pass, she had gone giddy with joy. They were Mexicans! Her own kind! Men who would help her. Men who would save her from the Apaches.

So without thinking, Maria had bolted past the White Apache and down the trail toward the burly man who led the six. She had shouted to alert them to their peril and been overjoyed when she'd reached the leader without taking a bullet in the back.

The events happened so quickly that Maria was astride the man's horse and fleeing down the mountain before she could collect her wits. Rather belatedly she realized that the man who had rescued her smelled badly. Besides that, he had a harsh air about him, even more cruel than that of the Apaches. His beady eyes actually scared her when he glanced back a few times as if to assure himself that she was indeed there.

And the man was a coward. When she was running toward him, she had seen his terror of the Apaches, a cringing terror the likes of which her father and uncle would never display.

They were bandits, Maria realized, and her heart sank within her. The horror stories she had heard about bandits rivaled those about Apaches. Having lived the sheltered life of a pampered senorita, she had never seen either until this fateful trip, and she hoped to high heaven she never saw either again, provided she lived long enough to get to somewhere safe.

Because there was nothing else to hang onto, Maria had to grasp the big man's bandoleers to keep from losing her balance on his mount. The man rode with reckless abandon, swerving wildly through tracts of trees and taking the slopes of gullies at breakneck speed. They were lucky the horse didn't break a leg and throw them both.

Then the leader reined up. But he stopped only long enough to tell one of his men to keep an eye on their back trail and bushwhack anyone who showed. The other bandit wasn't happy about being the one picked to cover their flight, but evidently his fear of the bandit leader was greater than his fear of the Apaches because he agreed and climbed down.

The big leader lashed his horse and they galloped along for over an hour, until they were well off the mountain and out on the desert to the east. The man had an amazing knack for finding gulches and arroyos through which to travel. It was as if he knew the lay of the land as well as he knew the lines in the palms of his hands.

Finally, when Maria was so tired and sore that she worried she would collapse and fall, the leader drew rein again in a dry wash rimmed by dry brush. There was a small spring, as close to dry as a spring could be and still be worthy of the name. The leader jumped down, dropped to his knees, and guzzled the water like a hog at the trough. Only after he had downed his fill did he let the rest of the bandits and the horses drink.

Maria, meanwhile, moved to one side, waiting her turn at the water. She craved a drink more than anything, but she did not care to get too close to her rescuers. In the back of her mind she hoped against hope they would simply ride on and leave her. But that feeble hope was dashed by the look the leader gave her, his hungry eyes roving over her as might the eyes of a starving man over a sumptuous feast.

The man hooked his thick thumbs in his gun belts and strutted over. His eyes glittered. Planting his dirty boots in front of her, he scratched his beard, then said, "I am Vargas, little one."

Maria kept her face as blank as a slate board, but her stomach churned. She had heard of this Vargas, a despicable killer whose list of innocent victims was longer than both her arms lined end to end. "You sound as if I should know the name," she said politely.

Vargas thumped his chest with a brawny fist. "Everyone in Mexico has heard of me."

"I haven't," Maria said, hoping he would believe her lie. She was not about to feed his exaggerated sense of self-importance and have him take the liberties he was sure to take if she showed that she was the least bit afraid of him. Her best bet was to keep him off guard and perhaps to persuade him to take her to safety despite himself.

"You must have," Vargas said. "From Ciudad Juarez to Cancun, from Mazatlan to Tampico, they know the name of Vargas."

"All I know is that you are the man who has saved me from the Apaches, and for that I am very grateful," Maria said, keeping her voice level. She had an idea that might result in her being reunited with her parents, and she put it into effect by saying, "My father will pay you a king's ransom for returning me to him—more money than you can carry in both your saddlebags."

The man's greed was as obvious as the oversize nose on his face. "Your father is rich?"

"Yes."

"What is his name?"

Maria took a few seconds to think. If she made up any old name, he might suspect she was lying. But if she revealed the truth, there was a chance Vargas had heard of her father and would take her at her word. "Martin Gonzalez."

"I know of him," Vargas said. "He has one of the largest ranches in all of Mexico. And his vaqueros are some of the toughest."

"Will you take me to my parents?" Maria asked. "I give you my word that you will be handsomely paid."

The bandit pursed his coarse lips and stroked his greasy mustache. "I must talk this over with my men."

"What is there to talk about?" Maria asked. "Surely you can use the money? And all you have to do to earn it is take me to my parents. There will be no questions asked, I assure you."

"We must talk," Vargas said and moved over to where the other bandits were huddled.

Maria took the opportunity to go to the spring. The water had been muddied by the men and the horses, but she had to quench her thirst. Cupping her right hand, she sipped gingerly, swirling the water to dilute the mud before each mouthful. The water tasted awful but it was cool and refreshing. When a shadow fell across her, Maria had to bite her lip. She refused to show her fear of the five bandits who approached her.

"Have you made up your minds?" she asked casually.

"We have," Vargas said. "And you will not like our decision."

Maria put both hands on the ground and tensed her leg muscles. If they intended to violate her, she would resist them to her dying breath. "What is it?"

Vargas grinned, exposing a black gap where four of his upper front teeth had once been. "We all know of your father. A few times we tried to steal some of his cattle but his damned vaqueros drove us off. He would not hesitate to kill any of us if we were to somehow fall into his hands. So it would be stupid of us to take you to him."

"But I give you my word—"

The bandit leader laughed. "Your word is not enough for us to risk our lives"—he paused and scratched under an armpit—"especially when we happen to also know that your father is the brother of Col. Jose Gonzalez. The good colonel has been after us for many years. He has vowed to spit on our graves one day."

Bloodbath

"But you can take me directly to our ranch," Maria said. "That way you will go nowhere near the presidio."

"I think not," Vargas said, leering. "Why do you think I have lasted as long as I have? I never take chances I do not need to take. And I do not need to take you back to your dear parents to make lots of money."

"What do you mean?"

"There are men who will pay many thousands of dollars for a pretty senorita like you."

"What kind of men?" Maria said, resisting the panic that threatened to engulf her. She knew the answer but she asked anyway to buy precious time. She had to think her way out of the terrible predicament her rash action had placed her in.

"The Comanches to the north pay in silver and gold for women such as you," Vargas said. "And there are slavers on the coast who would drool at the sight of such a lovely young thing."

Forgetting herself, Maria said, "What manner of pig are you that you would subject a woman to such a fate? Have you no decency at all?"

The leader's beady eyes glittered like the tips of bullets. "It is not very smart, senorita, for you to insult the man who has your life in the palm of his hand. But I will forgive you this time. You are too valuable to us for me to slap you around. However, a word to the wise. I will not be so merciful if you make the same mistake again."

Some of the bandits laughed the hard, brittle laughter of men who did not know the meaning of compassion or honor. In that brief moment when they were distracted, Maria made her move. She darted between two of them and ran to the

95

nearest horse. The heavy tread of footsteps behind her lent speed to her feet.

Maria vaulted into the saddle on the fly. A hand clutched at her leg but she jabbed her heels into the bay and it broke into a gallop, heading back down the dry wash. Curses and shouts laced the air.

At the first bend, Maria looked back. The bandits were all after her, Vargas in the lead, two of them riding double. She flailed the reins to get her mount to go faster but it was already going as fast as it could.

Once around the corner, Maria reined to the right and went up the sharp incline. Loose dirt and stones spewed out from the animal's flying hooves. For a few seconds she fretted that the horse would lose its footing and crash to the bottom of the wash, but it made it up and out. She rode across the flatland, bearing eastward since in that direction she would find the nearest towns and settlements.

When next Maria checked over a shoulder, she was appalled to see Vargas gaining on her. His big black horse moved over the ground as if it had wings. She regretted that she had not taken it instead of the one she was on. Vargas, being the bandit leader, would naturally have kept the best horse of the many they had stolen.

Maria settled down to a grim race for her life and honor. For several years she had sought out the company of handsome men as discreetly as a maiden should, dating and dancing to her heart's content. It flattered her to no end that she was sought after by some of the most eligible bachelors in Mexico. But at no time during her many dates had Maria allowed any man to claim the prize that would be her husband's by virtue of their marriage.

The horse she rode seemed to sense her fear and exhibited stamina she would not have guessed that it possessed. Yet even though the animal gave its all, Vargas caught her.

It happened as Maria was going flat out on a baked stretch of earth, her hair whipping in the wind, her dress hiked well above her knees. She heard the growing drum of hooves as the bandit's horse came closer and closer.

"No!" Maria cried and tried again to spur her horse into performing a miracle. Something snatched at her dress and she shifted to see Vargas a few yards from her, bent forward so he could grab hold. She yanked her leg forward, causing him to miss. Cursing, he pulled nearer, his outstretched fingers inches away.

Frantically Maria cut to the left, gaining ground, but not for long. Vargas wore a mask of fury as he gradually overtook her.

Maria suddenly realized there was a rifle in the saddle boot. She gripped the stock and heaved, but not quite hard enough to pull the rifle all the way out. Before she could heave a second time, Vargas was at her side. His hand flicked out and closed on the rifle. He pulled, but she clung on until he was pulling so hard his face had turned red. Then she let go.

It was a clever ruse, and more was the pity that it failed to work. Vargas was flung backward and almost fell. With the tenacity of a gorilla clinging to a tree limb, he clung to his saddle horn and righted himself. And now he had the rifle.

Maria hunched low, resuming her flight. She dreaded being shot, but no bullets rang out. The only possible reason chilled her to the core. The bandits did not want damaged goods. They wanted her in one piece so she would fetch a higher price when she was sold to the Comanches or the slavers.

For the third time Vargas narrowed the gap; he was right beside her. Maria swung her fist in vain. All he did was cackle as if at the antics of a child.

"Stupid bitch!" he said.

Maria saw the Winchester barrel sweep toward her head but there was nothing she could do. She had no time to duck, no time to turn her horse, no time to do anything other than brace herself a fraction of an instant before the barrel slammed into her temple.

Pinwheels of light exploded before Maria's eyes. Pain such as she had never known lanced her from ear to ear. A black cloud engulfed her, smothering the pinwheels, and the last sensation she experienced before the cloud claimed her consciousness was that of flying through the air.

The dust raised by over 200 horses was enough to choke the air for half a mile behind the long column of soldiers and pack animals.

At the forefront rode Col. Jose Gonzalez in full dress uniform, a glistening saber at his side, a shiny new pistol in his holster. He rode a white pacer that put the other horses to shame with its high-spirited gait. His saddle, unlike the plain rigs of the troopers, was adorned with enough silver to start a mine. He was a glorified image of spit

Bloodbath

and polish, and Jose Gonzalez reveled in it.

The column was hours out of Janos, on a winding road that would bring them in due course to the Sierra Madre Mountains, well north of the Janos to Hermosillo road.

Capt. Mora, one of the six junior officers who followed the colonel, had noticed that fact. "Permission to speak, Colonel."

"Granted," Gonzalez said, his gaze never leaving the six point men a quarter of a mile out.

"Since your brother was attacked at Adobe Wells, shouldn't we be going there?"

"And why would we do that, pray tell?"

"To track the red devils. To rescue your niece."

"Believe me, Captain, saving dear Maria is uppermost on my mind," Gonzalez said. "But you heard Pvt. Batres. My brother and Capt. Filisola are hot on the heels of the Apaches. We would be duplicating their efforts, would we not, if we went to Adobe Wells? It would be a great waste of time." The colonel paused to flick a speck of dirt from his sleeve. "No, Captain, to rescue my niece we must think like the savages who stole her. We must answer certain questions. Where will they go now that they have her? Which route will they take to reach their destination?"

"Do you have the answers, sir?"

"Of course," Gonzalez said matter-of-factly. "Since we are dealing with renegades, we know they will make for either the Dragoon or the Chiricahua Mountains north of the border. And knowing Apaches as I do, I believe that they will take the most direct route."

"Which would be, sir?"

"North from Adobe Wells to Roca Pass. Over

the pass to the east slope, and then north to Caliente Springs. From there it is only a day's journey to the border and safety."

Mora was a highly competent officer. He had spent over an hour trying to deduce the route the Apaches would take. After carefully considering all the options, all the known trails and even those rarely used, he still had not been able to form a mental map of the course the renegades would follow. But the colonel laid it out as plainly as if he had been told by those they chased, and Capt. Mora knew his superior was right.

"You never cease to astound me, sir," Mora said. "How is it that you can think like Apaches? Are you part Chiricahua or Mescalero yourself?"

The colonel chuckled. "God forbid that I should have any red blood in my veins. I don't think like them, Captain. I outthink them. You too must learn to outwit your enemies if you ever hope to advance high in rank."

"I try, sir, but I have a long way to go before I will be as good as you are."

Col. Gonzalez liked it when his men flattered him, so long as the flattery was sincere and truthful. Grinning, he motioned, and his four captains drew alongside him. "Soon we will come to a parting of the ways. At the next junction we will split the command into four parts."

"Is it advisable to split our forces, sir?" Capt. Bonita asked.

"We are up against five Apaches, not five hundred," Gonzalez replied. "You, Bonita, will take forty men and head due west as far as Roca Pass. If you do not strike the Apaches' trail, you will head straight for Caliente Springs. That is

Bloodbath

where we will all regroup, come what may."

"As you wish, sir," Bonita said.

Gonzalez jabbed a finger at another captain. "You, Ortega, will swing twenty miles to the east in case I am wrong and the Apaches we are after are really Lipans who are making for Texas. Ride due north until you are east of Caliente Springs. If you strike their sign, you are to send men to notify me at once while you try to bring them to bay."

"Yes, Colonel."

"Capt. Hildago, you will take your patrol toward Agua Prieta. The same applies to you."

"Sir!"

"I will take the remaining men and strike out directly for Caliente Springs, with Capt. Mora as my adjutant. No matter what happens, gentlemen, I expect to see the command reunited within two days. Are there any questions?"

No one had any, but Mora did have a comment to make. "I see what you are doing, sir. You're launching a four-pronged pincer movement with the idea of catching the Apaches between two of the prongs."

"There's hope for you yet, Mora," Gonzalez said, and they all shared a chuckle. "In case that plan fails, I fully intend to reach Calienta Springs before they do and set up a suitable reception."

"We will have to push the men harder than we ever have before to get to the Springs in time," Capt. Mora said.

"We are going to ride straight through," Gonzalez said. "Spread the word among those who will go with us. And inform the packmaster that he must urge the pack animals on as swiftly as he can. I cannot afford to slacken my pace to suit his beasts of burden."

"Right away, Colonel."

"One more thing," Gonzalez said, and he slowed to give each of them a meaningful stare. "No matter which one of us stumbles on the Apaches first, one consideration is paramount. You must do whatever is necessary to save Maria. Do I make myself perfectly clear?"

The junior officers answered in the affirmative, and Capt. Mora went to turn his mount.

"Apparently I must elaborate," Gonzalez said curtly. He verified that none of the soldiers in the main column were close enough to overhear, then lowered his voice anyway. "These words are for your ears alone. In the event that one of us gets close enough to the Apaches to open fire on them, but not close enough to stop them, I expect whoever is in charge to do the right thing by my niece."

Mora and the other captains shared puzzled expressions. "Sir?" Mora said.

"You must not let the Apaches take her. No matter what."

"I'm not certain that I understand," Mora said.

"Are you deaf? If it appears to you that the Apaches are going to escape with Maria, you are to deprive them of their captive."

Again Mora and the rest exchanged looks, only this time they were much more grim. It was Mora who had the courage to speak the words uppermost on all their minds. "You can't be saying what we think you are saying, Colonel."

"Must I spell it out for you? If we are unable

to save her, we must spare her the ordeal of being a captive for the rest of her days." Eloquent appeal lit his eyes. "If you are left with no other option, put a bullet through her brain."

Chapter Eight

Clay Taggart lost the trail an hour before sunset. The wily bandits had been able to reach the Baked Plain, as the locals called it, a seemingly endless expanse of arid earth which had been baked rock hard by the scorching sun. The ground was so hard that men on foot left no tracks whatsoever, while men on horseback left tiny scratches and nicks if they left any sign at all.

Only the very best of trackers could trail anyone across the Baked Plain. And although Clay had learned enough about the craft from the Apaches to qualify him as competent, he wasn't as good as they were and he knew it.

Consequently, on reaching the plain, Clay was forced to scour every yard of ground carefully for the telltale signs so crucial to his finding Maria Gonzalez. Even as he sweated and toiled, losing precious time with every minute of delay, his conscience waged a tug-of-war with his common sense.

It was stupid of him to be going to all this trouble, Clay kept telling himself. Maria meant nothing to him. She was a captive, not a friend. He would be better off if he turned around, rejoined the Chiricahuas, and let her suffer the fate in store for her. What did it matter to him?

But Clay forged on anyway. He couldn't say why exactly. It was not as if he cared for her, not as if she meant anything to him. He preferred to think that he was going to so much trouble on her behalf simply because the bandits had gotten the better of him by whisking her away right out from under his very nose, and he did not like for anyone to get the better of him.

Then Clay lost the trail. He was several miles into the Baked Plain when the signs petered out. There were no more faint hoof marks, no more scratches to go by. He made a circuit of the immediate area and still found nothing. It was as if the bandits had vanished off the face of the planet.

But Clay knew better. He suspected that the bandits had thought to wrap the hooves of their mounts in strips cut from a blanket, leaving him with no idea which way the vermin were headed, and the sun was fast dipping toward the western horizon.

Clay had a decision to make. Should he do what was best and go back? Or should he try to outguess the bastards? Since the bandits had stuck to a straight easterly course since entering the Baked Plain, the logical conclusion was that they were still bearing due east.

But if that were the case, Clay reflected, why had they all of a sudden bothered to wrap the hooves of their horses? He figured it was because they had changed direction and didn't want possible pursuers to know the fact. If so, which way should he go?

West was out of the question. Clay had come from the west and would have seen them. By the same token, the northwest and southwest were not likely choices as both would take the bandits back toward the mountains and the Apaches. Since Clay doubted the bandits were still heading due east, that left him two directions to pick from: the southeast or the northeast.

Clay picked northeast. Miles to the southeast lay the presidio of Janos, and no bandit in his right mind would go anywhere near it. He put the horse into a distance-eating lope, watching the animal's shadow steadily lengthen as the sun sank steadily lower.

In due course darkness claimed the Baked Plain. Clay navigated by the stars, a trick he had learned long before he had met Delgadito. All a man had to do was locate the North Star, which was done by first locating the Big Dipper. The two stars that formed the side of the dipper farthest from the handle always pointed at the North Star.

Once the sun was gone, a cool breeze swept across the plain, bringing welcome relief. Clay stopped often to look and listen. The bandits might have stopped for the night and he didn't care to blunder into them.

It was almost midnight when Clay spied a flickering dot of light far ahead. He closed his eyes and rubbed them, then looked again to confirm his weary senses weren't playing a trick on him. The light was still there.

About the same time Clay noticed brush and weeds on either side of him. He had crossed the plain.

Circling to the south, Clay came up on the fire as stealthily as a mountain lion stalking prey. He dismounted and ground hitched the horse several hundred yards off so the animal wouldn't catch the scent of other horses and whinny to them.

Clay held the Winchester in his left hand as he padded through the brush, avoiding spots where twigs lay and trying not to step on brittle rocks that would crack and alert the bandits. He was some ways from the camp when their gruff laughter and lusty curses reached his ears. He did not hear Maria's voice.

Going faster, Clay was soon close enough to distinguish bulky shapes seated around the fire. He flattened and snaked to a cactus. Peeking past the spines, he counted five outlaws. The big, bearded leader was talking.

"We'll go to Monterrey next. I know a man there who would be all too happy to take Ramon's place. Those stinking Apaches!"

"Poor Ramon," another said. "Just this morning he was joking about the time we strangled that old prospector and the bastard's mule kicked me when I tried to open the packs on its back."

"I remember," a third man said. "We killed that worthless old fool for nothing. All he had on him were a few pesos and sacks of fool's gold."

"The desert scrambled his brains," a fourth said. "It does that, you know."

Clay shut out their banter and scanned the area. He saw their horses tethered in a row to the north of the fire. Saddles and packs had been deposited at random. Maria Gonzalez was nowhere to be seen, making Clay wonder if the cutthroats had already had their fun and disposed of her. Then his ears pricked up with interested.

"I hope it does not take us long to contact the Comanches," Vargas said. "With the gold we get for the girl, we will have a grand time in Monterrey."

"I can't wait to be in a city again," a lean bandit said. "I am going to buy a different whore every day the whole time we are there."

"You and your whores. One of these times a whore will leave you with a memento of her affection, and we will have to listen to you moan every time you take a leak."

Their rowdy laugher was Clay's cue to crawl closer. He had no cover, but it couldn't be helped. Holding his face low to the ground, he sought Maria in every shadow.

"Speaking of women," one of the cutthroats said, "what about the bitch? Comanches don't care if the merchandise is damaged a little. Why don't we all take turns?"

"I agree with Louis," the lean one said. "It has been weeks since we treated ourselves. How about it, Vargas?"

Clay recognized the name. Vargas's fame had spread north of the border after his gang waylaid a wagon train bound for Tucson and made off with every last valuable the pioneers possessed. Lawmen had chased Vargas to Mexico, but did not go beyond their jurisdiction.

Bloodbath

"I suppose we should," Vargas said. "To be fair, we will draw twigs. Whoever gets the short one wins the honor of tasting her nectar first, eh?"

"Who holds the twigs?" the lean one asked.

"I will."

By the looks the bandits gave their leader, it was clear they trusted him about as far as they could heave him. But such was the fear Vargas instilled in them that not one complained.

Clay watched Louis stand and walk to what appeared to be a pile of blankets and tack. Louis bent down to grab hold of something, and when the bandit straightened, the blankets uncoiled to reveal Maria Gonzalez. The firelight showed dried blood plastered to the right side of her head. Her hair was matted and slick. She moved awkwardly when Louis pushed her toward his companions.

"Move it, damn you," Louis grumbled.

Stumbling, Maria shuffled over and stood swaying near Vargas. Her clothes were in the same deplorable state as her head, coated with dirt and grime as well as being badly torn and wrinkled.

"Ah, my little flower," Vargas said sarcastically, "did you enjoy your nap?"

Maria gazed blankly at him. Like a striking serpent, Vargas swung, viciously smacking her across the cheek. Maria staggered, but did not go down. Her cheek was split, blood trickling to her chin.

"The next time I ask you a question, bitch," Vargas said, "you will answer me or I will knock out a few of your teeth to teach you better manners."

The bandits thought their leader was hilarious.

"Now did you enjoy your nap?" Vargas repeated.

"Yes."

The word was croaked, barely audible to Clay as he crept ever nearer.

"Excellent," the bandit leader said, taunting her. "We have decided that we want to be entertained tonight. Can you guess who will provide the entertainment?"

Maria marshaled the energy to spin and flee, but she hardly took two steps when Louis pounced and held her in place despite her feeble attempts to break loose.

Vargas winked at the others. "A man would think she was playing hard to get. Or maybe she is the shy type."

"Perhaps she is a virgin," another said.

Clay saw the wicked delight that came over the five of them. They were all so intent on their victim that he had been able to crawl within 15 feet of the fire and still not been spotted. He drew the rifle close to his chest and curled his thumb around the hammer. Soon, he would make his play.

"If only she was!" Vargas declared. "It has been ages since I had a virgin. They are getting harder to find the older I become."

"That is because the only women you bed anymore are whores," Louis said. "If a man wants a virgin, he must take up religion and attend church. Virgins like to kneel in pews, not sit in bars."

"Since when have you become such a philosopher?" Vargas asked.

"It is a fact of life," Louis insisted. "A woman

Bloodbath

does not spend all her free time at a cantina if she wants to remain a virgin."

"Who cares?" the skinny one said. "Why are we doing all this talking when she's ripe for the plucking? Someone find twigs for us to use."

Clay had no forewarning. One of the bandits suddenly stood and came straight toward him, scouring the ground for twigs. In another few seconds the man would spot him. Under the circumstances there was only one thing he could do, and he did it.

Sweeping onto his knees, Clay centered the Winchester on the bandit's chest and stroked the trigger. The slug flung the man back and he crashed down on top of the fire, sending flames and a shower of sparkling embers in all directions. For several heartbeats the startled bandits sat there gaping.

Clay took prompt advantage of their reaction. Pivoting, he vented a war whoop while aiming at a second man; then he fired. The impact lifted the bandit clean off the ground and left him sprawled on his back with a red hole oozing gore in the middle of his forehead.

Belatedly, the bandits roused to life, all three palming pistols and blazing wildly away.

Bullets whizzed by overhead as Clay rose and ran to the right. He fired on the fly, working the lever smoothly. His shots thudded into a saddle vacated an instant before by Louis.

The bandits were scrambling toward their horses, shooting as they retreated, their shots poorly aimed.

Clay imagined that they thought there was more than one warrior. He lent credence to their assumption by continuing to move in a circle and firing every few steps.

Vargas leaped up, knocking Maria aside. Endowed with the longest stride, he reached the string first. There he vaulted onto the biggest animal without missing a beat, tore at the tether rope, and wheeled into the night. He did not stay to help his friends.

A clear shot at Louis's back presented itself. Clay could no more pass it up than he could stop breathing. But as he fired, the third and last bandit cut around behind Louis to get to one of the horses. The slug shattered the man's spine and he fell to the dirt.

Meanwhile, Louis dashed around to the far side of a chestnut and swiftly swung astride the animal. He had the presence of mind to bend low as he turned the horse to flee in the wake of the bandit leader.

The Winchester lever made a rasping noise as Clay worked it forward and back. He tried to get a bead on either rider, but they were lost amidst the black veil of nocturnal gloom before he could shoot.

In baffled annoyance Clay jerked the rifle down. He made sure the hoofbeats receded into the distance before he darted to the young woman's side and lightly clasped her elbow. She stared at him without a glimmer of emotion.

"Maria, it's Clay. What did they do to you? How badly are you hurt?"

"Clay?" she said. On seeing his face she took a step back in terror and wailed. "You're the White Apache! You want to rape me, just like they did!"

Bloodbath

Again Clay had no warning. Maria flew into him with her nails hooked to claw out his eyes. It was all he could do to bring his arms up to protect himself. In her panic she screeched like a wildcat and kicked at his shins.

"Stop!" Clay shouted, but to no avail. He backed up under her onslaught, trying his utmost not to hurt her, but at the same time not willing to let her harm him. Her features were those of a person gone berserk. She didn't seem to care that he was heavily armed and the only weapons she had were her fingernails.

Clay felt a searing pain in his forearm. He knew that he couldn't hold her at bay much longer. For her own sake he had to stop her, and with that end in mind he gripped the Winchester in both hands in preparation for ramming the stock into her stomach. To his consternation, Maria abruptly halted, gave a little cry, and keeled over.

Vargas was certain that a dozen savages had swooped down on his band. He raced blindly on into the moonless night, whipping his reins and using the rowels on his large spurs to their full advantage. Unlike American cowboys who filed the sharp points of their rowels down in order not to hurt their animals, Vargas had used a file to sharpen his. When he applied his spurs, the horse knew it.

Soon Vargas became aware that someone was after him. He glanced over his shoulder and spied a dim figure galloping a score of yards behind him.

An Apache! Vargas thought. He was not about to let the red demon carve his heart out. Pointing his pistol, he tried to aim but it was impossible to hold the six-gun steady. He fired anyway, thinking he might at least make the Apache break off the pursuit.

"Vargas! It's Louis! For God's sake, don't shoot!"

Most men would have been embarrassed by the mistake, but not Vargas. "Why the hell didn't you let me know sooner? "I could have killed you!" He slowed to allow Louis to catch up. "Is there no one else? What about Alfredo?"

"Shot dead near the horses."

"Damn those Apache bastards all to hell!" Vargas raged.

"Maybe you should not yell so loud," Louis said. "They might still be after us."

The reminder scared Vargas into knuckling down to a long, hard ride. Neither of them spoke again until, five miles later, they stopped on top of a small knoll to give their horses a breather.

"I don't see any sign of them," Louis said.

"Idiot. Haven't you learned anything?" Vargas said. "A man never sees Apaches until it is too late. Look at what just happened. We were nearly wiped out before we knew what hit us by fifteen or twenty of those sons of bitches."

Louis gave a little cough. "I don't think there were quite that many, amigo."

"How many then?"

"One."

Vargas did not suffer fools gladly. He gave the smaller man the sort of look that had caused many a fool to cringe, but Louis refused to be intimidated.

"Think about it. Count the number of shots that

were fired. I would say it was one warrior with a rifle."

"You're loco," Vargas said. Yet when he reviewed the attack, he had to admit that there might well have been a lone attacker. The insight flushed him with pulsating rage. He disliked being made a fool of even more than he disliked fools.

"So where do we go from here?" Louis said. "Monterrey or another city? We need to find three or four good men now, not just one."

"First we need to get the bitch back."

Louis's neck had a way of cracking like a whip when he snapped his head around. "You have a poor sense of humor."

"Who's joking? If there's only one Apache, as you believe, then it shouldn't be too hard for us to hunt him down and pay him back for all the grief he has caused us," Vargas said. "And must I remind you that now more than ever we need whatever the Comanches will give us for the girl?"

"But this is an Apache we're talking about. Who cares if there is just one? He killed three of us in twice as many seconds. Let him have the girl and good riddance."

"I am going to get her back." Vargas refused to change his mind. Once he came to a decision, he stuck to it as tenaciously as glue. "You can come or you can ride off and hear about your cowardice in every cantina between here and the border."

"You wouldn't."

Vargas rode to the bottom of the knoll without answering. Humiliation was sometimes as potent as fear in persuading others to do something against their will.

In a minute Vargas heard the sound of Louis's horse as it overtook his. He pretended not to notice and refrained from smiling smugly so as not to antagonize Louis. The truth was, Vargas needed to have Louis along. He had small hope of slaying the Apache on his own.

"You are going back there right this minute?" the other bandito asked.

"Yes."

"Can't it wait until morning?"

"Think about it," Vargas said. "He thinks that he has driven us off. The last thing he would expect is for us to return before daybreak. With the bitch hurt, he might even stay at our camp until first light. We cannot let the chance go by."

"I hope you know what you are doing."

"Don't I always?" Vargas said, although both of them were fully aware his long string of successful robberies, murders, and raids was due more to an incredible run of luck than to any genius on his part.

The jeopardy into which they were placing themselves made both men somber. They held their mounts to a brisk walk, slowing when Vargas figured they had less than a mile to go. Among a stand of mesquite they finally halted and dismounted.

"It is not too late to change our minds," Louis said.

"You can stay here with the horses if you want," Vargas said scornfully, although inwardly he hoped Louis would do no such thing. Hunkering down, he removed his spurs and placed them in his saddlebags for safekeeping. He looked at

Bloodbath

Louis and was glad to see his example being followed.

In the distance, gleaming palely, was the campfire. Vargas headed toward it, hunched low, trying to move quietly. He stopped frequently. Deep within him a tiny voice screamed that he should turn around and give up his insane notion before he paid for his stupidity with his life. But he had always been a proud man and he was not about to shame himself by turning yellow at the last minute. This unexpected bravery surprised him immensely. He was at a loss to explain it.

A gulch 200 yards from the camp gave Vargas a spot to lie low while the fire did the same. He sought signs of the Apache and the woman, and he thought he saw one of them moving about. That would be the savage, he reasoned.

Louis said nothing and did nothing but stare bleakly off into the darkness as if his certain death was imminent. He started when Vargas touched him and motioned for them to go on.

Vargas fed a round into the chamber of his rifle. Slipping from bush to bush, he closed on his prey. He expected to hear the crash of a gun but apparently the Apache believed himself to be safe. It was a fatal mistake, Vargas thought.

The bandito leader and Louis knelt behind a wide bush 30 feet from where their friends lay in the dust. Vargas took a deep breath, nodded at Louis, reared upright, and charged.

In concert, they aimed their rifles. In concert, they opened fire, shooting as rapidly as they could, emptying their weapons as they closed.

Nothing could have survived their volley of hot lead.

And nothing did.

Chapter Nine

"We should have gone with him," Cuchillo Negro said. When none of his fellow Chiricahuas responded to his statement, he said it again, adding, "He has stood by us through our hard times. We should stand by him."

The band had stopped for a rest at a small tank only Apaches knew about. It resembled a stone cistern and was halfway up the slope of a boulder-strewn hill situated in the middle of a parched stretch of landscape.

Fiero had just finished drinking. He made the sort of a sound a buffalo might make while cavorting in a wallow, then said, "I do not understand this strange concern of yours. So what if he has helped us? We have helped him. We owe him nothing."

"And he is a grown man, not a boy," Ponce said. "Men live or die by their own decisions, and it was his decision to go after the bandits."

None of the other warriors saw fit to comment on the fact that the youngest of them, whose claim to full manhood could be measured in moons instead of winters, was lecturing them on the nature of being a man.

Delgadito spoke next. "We have long prided ourselves on being able to do as we want when we want. We answer to no one but ourselves. Whether in times of peace or war, a warrior can walk the path that he sees fit to walk."

"That is part of our problem," Cuchillo Negro said.

Now the others all looked at him, and Fiero asked, "Since when is being free to do as one pleases a problem?"

"When it results in an entire people being conquered by another," Cuchillo Negro said. "Look at what happened to our people in our war with the white-eyes. They were able to beat us in our own land, in the mountains and deserts we have claimed as ours for more winters than anyone can remember. And why? Did they know our own land better than we did? No. Are the white-eyes better fighters than we are? No. They beat us because they have learned how to live and fight together, to put all their minds to one purpose and to see that purpose through to the end. That is the secret of the white-eyes. That is why they have been able to beat everyone who opposes them."

No one else commented. Secretly, they were all surprised. None of them had ever heard Cuchillo Negro say so much at one time. And he wasn't done.

"We have leaders, yes, but we do not make their will our will in all respects. As Fiero is so proud of pointing out, we do as we please. We go every which way. And because we do not know how to work together, we were weaker than the whites. It is not right to say that they shamed us by beating us. We shamed ourselves because our own weakness beat us."

"What would you have us do?" Fiero asked. "Become like the whites-eyes?"

"Yes."

"The heat has affected your brain," Ponce said.

"Because I want to see our people shake off the shackles of the Americans and go on living as we have always lived?" Cuchillo Negro said. "I tell you here and now that unless we learn to mold our wills to a single cause, as the white-eyes do, our people will never know true freedom again."

At this Delgadito's eyes narrowed. "So this is why you watch over Lickoyee-shis-inday like a mother dog over a pup. You hope he will teach us the secret of being of one mind in all things so that we can turn the white-eyes's strength against them and reclaim our land as our own?"

"A wise man learns from his enemies as well as his friends," Cuchillo Negro said.

Fiero uttered his customary snort. "We do not need to think like whites to defeat them. They conquered us because they have more men and more guns. All we need to rise up against them are more warriors who think as we do and more guns. It's as simple as that."

Cuchillo Negro rose and stepped into the sunlight. He knew it would be a waste of his time to argue the point with the firebrand, and he doubted very much that Ponce would come around to his way of thinking either. But he had hoped Delgadito would agree since, of them all, Delgadito was the deepest thinker. Maybe Delgadito did, he mused, but was unwilling to admit it.

As the warrior idly surveyed the horizon he glimpsed a pinpoint flash of light, then another and another until there were dozens, like stars sparkling low in the daytime sky. Only Cuchillo Negro knew better. At a low call from him, the others came into the open.

"*Nakai-yes*," Delgadito said. "Soldiers. Many soldiers."

"They must be after us," Ponce said.

"If so, they will never catch us," Fiero said. "The day I cannot elude a whole army of Mexicans is the day I take up basket weaving."

Delgadito had been studying the position of the pinpoints. "It is not our trail they follow," he said. "They are too far to the east."

"It does not matter," Cuchillo Negro said. "They are coming straight toward this hill. We must not be here when they arrive."

"So what if we are?" Fiero said. "The *Nakai-yes* have the senses of rocks. They will never spot us."

"But their horses might pick up our scent," Cuchillo Negro said. "And the four of us would be no match for as many soldiers as there appear to be. I, for one, do not intend to throw my life away needlessly."

Hefting his Winchester, Cuchillo Negro jogged to the bottom of the hill and swung to the northwest. They would be at Caliente Springs by morning; there they would rest up during the day. If Clay did not show by sunrise, the others would want to press on across the border. And he knew of no way to dissuade them.

Clay had better show up on time or he would find himself on his own.

The gurgle of rippling water brought Maria Gonzalez back to consciousness. She lay still, trying to recall where she was and what she had been doing last.

In a rush of harrowing memories, Maria remembered being taken captive by Apaches, fleeing with the bandits, trying to escape, and being hit by Vargas. She also recollected the attack on the camp and confronting the White Apache. Then what had happened?

"You can open your eyes if you wish. I have coffee ready."

Maria realized that there was indeed a strong scent of boiling brew in the air. The delicious odor made her stomach growl and her mouth water. She opened her eyes and saw the White Apache seated across a small fire from her, his elbows propped on his knees.

"I treated your wound with a poultice."

Reaching up, Maria found a crude compress on her head. She probed with her fingertips, assuring herself that she wasn't bleeding any longer. Encouraged, she went to sit up but was overcome by a wave of dizziness, not to mention intense pain in her back and her temple.

"I'd take it easy if I were you," Clay said. "You've been out for the most of the day but I doubt you're well enough yet to travel."

"Half the day?" Maria said. A glance to the west

123

confirmed the time. It also showed that they were in the shade afforded by a grove of cottonwoods on the bank of a narrow, shallow river. "Where are we? What happened to your four friends? And what do you plan to do with me now?"

Clay leaned back and arched an eyebrow at her. "You're welcome."

"What?"

"Where I hail from, it's polite to thank folks who have pulled your fat out of the fire. If I hadn't come along when I did, those bandits would have had their way with you and sold you to Comanches."

It would never have occurred to Maria that a man reputed to be a bloodthirsty renegade could have his feelings hurt by a failure to show proper gratitude, but that was the impression she had. "My apologies," she said stiffly. "I do thank you for what you've done, but I can't help but suspect you had an ulterior motive. You want me for yourself."

Clay bent forward to pour coffee into a battered tin cup he had found in the saddlebags of the bandit who had tried to bushwhack him. "I stole you from your parents. That makes you my responsibility."

"I thought as much," Maria said in contempt. "You did not go to so much trouble on my behalf."

"As for your questions," Clay said, "we're camped next to the Rio de Bavisque. My four friends, as you call them, wanted nothing more to do with you. And my plan is the same as it's always been. I aim to take you to Arizona Territory."

Bloodbath

Maria closed her eyes, despondent. It seemed her grueling ordeal would never end. She was losing hope that she would ever see her mother and father again. Twisting her head, she looked down at herself and felt tears well up. Her clothes were in the worst shape of any clothing she had ever worn, and she was no better off. Dust clung to her from head to toe. Dried blood clotted her hair and stuck to her tattered dress. She was in dire need of a bath. If she had the choice, she would have given anything to be back on the family hacienda attended by her devoted servants.

Clay Taggart noticed the senorita's sadness, but did not let on. Regret came over him, regret which he promptly shrugged off. He had no business feeling sorry for her. A true Apache wouldn't, and he was trying to pattern his behavior and attitudes after those of his Chiricahua pards.

He carried the cup around the fire and handed it to her without saying a word. Her eyes lingered on him as he took his seat.

"May I ask you a question?" Maria asked.

"I'd be surprised if you didn't."

Cradling the cup gingerly, Maria took a few short sips and sighed as the hot brew washed down her throat. "I would very much like to know why you are the way you are. Once you mentioned getting revenge on someone who had wronged you. Does it have something to do with why you have taken up with Apaches?"

"You want my life's story, in other words," Clay said dryly. "Sorry, ma'am. I happen to believe that a man's past is his own business and no one else's. If you're digging for something that would get me to change my mind about you, you're plumb out of luck."

"It must be nice to know everything," Maria said, acid in her voice.

"I wouldn't last very long if I was an idiot," Clay said, leaning on an elbow and taking a sip from another cup. It had been a while since last he had enjoyed coffee and he had forgotten how well it hit the spot after a long day in the saddle.

"I would guess you have a lot of hatred pent up inside of you," Maria said.

"Why? Because I kidnapped lovely women?"

"Because you will let no one get close to you except your Apache friends. It is as if you have built a wall around yourself so that none can see into your soul."

Clay said nothing. He had to hand it to her though. For such a young filly, she was terribly shrewd—and desperate. She would do anything to keep from being taken across the border, and he made a mental note to watch her closely from then on out.

Weakness put a stop to Maria's chatter. She finished half the cup, then set it aside and lay back down. She needed her wits more than ever, and they were denied her by the severe loss of blood she had suffered. A good night's sleep would restore some of her strength but it was too early to doze off and she did not want to anyway.

Horses nickered nearby. Maria turned her head and saw three tied to cottonwoods. She toyed with the idea of sneaking to them after dark, but doubted her nerves would be equal to the occasion.

Bloodbath

As if the White Apache could read her mind, he said, "Don't be getting any silly notions, senorita. We're miles from nowhere and it would be easy as pie for me to catch you again."

Clay slowly polished off the cup and refilled it. Coffee was a luxury he wasn't about to pass up. The Chirichuas had little use for it. They'd drink it on occasion, but they weren't addicted, like most whites. Delgadito's bunch even refrained from mescal and tizwin, hard drinks most Apaches favored.

As Clay drank, he thanked Lady Luck for smiling on him back at the bandito camp. He had intended to stay there the whole night through, but then had taken to thinking about the pair who slipped away. It wouldn't have been at all out of character for the murderous twosome to circle around and shoot him. So he had saddled three horses, loaded as many supplies as he could onto one, draped the woman over another, and ridden off.

He hadn't traveled more than a quarter of a mile when the night had rocked to rifle fire. The bandits had done just as he'd figured they would. He'd grinned, wishing he could have heard their lusty curses when they had aired their lungs over his absence.

Clay had given the bandits the slip, and he could relax until he was reunited with Delgadito. Well, not relax entirely, he mused, since he was in a region where bandits were as numerous as fleas on an old hound dog. Plus there was the threat of scalphunters, scum paid by the Sonoran government to exterminate any Apache caught south of the border. They earned their bounty by showing Apache scalps as proof of their performance. And the government didn't care if the scalps were those of warriors, women, or children. So long as they were Indian scalps, the scalphunters received their blood money.

Which had created a new problem in itself. Scalphunters were not notorious for being the most scrupulous of men. When Apaches were scarce, they took to killing any Indians they could find. Friendly tribes such as the Pimas and Maricopas lost many of their number who went off to hunt or fetch water or gather roots and were never seen again. It took a while for the friendly tribes to put two and two together, and henceforth they never went anywhere except in numbers sufficient to deter the greedy scalphunters.

A faint sound brought Clay's reverie to an end. It was so faint that for a full ten seconds he wondered if he had really heard the dull thud of a hoof. Then he heard another and knew someone was sneaking up on their campsite from the southeast.

Rolling to his feet with the Winchester in hand, Clay peered through the cottonwoods and spied several riders approaching. He had been careless! He had gone and built the fire too big, a mistake no true Apache would ever make. The column of smoke was probably visible for miles.

Clay had to think fast. There was no time to put out the fire, hide the charred limbs, load up the gear, and get the hell out of there.

Maria, he saw, had fallen asleep. He took a step closer to awaken her, but changed his mind. It might have been a blessing in disguise.

Bloodbath

Quickly Clay melted into the cottonwoods and knelt in a clump of brush. The four riders were close enough to note details. Their dusty uniforms revealed they were soldiers. Since there were too few to constitute a patrol, Clay deduced they had been sent on ahead of a large column.

As Clay watched the troopers warily approach the camp, he studied them as would an Apache, noting which one was the most alert, which appeared the most dangerous, which would be the easiest to slay. He stopped thinking like a white rancher and instead thought like a Chiricahua warrior.

When the patrol drew rein a few dozen feet from Maria, it was not Clay Taggart, rancher, who raised a rifle to his shoulder, but Lickoyee-shis-inday, Apache.

A corporal led the patrol. He had spotted Maria, and it was clear that he did not know what to make of the situation. To find a woman sleeping peacefully by herself in the middle of nowhere was not a common occurrence.

The corporal whispered orders. All four soldiers dismounted. Fanning out, they converged on the camp, moving slowly, raking the undergrowth for evidence of hostiles.

Clay let them come nearer. He was so well hidden that they would have to be right on top of the bush to notice him and he was not going to let them get that close. Since the corporal was the one the others would rely on in a crisis, he targeted the corporal first, centering the sights squarely on the man's torso.

But as so often happened in life, the unexpected reared its head in the shapely form of Maria

Gonzalez, who choose that particular moment to snap out of her slumber. Whether she heard or sensed the soldiers, she sat bolt upright, and on seeing them she screeched in Spanish, "Look out! The White Apache is here!"

The corporal dropped into a crouch just as Clay applied pressure to the trigger and the bullet took off the man's hat instead of his head.

The bush hid the muzzle flash but the four soldiers had a good idea of where the shot had come from and they cut loose with military precision.

Slugs zipped past Clay, clipping the bush, nicking an arm. He tracked the corporal as the man rose and ran to Maria. She started to rise, her hand reaching for the corporal's. Clay drilled the man as their fingers touched.

Maria's scream rivaled the din of the gunfire.

Shifting, Clay shot a second trooper. The last two elected to preserve their lives and sprinted toward their horses. Clay elevated the Winchester.

To a Chiricahua, horses were animals. No more, no less. They were not viewed as pets, never regarded with affection. More often than not, horses were eaten. Every boy knew that to become attached to one was the height of folly.

Clay Taggart had been reared differently. As a rancher, he had ridden horses daily and worked with them from dawn until dusk. There had been several he had liked immensely.

But since he had joined with the Apache, Clay had learned to harbor no such sentiments. Horses were horses, and in this instance, when they were the means his enemies would use to bring even more enemies, they had to be dealt with accordingly. In rapid order he dropped three of them with slugs through the head. The fourth, however, heard its fellows whinny as they fell, and it fled.

The two soldiers were left stranded. One darted in among the trees. The other whirled and fired at random, a man whose reason had been replaced by riveting fear.

Working the lever, Clay aimed and fired. He had such confidence in his marksmanship that he didn't wait to see if the man went down, but leaped to his feet and raced after the soldier who had fled.

Crashing in the growth ahead told Clay which direction to take. Like a black-tailed buck he bounded through the cottonwoods at a speed no white man or Mexican could equal. But the soldier was fleeing for his life, and fright was known to lend strength and speed to ordinary limbs. It took over a minute of hard running before Clay spied his quarry. The soldier also spied him.

Clay had to throw himself to the ground as the trooper's carbine cracked. Flipping to the right, he rose and went to fire but the man had already whirled and run off. Too many trees were between them.

Swinging to the north, Clay pumped his legs, taking a course parallel to that of the soldier. He had gone over 50 feet when he realized the cottonwoods had fallen completely silent. Instantly he stopped and crouched.

The soldier was crafty. He had gone to ground in the hope of flushing the White Apache out.

It wouldn't be that easy, Clay reflected as he

stalked to a tree with low limbs. Climbing ten feet, he paused. From there he had a bird's-eye view of the area where he had last seen the trooper. The man lay in high grass, facing toward the camp, the carbine tucked to his shoulder.

Clay braced the barrel of his Winchester against the trunk, held the bead steady for a three count, and fired. The slug penetrated the rear of the soldier's head and exploded out from his forehead in a rain of flesh and brains.

Jumping down, Clay made for the camp. He didn't know how close the main column was and had to consider the likelihood that the shots had been heard. It was imperative he get the woman out of there.

There was only one problem.

When Clay emerged from the vegetation at the edge of clearing, he discovered that Maria Gonzalez was gone.

Chapter Ten

Their camp had been established for the night. The horses had been tethered and perimeter sentries posted.

Col. Jose Gonzalez and Capt. Mora were seated by one of several fires, drinking coffee and discussing the route they would take the next day, when one of the sentries yelled that a horse was fast approaching. Moments later a riderless horse burst into the encampment and halted, its sides heaving.

Soldiers leaped to their feet, carbines at the ready. The colonel and his aide rushed to the horse and Capt. Mora seized the reins. But there was little chance of the animal running off. It was too exhausted to lift a leg.

"This is one of ours," Mora said, smacking the regulation-issue saddle. "But whose?"

"I recognize the blaze on its chest," Col. Gonzalez said. "This is the mount issued to

Cpl. Hildago. He was sent ahead to see how close we are to the Rio de Bavisque. He must have been ambushed, either by bandits or the Apaches we are after." Spinning, the colonel rasped out orders. "Break camp immediately! Douse those fires! I want every man mounted and ready to ride in five minutes."

A flurry of activity ensued as every man rushed to obey. Unlike lazier commanders, who were content to spend all their time behind their desk while their men languished in barracks, Col. Gonzalez drilled his troops daily. There was no more efficient unit in all of Mexico, which the men proved by being in the saddle in the time stipulated.

Col. Gonzalez swung into the leather, rose in the stirrups, and whipped his arm forward. Capt. Mora issued the order to move out, and 40 horses were rapidly brought to a canter.

They wound northward along a dusty ribbon. Mora stared at the inky sky and said, "Would it not have been advisable to have waited until morning, Colonel? We can not see a thing in this soup."

"The missing troopers are all that matter. Some of them might still be alive," Gonzalez answered. "Always put the welfare of your men above all other considerations, Captain. It is the earmark of a genuine leader."

"I wholeheartedly agree, sir. But how will we locate them if we cannot track them?"

"We will trust in Providence. If nothing else, even if we do not find any trace of them, we will have done our duty. Our men will respect us for that. And never forget that earning the respect

134

of those you command is the first step toward earning their loyalty."

From then on, they knuckled down to the business of riding. In due time they bore to the northwest. It was over two hours later that a band of trees materialized in the distance. And where there were trees, Capt. Mora knew, there was usually water.

"The river," he said.

"Look," Col. Gonzalez said, pointing.

A mile or more away glittered a yellowish-orange finger of flame.

"We have them!" Mora said.

At that very moment other eyes were on the same fire. Martin Gonzalez reined up on a ridge to the west and pushed his sombrero back on his head. "Could it be? Would they be careless enough to make a fire with us on their trail?"

"Maybe they think that we have given up," Capt. Filisola said. "Or it might not be them at all."

"Maybe we should send Pedro and Sgt. Amat on ahead to scout out the situation," Martin said. "We don't want to ride into a trap."

"It's best if we all stick together," Filisola said. "If it is the Apaches, with a little luck we can surround them. And for that we'll need every man we have." He assumed the lead and carefully picked his way downward. Truth to tell, he was elated by the sight of that distant camp. It inspired his flagging hope. As hour after hour had gone by with no sign of the savages or their captive, he'd had to confront the very real prospect that he would never set eyes on the lovely senorita again. A pall of gloom had seized his soul and refused to let go.

Now, Capt. Filisola felt like a man reborn. Perhaps there was a prayer after all. Perhaps he would get to have the wonderful pleasure of Maria Gonzalez's company, not once but many times. And if she wound up being as enamored of him as he was of her, well, who was to say what might happen?

Filisola grinned. Maybe it was time he gave serious thought to giving up the bachelor life. His looks and charm would not last forever. And there were much worse fates than marrying into one of the richest families in Mexico.

Martin Gonzalez was equally elated. He had about given his precious daughter up as lost to him forever, a calamity he did not know if he could endure.

Martin often thought of a friend whose own daughter had been abducted. Later the friend had learned that she had been made the wife of a notorious Apache. Through intermediaries, the friend had tired to buy her, but the Apache refused. The friend had offered to trade for her, to give as many guns and horses and whatever else the Apache might want. Still the Apache declined.

In despair the poor father had put the barrel of a cocked pistol in his mouth and pulled the trigger. The very next day a messenger had arrived, sent by the warrior to say that he had changed his mind and was willing to trade. When the Apache found out the father had killed himself, the warrior slew the daughter because he did not want a wife who came from a bloodline of weaklings.

Many times since Maria had been taken, Martin

wondered how well he would hold up if he failed to save her. His grief might tempt him to commit the same act as his friend. But he couldn't. Theresa would need him more than ever.

Capt. Filisola swung to the northwest to approach the fire through the cottonwoods. He had the men dismount and advance in skirmish order. They had gone 50 yards when he realized the camp was on the other side of the Rio de Bavisque.

Meanwhile, Col. Jose Gonzalez led his own men in a skirmish line from the southeast. He strode at the center of the line, his pistol in one hand, his saber in the other. The fire, he saw, had burned low. Near it, he could just make out the outlines of men asleep.

The colonel whispered an order to Capt. Mora, which was relayed down the line in both directions. The ends turned inward, making a horseshoe formation, which resulted in the camp being ringed on three sides. Advancing silently, their every nerve on edge, the troopers closed in on their age-old enemies.

On the north bank, Sgt. Amat turned to Capt. Filisola and whispered, "I see men moving in the dark beyond the camp, sir. Many men."

Filisola squinted and saw figures creeping toward the river. It excited him. His racing mind hit on the obvious conclusion: the White Apache and those with him had joined up with a larger band of renegades, and the savages knew that a small party was trying to sneak up on them.

"Who are they?" Martin Gonzalez asked. "What do we do?"

Before Filisola could answer, one of the nervous troopers in his patrol spotted the figures, jumped to the same conclusion he had, and did what any other man might have done under the same circumstances. Without thinking, the trooper aimed his carbine and fired. His shot inadvertently served as the signal for all the soldiers and vaqueros on the north bank to open fire. Few had clear targets but they fired anyway. When dealing with Apaches, every man there had learned long ago that those who lived longest were those quickest on the trigger.

The initial volley tore into the soldiers moving toward the dwindling fire. Col. Gonzalez and his men were concentrating on the prone forms near it. The first inkling they had that there was anyone else within ten miles of the spot came when slugs tore through the air around them. Two troopers fell, one howling in agony at the burning lead in his gut.

Col. Gonzalez reacted as would any seasoned commander. He saw the muzzle flashes on the other side of the Rio de Bavisque and bellowed, "More Apaches! Fire at will!" Then he proceeded to blast away with his pistol.

All along the line, soldiers crouched or knelt and shot round after round at the north bank while those on the north bank did the same at the south bank.

Men fell on both sides. Here a trooper toppled over, screaming. There a vaquero went down, cursing Apaches with his drying breath.

It soon became apparent to Capt. Filisola that he was greatly outnumbered. He rose to order a retreat and felt a searing pang in his right shoulder. The impact spun him around, and in the act of spinning, his left boot caught in the bush he had been behind. His leg started to sweep out from under him. Frantically the captain tried to right himself but all he succeeded in doing was throwing himself more off balance, and the next thing he knew, he was tumbling down the bank to the water's edge.

Filisola heard bullets thud into the earth beside him. He was completely exposed and lying there helpless in the open. Propping his hands under him, he scrambled for cover.

On the south bank, Col. Gonzalez had seen a figure spill from the undergrowth. He couldn't credit the testimony of his own eyes when he saw that it was someone in uniform. For a few moments he thought it might be an Apache. Then the figure glanced toward the south side of the river, and despite the distance and the dark he knew immediately who it was.

Striding into the clearing, Col. Gonzalez raised his saber on high and thundered in the voice that could be heard by everyone, "Cease firing! Cease firing this moment, idiots! Cease firing!"

Capt. Filisola, in the act of clawing up the bank, froze, too stupefied to speak. The awful truth dawned and he wanted to burrow into the ground and cover himself with a ton of dirt so no one would ever find him.

The sight of the colonel shocked both sides into lowering their weapons. Martin ran down into the river and stood in the shallows, gaping. "Brother! I am so sorry! We thought that you and your men were Apaches."

"The same applies to us," Col. Gonzalez called

out. "Come across and we will tend the wounded."
He turned to issue directions to his own men
and noticed the forms that he had assumed were
slumbering Apaches. To his consternation, they
were dead soldiers, members of the patrol sent
out with Cpl. Hildago.

Others were soon arranged in rows beside
them. The battle had resulted in the deaths
of four men, one of them a vaquero, and the
wounding of seven others. Most of the wounds
were minor.

Capt. Filisola sat glumly while his shoulder
was being bandaged. He was convinced that his
military career was at an end. The colonel was
bound to report the incident. Filisola wouldn't
be surprised if a military tribunal was called and
he found himself on trial. Given the nature of
his offense—firing on his superior officer—he'd
be lucky if he got off easy with a life sentence.

Suddenly the moment Filisola dreaded was
upon him. The colonel walked over and shooed
all those within earshot away. "How bad is it?"

"I lost very little blood, sir," Filisola said. "In
three weeks I should be as good as new."

The colonel sat down on the same log. "Well,"
he said softly, "we sure made a mess of things,
didn't we? This is the first blemish on my record.
I wouldn't be surprised if I'm recalled to Mexico
City to answer an official inquiry."

"I will be right there with you," Capt. Filisola
said. Impulsively, he gripped his superior's arm.
"Please forgive my stupidity, Colonel. I should
have stopped my men from firing until I had
determined who we were shooting at."

"I made the same blunder," Col. Gonzalez said.

Bloodbath

"And while we were justified to a degree by the circumstances, those fat generals in Mexico City who have never served a day in the field can hardly be expected to appreciate the position we were in."

"True, unfortunately, sir," Filisola said, more depressed than ever.

"So perhaps it is best if they never have to sit in judgment on us," Col. Gonzalez said quietly.

"What are you saying?"

"Since we thought we were fighting Apaches, that is how our reports should read," the colonel said. "We came on an Apache camp we presumed to be deserted and were ambushed."

It would not have shocked Vicente Filisola more had the Pope decreed that the Bible was nothing more than a collection of old fables. "You are saying we should lie, sir?" he asked in a stunned whisper.

"I'm saying that sometimes a soldier must do that which is most expedient, not only on the field of battle, but in dealing with those higher in rank who are not in a position to understand the underlying facts of a particular case."

"Yes, sir," Filisola said, not entirely convinced. A lie by any other name was still a lie in his book.

Col. Gonzalez was a shrewd judge of men. He would not have risen so far if he were not. "What would you have us do, my good Captain? Ruin both of our careers over a mutual blunder? Our duty is first and foremost to our country and the people of Mexico, but would either be served by the scandal that would result? No, on all counts. It would be a shame for you to have your head put on the public chopping block so soon after your promotion." Sighing, the colonel rose and went to leave.

"What promotion?" Filisola asked.

"Didn't I tell you?" Col. Gonzalez said casually. "For being clever enough to figure out that the Apaches were going to attack my brother's party and the courage you displayed in rushing to his aid, I decided a promotion was in order. Before leaving the fort, I sent a dispatch to Hermosillo. In it, I informed them that you were the recipient of a field promotion to the rank of major." He stretched, then took another stride.

"Colonel," Filisola said, overcome with gratitude.

"Yes, Major?"

"I agree that it would ill serve our country for us to be punished for a simple mistake. But what about the men, sir? They will tell stories—"

"Show me a man with any brains who will stand on a rooftop and shout to the world that he is an idiot," Col. Gonzalez said. "As far as we are concerned, the only ears that matter are those in Mexico City. And in my capacity as Commander, I can guarantee that the only reports that will cross their desks are those we submit and that which Maj. Mora is required to file. But you need not worry about him. We just had a talk, and he is as pleased with his new promotion as you are. Trust me. I have been at this much longer than you have."

"I trust you with my life, Colonel."

Col. Gonzalez smiled and walked off. A little adroit maneuvering and he had turned a potential disaster into two promotions and added to his sterling record. The account he planned to submit would make it clear that were it not for his brilliance, the Apaches would have overwhelmed his unit.

The colonel thought of the shocked look on the captain's face at the suggestion they should lie. That was always the way with the young ones. They were too idealistic for their own good. They had yet to learn that, in the dog-eat-dog world into which they had been born, the biggest bones went to those dogs willing to fight for what was theirs.

And Col. Jose Gonzalez was too fond of being at the head of the pack to settle for anything less.

Half a mile to the east, four stocky, bronzed figures stood under the starlit sky waiting to see if the gunfire would resume.

"We must investigate," Cuchillo Negro said. "Clay might need our help."

"He can take care of himself," Ponce said.

They had been traveling fast and hard ever since they had spotted the soldiers earlier. So it had come as a considerable surprise when the sounds of the battle had risen to their ears— sounds that told them more soldiers were to the west of their position.

"This country crawls with *Nakai-yes*," Delgadito said. "If it is not bandits we run into, it is soldiers. The longer we remain, the bigger the risk we run."

"Risks are the spice of life," Fiero said. "For once I agree with Cuchillo Negro. We should go see what all the shooting was about. Even if Lickoyee-shis-inday is not involved, there might be Mexicans to kill, plunder to take."

"You never can turn your back on a good fight," Delgadito said. "And I was only mentioning the risk, not using it as an excuse to keep from doing what must be done. We will go."

Spreading out, the quartet flowed over the ground like living wraiths, making no more noise than the passage of the wind itself. In practically no time they were among cottonwoods, and they slowed down to get their bearings. Through the trees came the murmur of many men and the sound of many horses.

Fiero, as was his habit, moved into the lead. When battle loomed, he liked to be first into the fray. From cover to cover he flitted until he saw several fires and dozens of soldiers moving about, engaged in various tasks.

For more years than either side could remember, Apaches and Mexicans had despised one another. The Mexicans claimed it was because Apaches were bloodthirsty demons who thrived on war, which was true to a degree. The Apaches claimed it was because the Mexican government had continued the Spanish practice of enslaving Apaches to work in mines and killing them for bounty. Neither had any compunctions about killing the other.

So as Fiero sank onto his stomach and made like an eel, he had one idea uppermost on his mind: How many Mexicans could he slay and still get away?

Cuchillo Negro was only interested in learning whether Clay was safe. He rated Lickoyee-shisinday as invaluable to the Chiricahuas and did not want anything to happen to him.

Bloodbath

Delgadito was also concerned but his reason was not the same. He needed Clay Taggart to help rebuild his band so that one day he could again rise to a position of leadership.

Of the four, only Ponce saw no sense in the peril they were courting. The Apache creed was to kill without being killed, and to that end, warriors went to extraordinary lengths when going into battle to make sure there was always a means of retreat if the worst should happen. In this instance, though, they weren't bothering to scout the area, to check all the avenues of approach, to assess the strength of their enemies. They were rushing blindly in, and Ponce, for one, was most displeased.

Not Fiero. A rare grin tugged at the corners of his mouth, as it always did when the time came to spill blood. He stopped behind a small bush, pulled his knife, and pried the bush loose at the roots. Replacing the knife, he held the bush in front of his face and went on.

Every Apache boy had to master the silent stalk. Fiero had been an adept pupil, and among his elders it had long been acknowledged that he was one of the best warriors who had ever worn a Chiricahua breechcloth. His only weakness was his headstrong nature. Too many times he allowed his lust for battle to cloud his judgment.

In this case, as Fiero inched nearer to the bustling camp, as his keen eyes roved among the soldiers and animals, he pondered how he might inflict the most possible damage. There were too many troopers for a frontal attack, and the horses would be so well guarded that stealing a few or running them all off would be next to impossible.

Then Fiero saw the officers, three of them. Long ago he had learned to pick out the leaders by the fancy braids—ribbons and insignia, as the *Nakai-yes* called them—that officers wore. Here were several ripe for the plucking.

The trio sat on a log beside a fire near the trees. Another man was with them. He had a beard and wore a sombrero, and Fiero remembered him as being with the carriage that day on the road to Janos and again at Adobe Wells, trying to prevent the senorita from being taken captive. He must be her father, Fiero guessed. Which meant the soldiers were there to track them down and rescue the woman.

Fiero stopped when one of the younger officers idly gazed toward him. He resumed crawling once no one was looking.

Based on which man wore the most braids and commanded the most attention, Fiero picked the individual in charge. That was the one he decided to kill.

It took over an hour for Fiero to get within 30 feet of the perimeter. He saw bodies of slain soldiers laid out, then covered with blankets, and he wondered who had killed them. Had Clay been there, as Cuchillo Negro suspected?

A long time passed before the camp quieted down. The soldiers fixed their supper and sat up late, talking and drinking coffee. Guards were posted, eight of them spaced at regular intervals. Two more were assigned to safeguard the horses.

Fiero raised his chin from his forearm only after most of the troopers had turned in. The younger officers yawned frequently, but made no move to go to sleep. They appeared content to listen to their commander and the bearded man babble on and on.

Fiero had no such desire. He was not going to lie there all night. Bracing the bush against a clump of grass, he grasped his rifle in both hands, wedged the stock tight to his shoulder, and trained the barrel on the Mexican with the most insignia. The man was laughing as Fiero touched his finger to the trigger.

Chapter Eleven

The Chiricahuas were not the only ones who heard the din of the aborted battle.

Clay Taggart reined up sharply and twisted in the saddle. He had ridden about a mile south from the campsite with Maria's horse and the pack animal in tow.

The crackle of gunfire puzzled Clay. A good judge of distance, he knew that the gunfire came from the vicinity of the abandoned camp. But he was at a loss to explain it.

The only possibility that made any sense was that the rest of the patrol had arrived on the scene and tangled with Delgadito and company, who must have shown up after he'd left. Yet even that scenario was highly unlikely since Delgadito wasn't fool enough to tangle with a large patrol unless the odds were stacked in his favor, and from the sound of things half the Mexican army was involved.

Clay shrugged and rode on. He was too far away to be of any help even if Delgadito were involved, and he had a pressing matter of his own to deal with, namely recapturing Maria Gonzalez.

He had to hand it to her. She had more grit than he had suspected, and she was almighty clever, to boot. While he had been occupied with the four soldiers, she had fled, but not just in any direction. She had waded into the Rio de Bavisque and hurried off, sticking to the middle of the river, where no one could track her.

Clay had been stumped for a minute, unable to decide which way to go. Maria could have gone north or south. But the latter seemed his best bet since it would take her closer to civilization instead of back toward the Sierra Madre Mountains.

After the shooting died down, Clay clucked his horse into motion and continued searching. Finding Maria in the dark with no tracks to go by was akin to finding the proverbial needle in a haystack, but he was not about to give up. Not because he wanted her as his captive so much as he was concerned for her safety. The wilderness was no place for a green snip of a woman who wouldn't stand a chance if she ran into any of the many beasts, both animal and otherwise, that roamed the vast untamed region.

The notion that he might care enough to be bothered about her welfare disturbed Clay. It went against all his Apache learning to give a hoot for a captive. A warrior was expected to steel his heart to his enemies, and technically Maria was an enemy of the Chiricahuas.

Maybe the problem, Clay reflected, was that he

wasn't as much of an Apache as he liked to think. Maybe the values of his white upbringing were too deeply ingrained for him to become just like a full-blooded warrior. Maybe, when all was said and done, he was just kidding himself.

The snap of a twig off to the right brought Clay out of his pensive state. Reining up, he listened, but heard nothing. Nor was there any movement in the brush bordering the river. Maria might be crouched 20 feet away and he would never know it.

In recent months Clay had learned that to survive in the wild a man had to rely on more than logic and common sense. Often intuition played a hand in whether someone lived or died. A man might be approaching a narrow draw and get a bad feeling about the place, or be riding along and have an uneasy feeling that he was being watched by hostile eyes. Those who failed to heed such feelings sometimes paid a fatal price.

Now a feeling came over Clay, not one of impending danger but a conviction that Maria was indeed hidden in that patch of brush and that if he went on by he would never find her. Acting on the impulse, he wheeled his horse and jabbed his heels. The animal snorted as it pounded up the bank and barreled into the vegetation.

Clay rode a score of yards, but flushed nothing. He slowed down and was turning to go back when a slim shape exploded from concealment less than five feet away. Releasing the lead rope, Clay gave chase. He saw her pale face when she glanced back and heard her cry of dismay.

Bending low, Clay pulled alongside of Maria and tried to grab her arm. She veered aside. He narrowed the gap again, but this time when he learned over, he shoved off and tackled her on the fly. They tumbled, winding up with her on top of him.

"I won't let you take me!" Maria said, swinging her small fists. Tears welled in her eyes at the thought of being recaptured after all the trouble she had gone to. She had pushed herself to the point of collapse. All her muscles ached. And in order to travel faster, she had removed her shoes back at the camp. Consequently, her feet were caked with mud and badly cut from the sharp stones on the river bottom and the thorny brush.

Maria had been congratulating herself on her escape when she'd heard a horse splashing down the river. Bolting into the brush, she had squatted, confident the White Apache would be unable to find her. But he had.

Clay Taggart had a frenzied wildcat on his hands. He seized her wrists and heaved to his feet, nearly losing an eye when she lunged, her nails raking his cheek and drawing blood. "Calm down, damn it," he said. "I'm not about to hurt you."

"I won't go! I won't!" Maria said, kicking at his shins.

"You don't have a choice," Clay said. He winced when pain shot up his right leg. "It's for your own good. You wouldn't last two days out here by yourself."

One moment, Maria was struggling and kicking. The next, she collapsed, falling against him, her tears turning into a torrent as all that had happened since her abduction finally took its belated toll. She had tried to be strong for as long as she could. Having her hopes dashed was the last straw.

Clay held her loosely, not quite sure what he should do. Half of him wanted to hold her and assure her that she would be just fine; the other half wanted to slap her around and tell her to quit being such a baby. He did neither. Instead, he waited while she cried herself out.

"You fit to ride now?"

Maria nodded dumbly and permitted him to lead her to his horse. She was thrown into the saddle and the horse was led to the river. There Taggart transferred her to the mount she had been riding before. She heard him urge her to hang on tight, but she didn't care whether she stayed on or not.

Life was too ridiculous for words, Maria decided. What had she done to deserve such misery? How could there be a loving God, as the priests claimed, if people were allowed to suffer so? Did it mean there wasn't a God? Or did it simply mean that God gave men the will to be good or evil as they chose and it had simply been her misfortune to fall into the clutches of the wickedest of all?

Maria was too dazed to think much. She half wished she would die right then and there to spare herself further grief. Life seemed pointless. She would never see her mother and father again, never see their hacienda. So many things she had taken for granted would be denied her forever.

Clay Taggart glanced back when his captive gave a stifled sob. He was going to tell her to be quiet, but suspected his harsh words would make her cry harder.

Bloodbath

The strip of brush along the river was too thick to suit Clay. He was constantly detouring around thickets and briars. Swinging to the west, he entered a line of trees. Far to the north lay Caliente Springs, where he was supposed to rendezvous with the Chiricahuas. He figured he would have to go even farther west in order to avoid whoever had done all the shooting; then he'd circle around to Caliente Springs.

For long minutes they heard nothing but night sounds: The chirp of crickets, the hoot of owls, and the squeak of a bat. All of a sudden, though, the woodland became as silent as a tomb.

Halting, Clay fingered his Winchester. Such profound quiet was unnatural. Predators were near, either animal or human.

The creak and jingle of tack told Clay which. He spotted riders moving along the Rio de Bavisque, five or six of them in all. He could not make out much detail, but he knew they weren't Apaches. The riders were 70 yards away, so there was a very small risk of being discovered.

Clay went on once the men were out of sight, but the woods did not come back to life, as they should have. He was extra vigilant from then on, so he heard the next batch of riders long before he saw them.

There were five, heading south to the west of the trees. Clay saw that they would pass within 15 feet of where he sat, so he moved among a cluster of willows. Maria was slumped over, her long tresses hiding her features. He was glad that she wasn't more alert or she might have yelled to attract them.

Their dusty uniforms stood out against the

backdrop of night. Now Clay had part of the answer, and it was an answer he didn't like. How many more groups of soldiers were in the area? And who were they after?

The second bunch had gone by and Clay was raising his reins to go on when that which he had suspected would happen did. Maria had seen the troopers and raised her voice loud enough to be heard clear down in Mexico City.

"Soldiers! Soldiers! Help me! The White Apache has taken me captive!"

Cursing, Clay fled, hauling hard on the lead rope. Coarse shouts confirmed the soldiers were in pursuit. Clay skirted a log and dashed between two willows. To the rear a carbine blasted and the slug bit into the willow on the left.

Clay was in a tight spot. Outrunning the soldiers was a hopeless proposition, what with him being slowed down by the other two horses. Nor would it be smart to make a stand. In addition to being outnumbered, he never knew when Maria might turn on him to keep him distracted so the troopers could finish him off.

Another complication reared its ugly head when from the northeast a man shouted in Spanish, "This is Maj. Filisola! We are on our way, Sergeant!"

Soldiers were all over the place. Clay cut to the northwest, pushing the horses as best he could. The crack of branches and the thud of hooves warned him the first bunch of soldiers were getting too close for comfort.

Shifting, Clay banged a shot at a vague target and was rewarded by a yelp of agony and the crash of a body hitting the ground.

Bloodbath

Striking northward again, Clay sought to outdistance the rest, but it was as he had thought it would be: they gained rapidly. And all the time, bearing down on him from the northeast, came the major and more troopers. He had to trust in luck and pray the soldiers would lose interest if he could give them the slip.

Unknown to Clay Taggart, Maj. Vicente Filisola was not about to ever lose interest. Not only was he anxious to save the senorita of his dreams; he was eager to avenge the death of a man he had looked up to as the best military mind in the Mexican Army.

Col. Jose Gonzalez had been shot smack between the eyes by an Apache lurking in the dark. He had died instantly, his mouth slack, his tongue lolling. The colonel had resembled a poled ox more than a distinguished commander.

The camp had been in an uproar. Enraged troopers had rushed every which way, seeking targets that weren't there. Filisola and Mora had rallied the panicked men and organized a thorough search of the immediate vicinity, but found no trace of the shooter.

There had been that one shot, no more. The two majors agreed that it had to have been the work of Apaches, who had melted into the night as silently as they had come.

But Filisola was not to be so easily thwarted. As senior officer, he had ordered a sweep of the area for miles around, with the goal of flushing the Apaches into the open. Deep down, he'd doubted it would produce results. Then, to his fierce delight, he had heard the sweet voice of the colonel's niece. Nothing short of death would stop him from saving her. In the bargain he would put an end to the depredations of the White Apache.

Clay Taggart had no idea he was up against four dozen vengeful soldiers spread out over a five miles radius. To him they were ordinary troopers, and ordinary troopers more often than not would run from Apaches rather than tangle with them.

From the sound of things, Clay knew the two groups would soon be on him. He had to act and act fast or he would never get revenge on Miles Gillett. He would die there by the Rio de Bavisque, unmourned, his body left to rot.

It would be a cold day in hell before Clay let that happen. Plunging into thick timber, he drew rein and jumped down. Maria attempted to resist when he grasped her wrist and pulled, but she was too weak and weary to keep from falling next to him. Streaking out his Bowie, he cut the lead rope to both her horse and the packhorse.

"What are you—" Maria said.

"Quiet," Clay said and rapped her lightly on the skull with the hilt of his knife. She slumped, dazed but not unconscious. Quickly Clay seized the bridle to her animal and swung it around so that it faced due south. Then he positioned the packhorse, facing it due north. The animals stood tail to tail.

Sheathing the Bowie, Clay stepped between the horses. He gave her mount a resounding smack on the rump, pivoted, and did the same to the pack animals. They promptly snorted and sped off, making as much noise as a herd of buffalo.

Clay crouched beside Maria and gripped the reins to his horse so it wouldn't get it into its head to join the others. He watched the other animals break from the timber and listened to yells from the soldiers and the boom of guns.

Would they take the bait? That was the crucial question. Clay observed horsemen racing in both directions and heard someone shout orders.

Clay stayed put until the hoofbeats faded. His ruse had bought some time, but not much. It wouldn't be long before the soldiers caught the riderless horses and realized they had been duped.

Hooking an arm around Maria's slim waist, Clay slung her onto the saddle as if flinging a sack of grain. He held her up with one hand while mounting in back of her. Then he turned to the west and departed.

So far, so good, Clay thought. Maj. Filisola and his men were being led on a wild-goose chase. If he could reach the foothills, he'd lose them. He selected grassy tracts that muffled his animal's tread and shied from open spaces.

More shouting filled the air, from the southeast this time. More troopers were coming. Clay angled to the southwest. He rode half a mile without encountering another soldier. Evidently his quick thinking had bailed his hide out of the fire.

Presently Clay looped toward the northwest. His original destination was the same. Delgadito would be waiting for him at Caliente Springs.

Three shots broke the silence. Clay surmised it was a signal but he had no inkling for what. Coming on mesquite, he prodded his horse into a trot. Maria swayed, still woozy, her shoulders bumping his chest. He thought that he heard her mutter a few words.

By all rights Clay should have been a bundle of nerves. Clay Taggart, the rancher, would have been. But Clay Taggart, the White Apache, found himself thrilling to the challenge of outwitting a company of soldiers. He exercised caution as an Apache would, relying on the skills he had honed under Delgadito's tutelage.

Some minutes passed before the wind brought him the sounds of three more pistol shots, the same signal as before, only farther away.

Taggart barely slowed down. He was positive he had given the soldiers the slip. By his reckoning he was well to the northwest of the river and could slant to a more northerly heading anytime he wanted.

"Please let me go."

The soft appeal caught Clay off guard. "I thought you were out to the world."

"Please," Maria said. "This is my last chance. You are my only hope."

"Then you don't have any hope," Clay said testily and regretted being needlessly cruel.

"What manner of man are you? You have turned your back on everything you knew and sided with the bitter enemies of your people. You have killed many innocents. And now you would send my soul to a living hell. Why? What have I ever done to you?"

"You ask too damn many questions."

Maria felt more tears fill her eyes and blinked them away. The time for tears was past. She must use her wits as she had never used them before. Appealing to his greed had not worked because he was one of those rare men who did not value money. But perhaps appealing to his conscience would have the desired effect. Buried somewhere under that hard exterior must be a shred of compassion. There had to be!

"You told me that you loved a woman once."

"I don't care to talk about her," Clay snapped. The reminder seared a red-hot branding iron of remorse into his gut.

"It's not her I want to talk about. It's love," Maria said. "Any man who can love another can't be all bad. You must have some decency left inside of you. I'm appealing to that decency. I'm begging you to let me go before we rejoin the Apaches."

"I can't."

Maria turned, her face inches from his. "Why must you be so stubborn? Why do you always let your pride stand in the way of doing that which you know to be right?"

"Be quiet."

"I will not," Maria said, defying him. "Not when all I hold dear is at stake. Didn't you have a mother and a father? How can you tear me away from mine? My mother will go crazy with grief. My father will wither away little by little. And all because you are playing at being an Apache."

Clay resisted an urge to smack her. "I'm not playing. The Apaches are my pards."

"Maybe so, but the truth is that they are Apaches and you are not. No matter how long you live among them, no matter how many of their ways you adopt as your own, deep inside you will always be white."

"That's where you're wrong. Being an Apache is more than dressing as they do and living as they do. I could never expect you to understand because I reckon I don't know quite how to put it into words. It has to do with thinking like them, with knowing that you're at the bottom of the barrel and have nowhere to go but up."

"And that gives you the right to go around killing people as you see fit, senor? That gives you the right to kidnap women who have never done you any harm?"

Clay cocked his head to listen. It was a grave mistake to let her divert his attention when there might be soldiers within earshot but he could not bring himself to clip her on the jaw.

"Can't you answer me because you know that you are in the wrong?"

"Who's to say what's right and what's wrong anymore?" Clay said. "I figured that I knew once, and then my whole world was turned inside out. My woman turned on me. My friends turned on me. Even my government turned on me. And it taught me a valuable lesson."

"Which is?"

"That when a man has nothing to lose, he'll try anything. That it's every hombre for himself, and the devil take the hindmost."

"You can't really believe that?"

"I believe this," Clay said and patted his rifle. "I believe in the law of the gun. I believe in the old saying about an eye for an eye, a tooth for a tooth. I believe that making those who have wronged you pay is better than turning the other cheek like a Bible thumper."

"If that is true, then I pity you."

"Save your pity for yourself."

Maria faced around. "You have lost your soul to the devil, Clay Taggart. I would not want to be in your shoes when you are called to account."

The wind picked up, knifing down off the Sierra Madres to rustle the mesquite and stir Clay's long hair. He shut her words from his mind, refusing to give them any consideration. Maybe she was right, maybe she wasn't. But he had picked the trail he aimed to follow and he intended to play his hand out, come what may. No matter what else was said about the White Apache, no one would ever be able to accuse him of being a coward.

Clay reined the horse to the north, guided by the North Star. He would reach Caliente Springs by noon if he didn't run into more patrols. From there it would be a clear shot to the border and safety. He rose in the stirrups once more to make a final survey of the country behind him. Satisfied he had outstripped any pursuit, he goaded the horse to a gallop, never knowing that he was wrong.

Mere seconds after the sound of the White Apache's mount faded on the breeze, a bulky silhouette detached itself from the mesquite. It was Pedro the tracker, who had gone off by his own to find the Apaches who killed the brother of his boss. He had wanted to hunt alone rather than be burdened with noisy soldiers who didn't know the first thing about stalking at night. And it had paid off.

Pedro stared after the renegade a few moments, then wheeled his horse and rode hell for leather toward the camp. He knew where the White Apache was going, and he smiled to himself as he rode.

"We have you now, butcher."

Chapter Twelve

The desert was an inferno. A golden cauldron dominated the sky, scorching all life below. Plants drooped, withered by the heat. Animals were sheltered in their burrows or wherever they could find tiny patches of shade.

Across the parched landscape plodded the White Apache's stolen mount. In the saddle sagged Maria Gonzalez, her face baked red, her chin touching her chest. She would have fallen off long ago had the White Apache not lashed her wrists to the saddle horn and her ankles to the stirrups.

Clay himself walked, leading the animal by the reins. The blistering oven, which once would have melted him as a flame melted a candle, hardly fazed him at all. Where once he would have been caked with sweat from head to toe, the only concession his body made to the scalding temperature were a few beads of perspiration on his brow below his headband.

Caliente Springs lay less than half an hour away. Clay had pushed the horse to get there because he didn't care to be left behind by the rest of the band. Whether the animal lived or died was of no consequence to him; he'd butcher the carcass, eat what he could, and dry some of the flesh for later use, just as any Chiricahua warrior would.

For over an hour Clay had tramped on, looking neither right nor left, his mind in a turmoil that his face didn't show. As would any full-blooded warrior, he was becoming more and more adept at hiding his feelings, at keeping his features as impassive as stone so that his true emotions were known only to himself.

He was in conflict with himself. His white upbringing raged fiery war with the Apache ways he had adopted, and neither was able to gain the upper hand. The internal war boiled down to one burning issue. What was he to do with Maria Gonzalez? The white part of him wanted to let her go so she could be reunited with her family. The Apache part of him wanted to keep her as his wife, maybe the first of several he would take, provided he let her live along enough.

For two bits he would have been tempted to throttle her senseless. Her words of the night before had started the conflict, and no matter how he tried, he couldn't put it from his mind. Was he as she claimed, white? Or was he, as he believed, more like an Apache? Or did the truth lie somewhere in between?

Clay had wrestled with the problem for so long that he was tired of thinking. He absently stretched and swept the horizon on all sides, a precaution every Chiricahua learned to make as much of a habit as breathing.

A spiraling cloud of dust highlighted the southern horizon.

Clay's jaw muscles twitched. He had been careless. He had been deep in thought when he should have been keeping his eyes peeled.

The size of the cloud indicated a large party on horseback. It had be soldiers, either the same bunch he had tangled with at the river or a different one. They were riding hard, from the look of things, unusual for troopers in broad daylight—unless they were after someone.

Breaking into a trot, Clay yanked on the reins to get the horse to keep pace. Maria snapped awake and looked sluggishly around, then sagged again, too fatigued to care about anything other than the rest she craved.

For 15 minutes Clay rode northward. At last a ragged ridge appeared. Caliente Springs was located in a narrow gap near the summit. The springs were so remote that few Mexican or white travelers ever visited them although they were used regularly by Indians.

Clay had visited the site several times. On the other side of the ridge stretched miles of chaparral laced by thorny thickets. Once there, the band would elude the soldier with ease.

The brown ridge grew in size. A threadbare path meandered up toward the gap, curving among a field littered with boulders of every size, shape, and description. The gap was shrouded in shadow.

At the edge of the boulder field, Clay stopped.

Bloodbath

Swiftly, he cut Maria free and lowered her to the ground. She came back to life and glared at him.

"What are you up to now, Senor Taggart?

He knew why she called him by his given name rather than the one bestowed on him by Delgadito, but he refused to be taken in by her tricks, refused to see himself as more white than otherwise. He also refused to answer. Gripping her wrist, he walked her between a pair of towering boulders spaced barely wide enough apart for a rider to pass through. "Don't move," he said.

Clay coaxed the horse into the space. One arm draped around the animal's neck to reassure it, he suddenly lanced the Bowie into the animal's throat and wrenched mightily. Flesh sheared, blood spurted. The horse tried to buck but was too exhausted.

Gradually the mount weakened. The ground was soaked a bright red when Clay let go and rejoined Maria.

Snorting and swaying, the horse tried to back into the open but its front legs buckled. It sank down right there, blocking the trail. Blood caked its chest and forelegs.

"How could you?" Maria asked. "That was a sadistic thing to do. There was no reason to hurt the poor creature."

"Oh?" Clay pointed at the dust cloud, now much closer and much larger.

Marie was all too aware what the cloud meant and became deliriously excited by the idea she might soon be rescued. She figured out that Taggart had killed the horse to block the trail and give them more time to reach the top. The devil didn't miss a trick, she mused.

Clay was about to leave when he remembered the Henry. Stepping around the spreading pool of blood, he plucked it from the saddle boot. Then, with a rifle in either hand, he nudged the woman and they started to ascend.

High above them four pair of dark eagle eyes watched with interest.

"He will not make it in time," Delgadito said.

"He will if he lets go of the woman," Fiero said. "I would, were I in his moccasins."

Out on the flatland, six dust-choked riders galloped toward the ridge in advance of the main body of troopers and vaqueros. Among them rode Maj. Vicente Filisola, who should have ridden with the main column as would any other commanding officer. But he was too upset about Maria, too worried the Apaches would spirit her away. So with Pedro, Sgt. Amat, and three of his best riders, he had gone on ahead of the column to see if he could slow Maria's abductor down.

The tracker was the first to spy a patch of light blue on the ridge. "Captain! That is the color of the dress the senorita wore."

Filisola looked and his blood raced like lightning. "Faster, men!" he said. "We must not let that devil get over the ridge or we will never see her again!"

Clay saw the six riders sweeping toward him. In the distance was a growing knot of soldiers. He was hopelessly outnumbered, but not about to give up without a fight.

Apaches were more than a match for their longstanding rivals. Normally soldiers fled rather than fought. But this time the honor and life of a young woman was at stake. And it has been forever true that in the breast of the most callous of men often beats a soft heart for a fair maiden in distress.

So the soldiers arrived on the scene bent on vengeance for the beloved commanding officer they had lost and determined to save his precious niece at all costs.

Clay climbed as rapidly as his captive's condition allowed. She stumbled so often that he suspected she was trying to slow him down and hauled on her arm so hard it nearly popped out of the socket. "No tricks," he growled.

Maj. Filisola came to the beginning of the trail and fumed when he saw the dead horse blocking the way. Vaulting to the ground, he waved his saber. "Upward, men! Before she is lost to us!"

Getting a running start, Filisola flew toward the dead horse and sailed over it in a single leap. He went on without looking back. Let the others come as they may, he reflected. He was going to rescue Maria.

The major saw a flash of blue above him. Tilting his head back, he spotted Maria and her captor. An icy chill rippled down his spine at the mental picture of the violation that would occur if he failed her. "I'm coming, Senorita! Have hope!"

Maria Gonzalez heard and remembered the dashing young officer. She dug in her heels. "Let me go! Please!"

Clay turned a deaf ear to her plea. Jerking her arm violently, he climbed higher. A rifle cracked below them and a slug ricocheted off a boulder to their left.

Below, Maj. Filisola spun and frowned at the smoking rifle in Pedro's hands. "Are you loco? You might hit her by mistake."

"We must slow him down until the rest get here," the tracker replied. "You know as well as I do that, if he gets over the ridge, all is lost."

Clay came to an open grade. On either hand were jumbled boulders, a treacherous maze the woman was incapable of negotiating. He had no choice but to go straight up. "Move quickly if you value your life," he said, giving her a shove. They went only a few feet, however, when the air rang with gunfire. Bullets smacked into the earth all around them. He felt a stinging sensation in his calf, another on his shoulder.

Throwing Maria behind a boulder, Clay brought his Winchester to bear. His first shot toppled a soldier and drove the rest to cover. They replied with a barrage of lead that kept him pinned down.

And all the while, the main body of soldiers galloped nearer and nearer.

Clay was fit to be tied. He was close to the summit, but it might as well be on the moon. He could readily escape, but not dragging a woman along. Still, he refused to leave her.

Filisola and his small group of avengers slowly worked upward. Glancing back, he saw Martin Gonzalez and Maj. Mora. In another few moments the ridge would be swarming with dozens of soldiers. The White Apache's days of pillaging and plundering were almost over.

The object of the major's bloodlust realized the same fact. Clay looked down at the woman at his feet, and she met his gaze defiantly. She was no longer the timid girl he had snatched at

Adobe Wells. The crucible of hardship had forged a miraculous change.

"Leave me," Maria said. Her flagging spirit had been revitalized by the appearance of the soldiers. Instinctively she knew they were her last, best hope of escaping. Her moment of truth had arrived, and she was ready.

"Never," Clay said and leaned against the boulder to feed cartridges into his rifle. He didn't hear her move, but he abruptly sensed that she had, and pivoting, he was just in time to ward off a brutal blow that would have caved in his skull had it landed.

Maria stepped back, the big rock she clutched poised to strike again. "I'll die before I'll let you take me!"

"That's what you think," Clay said. Feinting a step to the right, he suckered her into swinging, and as the rock cleaved the air, he delivered a solid hit to her stomach with the butt of his rifle. She collapsed, breathing heavily. The rock fell from her limp fingers.

"Damn you! Damn you all to hell, White Apache!"

Another volley blasted below. This one was twice as loud and lasted twice as long. Leaden hornets buzzed overhead and spanged off the boulders.

The rest of the soldiers had arrived and were fanning out, firing as they ran. Clay saw the same bearded man in a sombrero whom he had seen at Abobe Wells. It was her father, he figured, and fixed a bead on the man's sternum. He had the man dead to rights. All he had to do was squeeze the trigger.

"If I had your knife, I would kill you!" Maria spat.

Clay smiled and fired.

Down the slope, Martin Gonzalez's sombrero went flying and he dived for cover.

"I would peel your skin from you like Apaches do to our people," Maria said spitefully. "I would rip out your tongue and feed it to the buzzards."

"I believe you would," Clay said. A pair of troopers drew his fire and both went down, sporting new nostrils. "You are my kind of woman, sweet thing."

"How dare you!" Maria cried, punching his leg. "It is true what they say. You are a monster!"

"I try."

So many soldiers dotted the ridge that crossing the open grade invited certain death. Clay grabbed her wrist and tried anyway, dragging her after him. Farther down someone shouted and the shots tapered off.

Then someone else yelled, "Don't let him take my baby!"

Smoke and slugs filled the air. To Clay, it was as if he stood in the middle of a rain of bullets that chipped the rocks at his feet and crisscrossed the air around him. How they all missed, he would never know.

Lunging to the sanctuary of the boulder, Clay pushed Maria down and crouched to take stock of the situation. The shooting tapered off, but didn't stop. He could see the summit and the gap 40 yards above him, but reaching it was impossible unless he could turn invisible to cross the grade—or if he had a shield.

Inspiration prompted Clay to pounce on Maria

and seize her from behind. Hooking his left arm around her waist, he said in her ear, "Now we'll see how much your father really loves you."

"What are you—" Maria began, bewildered. Terror gnawed at her vitals but she suppressed it. She knew that now was not the time to give in to her fear or she wouldn't live long enough to see the next dawn.

Clay sidled into the open, holding Maria in front of him, facing his enemies. He contrived to contort himself so that the only target the soldiers and vaqueros had was his captive. Backing slowly, he began to climb the grade again.

Maj. Filisola tingled with horror at the sight of the lovely woman he had come to adore being used so callously. He heard carbines being worked and men rising to shoot. "Hold your fire!" he roared. "Anyone who pulls a trigger faces a firing squad! So help me!"

Nearby, Martin Gonzalez paused with his rifle leveled. "She is my daughter, Major," he called out. "I have the final say, and I say that we must not let him get away with her. Under no circumstances. Do you understand?"

"No one fire!" Filisola repeated.

"Didn't you hear me?" Martin said. "Even if it means her life, we can't let her fall into Apache hands."

"Your brother felt the same," Filisola said. "I did not agree with him, and I do not agree with you."

For moments that seemed like an eternity, there was a stalemate. Clay continued to back upward, Maria frozen in his grasp, while the soldiers and vaqueros watched, uncertain what to do. Many

had risen in their eagerness to shoot. Filisola
held his breath, willing Maria and the renegade
to reach safety swiftly, aware a nervous twitch
would result in a bloodbath.

It was at this instant that another element
entered the fray. Delgadito, Cuchillo Negro, Fiero,
and Ponce had descended to the top of the grade
without being seen. Cuchillo Negro had started
down first and the rest had followed. Now, as
one, they showed themselves, fired several shots
apiece, and ducked down again.

Caught completely off guard, the soldiers and
vaqueros lost six of their number and half again
as many were wounded before the others got over
their shock and cut loose with reckless ferocity.
Carbines, rifles, and pistols blended in a lethal
litany that rivaled the crash of thunder.

"No!" Maj. Filisola said. "For God's sake, stop!"

But no one listened, not even the few who
heard him over the din. Their mortal enemies
were above them. There wasn't a man present who hadn't lost a relative or a friend to
Apaches. They fired and fired and fired, then
reloaded when their guns went empty. Many
charged.

Caught in the middle were Clay and Maria
Gonzalez. Slugs peppered the area around them,
zinged off rocks, nicked their bodies. He went
faster but the lead followed them as if drawn by
a magnet.

Maria was panic-stricken. She didn't want to
be. She wanted to be brave and to hold her
chin high. But the knowledge that she was a
heartbeat from death shattered her newfound
courage and left her cringing in fear. She made

a tremendous effort to marshal her courage. Then she was struck.

Clay heard her cry, felt her buckle, and saw the red splotch on her left thigh. They were almost to the top of the grade. A few more steps, and her father would never set eyes on her again. The Apaches were shooting steadily, trying to stop the onrushing Mexicans, but there were too many.

Suddenly Clay reached the top. Bullets were as thick as hail. They chewed into the ground and bit into boulders. A short jump would carry them out of reach, and he girded his legs.

Maria's agony had dispelled her fear. She twisted, realized she was yards away from certain captivity, and threw herself forward, attempting to unbalance her captor.

The trick nearly worked. Clay dug his soles into the soil and clung to her, his biceps rippling. He fell to one knee for added purchase.

Fighting like a wildcat, Maria tried to break free. She screamed when he pulled her higher despite her frantic struggling.

Clay surged upward, hauling her over the rim. Maria tried to turn and scratch his eyes out. He gave her a cuff that brought blood to her lips, then locked her arm in a vise of iron and hastened upward.

When Maj. Filisola saw Maria vanish, his mind went blank with dread. He forgot his military training, forgot every rule he had ever learned about engaging Apaches in combat. Raising his saber on high, he sprinted up the ridge. "After them, men! Save the senorita!"

The Chiricahuas had held out as long as they

dared. With soldiers coming at them from several directions, they had to get out of there. Delgadito melted into the boulders and was immediately joined by Fiero and Ponce. Cuchillo Negro delayed long enough to drop a vaquero; then he too made for the summit with the speed and agility of a mountain sheep.

To steal without being caught. To kill without being killed. Those were the Apache creeds. None of the warriors, including Cuchillo Negro, were willing to sacrifice themselves needlessly. They had done what they could to help Lickoyee-shisinday. Whether he made it to the summit was entirely up to him.

Clay wasn't far behind them. Maria had gone limp with shock and offered no resistance. Slugs zipped by now and then but none came close enough to pose a threat. He knew he had won, knew she was as good as his, and his smile returned.

The last stretch appeared, a tunnel of sorts formed by massive slabs that had toppled and leaned against one another. Clay ran through to the sunlight beyond. A few more strides brought him to the gap. He was ten feet below the summit. The Chiricahuas were already halfway to the other side. Cuchillo Negro beckoned him to hurry.

Troopers and vaqueros choked the trail. In the forefront was a young officer brandishing a saber, the look of a madman on his face.

Clay faced Maria. Tears ran down her cheeks and her shoulders shook in convulsive sobs.

"I hate you! I'll hate you forever!" she said.

The White Apache knew differently. She would

be just like other women taken by the Apaches. At first she would be moody and refuse to do as she was told. In time, though, she would realize her plight was hopeless and accept her fate and settle into the routine of Apache life. Much later, she might even come to enjoy living again.

Clay glanced at the warriors, then at the Mexicans. He reached out and caressed Maria's chin. "You are mine, woman—if I wanted you."

So saying, he kicked her in the stomach, knocking her off her feet and sending her tumbling down the slope. He lingered long enough to see the shocked amazement on her face when she sat up. Then he spun and ran.

The warriors were waiting. For once their emotions showed. Each wore a quizzical expression, and it was Cuchillo Negro who voiced the question uppermost on all their minds. "Why?"

"She was too weak to make a fitting wife," Clay said. Taking charge, he led them toward the chaparral, where they would disappear as if the earth had swallowed them, while over the crown of the ridge came cries of joy.

BLOOD TREACHERY

Chapter One

Cpl. Jim Ralston was a dead man but he didn't know it yet.

The day had started the same as the past five. The young soldier had risen at the crack of dawn, downed several cups of scalding black coffee, chewed a few tangy pieces of beef jerky, and climbed on his mount as the blazing sun cleared the golden eastern horizon.

Once again Ralston rode steadily deeper into the Chiricahua Mountains. Common sense told him that he should turn around and hightail it back to Fort Bowie. Simple logic made it plain that a lone trooper had a snowball's chance in hell of tracking down the most feared renegade in all of Arizona Territory. But then he thought of the ten-thousand dollars being offered for the White Apache, dead or alive, and he shook his head to dispel his doubts.

Ten-thousand dollars was more than Ralston

could expect to make in a lifetime. Having that much money meant he could say adios to the stark military life he had lived for seven years. He could head back to the States and set himself up in a fine house. Maybe he'd even find himself a pretty woman who would be willing to settle down and spend the rest of her nights giving him back rubs and her days darning his socks.

Of such fancies are dreams made. And Cpl. Ralston's dream explained why he had taken the two weeks' furlough he had earned, loaded up a pack mule, and headed into the Chiricahua Apache Reservation.

The trooper knew he had disobeyed a standing order. Headquarters, Fifth Cavalry, had sent a dispatch to all commands. Under no circumstances were soldiers to enter the Reservation without the express consent of their superiors. Anyone who violated the edict stood the risk of being court-martialed.

It had taken a score of years and the loss of many lives before the U.S. government had been able to bring the fierce Chiricahuas to bay. The tribe had only agreed to live on a reservation after their revered leader Cochise wrangled a promise from Washington; the heart of Chiricahua country, the Dragoon and Chiricahua Mountains, was to belong to the Chiricahuas for all time.

Since the treaty had gone into effect, there had been scattered incidents. Many of the younger warriors resented living under the white man's yoke. A few had turned renegade and many more would if provoked, so the government bent over backwards to insure they weren't. Whiskey traders were kept off the reservation—but managed to smuggle their wares in anyway. Prospectors were barred from looking for color in the mountains—

but scores did so and were rarely caught. And soldiers were to fight shy of the Chiricahuas or suffer the consequences.

But how could anyone in his right mind pass up a crack at ten-thousand dollars? Ralston asked himself as he crested a barren ridge. He certainly couldn't, and he knew of other soldiers who felt the same way but lacked the grit to try and claim the money.

Besides, the corporal doubted the government would raise much of a ruckus if someone rode into the fort with the body of the White Apache draped over a saddle. Washington didn't care how the terror of the Southwest was brought down, just so someone made wolf meat of him before he stirred the Chiricahuas up enough to incite them to out-and-out war.

No, sir, Ralston mused. The man who brought in the savage killer would be hailed as a hero, no questions asked. His story would be in all the papers. He'd be famous in no time. So what if a few rules were bent in the doing of the deed? It was the result that counted.

The burning sun had bought beads of sweat to Corporal Ralston's forehead. He wiped the back of his sleeve across his brow, pushed his hat back on his head, and unslung his canteen to take a sip. As he raised it to his parched lips, he caught a glimmer of light on the rocky slope to the west, no more than a pinpoint flash.

Instantly replacing the canteen, Ralston moved behind a boulder the size of a log cabin. Twisting in the saddle, he opened his saddlebags and took out a small spyglass he had bought at the sutler's. He unfolded the telescope and pressed it to his right eye.

Nothing moved on the slope. Whatever had

caused the flash was either gone, or so well hidden as to be invisible.

Ralston suspected the latter. The glimmer had been caused by sunlight reflecting off metal, most likely a rifle or a knife. And odds were that the rifle or knife had an Apache attached to it.

Wedging the spyglass under his wide leather belt, the corporal drew his carbine from the boot and fed a round into the chamber. He had to remind himself not to do anything rash. It might be a tame buck out hunting, although the odds were slim given that he was so far into the wilderness and the tame bucks liked to stay closer to the reservation proper.

Deciding to play it safe, Ralston rode back over the crest of the ridge and along it to a point directly across from the spot where he had seen the flash. He drew rein, dismounted, and ground-hitched his animal. The mule he tied to a manzanita, since it had a tendency to wander off.

The corporal stuffed extra ammunition into his pockets, then climbed to the top. He eased onto his belly behind a small boulder and scanned the vicinity. To his left a lizard scuttled across the baked earth into the shade of a cactus. It was the only sign of life to be seen.

Arizona was a hard land and it bred hard men, white and red. Ralston wasn't fooling himself. He realized that he was up against one of the most dangerous men alive. And it would take dumb luck, as much as anything else, for him to put an end to the White Apache's rampage.

According to the post commander, the White Apache had once been a respectable rancher named Clay Taggart. He had gone bad, though, in a big way. First he'd tried to rape the wife of a neighbor and killed one of the hands who came to her rescue. Then, on the run from the law, he'd hooked up with Delgadito, a genuine Apache renegade who had been the most wanted savage in the Territory until Taggart came along.

It was hard for Ralston to imagine. He couldn't see any white man pairing up with any red devil. In his eyes it was a crime against human nature, a perversion of all that he believed in. Apaches were little better than animals. Everyone knew that. Which made any white who would side with them a traitor to his own kind.

The corporal shut such thoughts from his mind and concentrated on the slope. When tangling with Apaches, the rule of thumb was to shoot first and think later. He brought the telescope into play again but the result was the same as before.

Minutes dragged by. The heat was stifling. Ralston's uniform clung to him when he moved. He would have given anything to enjoy a nice, long cold bath—and he wasn't a big believer in baths. Once every three months or so was enough to keep him clean and in the flush of health. Take baths too often, his grandpa used to say, and a body would wind up sickly.

Ralston frowned, certain he was wasting his time. He figured the Apache was long gone. He would be better off forking leather and riding on. Putting his hand down, he pushed to his knees and started to turn. As he did so, he saw an Apache standing less than ten feet away with an arrow notched to a sinew bowstring.

The trooper acted on sheer instinct. Throwing himself to the right, he leveled the carbine and snapped off a shot while in midair. More by luck than design the Apache was hit squarely in the chest and staggered backward.

Even as Ralston hit the ground he clawed at his revolver. He rolled a few feet in case the stricken warrior managed to loose the arrow while thumbing back the hammer of his Colt. Suddenly stopping, he saw the warrior sinking to the ground as if mortally wounded. But Ralston was taking no chances. He fired three times. The blast echoed off the nearby mountains, resembling a cannonade.

At each retort the Apache jerked with the impact of the bullet. With the third shot, he pitched onto his face and lay as still as a log.

Ralston slowly rose, keeping the warrior covered. His blood raced, his temples pounded. It had all happened so fast that only now did his brain begin to function as it should. Walking over, he nudged the dead Apache with the tip of his boot. When there was no reaction, he bent and flipped the warrior over.

Only then did Ralston realize it was a boy, no more than fourteen or fifteen years old. The boy had no knife, no tomahawk. The bow was old. The arrow lacked a barbed tip, and it was the only shaft the boy had. Belatedly, Ralston recalled that the youngster had not held the bow ready to shoot but rather had held it low down, at his side, with the arrow angled at the ground.

Ralston slowly holstered the pistol. It occurred to him that the boy wasn't a renegade, that he had just slain a young tame buck out hunting.

Some men would have felt deep remorse. Many would have regretted what they had done. The corporal merely kicked the boy in the side and muttered, "You damn redskin. That's what you get for sneaking up on me the way you did."

Abruptly, Ralston had a troubling thought.

Blood Treachery

What if the youngster had been a member of a hunting party? Crouching behind a boulder with his carbine in hand, he surveyed the length and breadth of the mountainous terrain but saw no reason for alarm. When enough time went by to convince him the youngster had been alone, he rose and hurried to where he had left the horse and the mule.

Stepping into the stirrups, Ralston set off at a brisk pace northward. He had to get out of there. The sound of the shots had no doubt carried a long distance and might prompt other Apaches to investigate.

For the better part of the morning the corporal forged his solitary way into the Chiricahua homeland. He marveled for the umpteenth time at the Apache ability to endure in a harsh, arid land fit only for sidewinders, gila monsters, and scorpions. It was no wonder the Apaches were noted for being as tough as the creatures with which they shared their land.

Shortly before noon, Ralston rode over a crest into a heavily forested tract bordering a narrow, fertile valley. It was a virtual oasis. He made toward a meandering stream with a smile of anticipation on his face.

At the water's edge, the corporal climbed down, knelt, removed his hat, and plunged his entire head into the cool, invigorating water. Rising up, he laughed lightly and shook himself to clear his eyes. Then he drank, gulping even though he knew it was wiser to sip slowly after blistering in the intense heat for so long. He couldn't help himself.

Once Ralston had slaked his thirst, he walked over to a tree and sat with his back to the trunk. His horse still guzzled greedily, as he had, but the mule had moved off a few yards to graze. Mules were smarter than horses in that respect; they never drank so much that they swelled up like a waterbag fit to burst and became too waterlogged to move.

Ralston toyed with the notion of going over and dragging his mount out of the stream, but he couldn't motivate himself to make the effort. Sitting in the shade with a faint breeze chilling his damp skin felt so glorious, he had no desire to budge. Besides which, he had decided on the spur of the moment to spend the night there. Sources of water were few and far between. He intended to make the most of this one while he had the chance.

Accordingly, after briefly dozing, Ralston stripped off his cartridge belt and his uniform, then waded into the stream in his birthday suit. A convenient pool, about knee-deep, gave him the perfect spot to plop down. The water rose to just under his chin, and for the first time in more days than he could remember, he wasn't sweating from head to toe. It felt wonderful.

"Almost makes a man wish he was a fish," Ralston said aloud to himself. He moved closer to the bank to be within quick reach of the carbine and the revolver, which he had placed at the water's edge.

Both the horse and mule were cropping grass. Neither betrayed any skittishness, as they would if they had caught the scent of an Indian or a beast.

Ralston allowed himself to relax fully for the first time that day. He leaned his head back onto the bank and closed his eyes, relying on the animals to warn him if a threat loomed. Off to the northeast a bird shrieked, prompting him to crack his lids and look. A red hawk soared high on the currents, wheeling in search of prey.

They had a lot in common, Ralston thought. They were both alone. They were both hunters. They both relied on their wits to survive. He watched the big bird soar for a while, then dozed off. A dream came to him in which he grew great wings and flew into the air like an avenging human hawk. Soon the White Apache appeared below. He swooped down and grasped the renegade in razor-sharp talons. Ripping and rending, he tore the White Apache to ribbons. The renegade died screaming.

Ralston came awake slowly, savoring a feeling of lassitude. Something pricked him ever so lightly on the left shoulder. It felt like the bite of a small insect. He idly reached up and ran his hand over the spot but felt nothing.

Once more the corporal was pricked, this time on the forearm. Reluctantly, he opened his eyes and stared at his wrist. He was surprised to see a tiny drop of blood.

A sharper prick lanced the side of Ralston neck. Immediately he slapped at himself, thinking that maybe a bee or a hornet was responsible. But then his hand was seared by a strange burning pain and when he lowered his arm, he discovered that two of his fingers were gone. Blood squirted into the stream, turning the water a murky rust color.

Startled, Cpl. Ralston twisted to see what was behind him and nearly passed out from shock. He tried to jump to his feet but his legs refused to cooperate. So stunned was he that for the moment he forgot about his missing fingers.

A man stood there, holding a Bowie knife. He

was tall, well proportioned, and superbly muscled. His body had been bronzed by the sun until it was the same hue as an Apache's. His long black hair was also typical of an Apache's, as were the breechcloth and style of moccasins he wore. Slanted across his chest, Indian fashion, was a bandoleer brimming with cartridges. Slung over his left shoulder was a Winchester. On his right hip, in a Mexican holster decorated with silver studs, rode a fancy nickel-plated pistol.

Unlike Apaches, the man wore a wide-brimmed brown hat such as prospectors favored, the front brim curled up so he could see clearly. And in marked contrast to any Apache who had ever lived, the man's eyes were a striking lake-blue.

Ralston knew who it was. Recognition shattered his shock and he turned to grab his Colt, which had been inches away. But the revolver and the carbine were gone.

"Are you looking for those, soldier boy?" the apparition asked in a deep voice, and pointed at the weapons that had been placed a dozen feet off, well out of his reach. "I moved them while you slept."

The corporal couldn't conceive of anyone being so light on his feet. He glanced at the horse and mule, which grazed on as if nothing out of the ordinary had taken place.

The man noticed and smiled. "I know what you're thinking. Calvary horses usually act up when they smell Apaches. But I'm not an Apache."

"I know who you are," Ralston blurted more harshly than he would have liked. It was then that sheer agony coursed through him as he belatedly felt the full effect of having his fingers sliced off. He pressed the stubs against his side and shuffled awkwardly to his feet, heedless of his nakedness. "What do you want?" he stupidly asked, well aware of the answer before he posed the question.

"Why the boy?"

"I don't know what you're—" Ralston began, and yipped like a gut-shot coyote when the Bowie leaped out and ripped a four-inch gash in his left shoulder.

"Why did you kill the boy?"

Ralston, grimacing, back-pedaled. Desperate for salvation, he looked to right and left for something he could use to defend himself.

"I heard the shots, blue-belly," the renegade had gone on casually. "I found the body and read the sign. You had no call to gun him down."

"I did!" the corporal responded, his voice strident with fear he could scarcely hide. "He was trying to kill me!"

"Liar. His name was Eskaminzin. His cousin, Ponce, rides with me and every so often Eskaminzin would pay us a visit. We tried to get him to join our band, but he always refused. He said that he didn't hate the whites as much as we do."

Ralston had gone the width of the stream. He halted, shut the torment from his mind, and willed his nerves to steady. "I tell you that he left me no choice!" he lied. "You have to believe me. I'm not one of those who go around making wolf meat of Apaches for the hell of it."

"What are you doing here, then?"

There was no earthly reason, other than hunting Apaches or prospecting, for any white man to be in that part of the reservation, and Ralston knew it. "I had some time on my hands," he said, "and I heard tell that there might be gold up in these mountains."

"So you're playing prospector, is that it?"

"Yes," Ralston said, nodding vigorously. The White Apache didn't strike him as being anywhere near as bloodthirsty as he had been led to believe. With a little luck, he was sure he could talk his way out of the fix he was in.

"That's mighty peculiar," the tall man said. "I don't see any prospecting gear on your mule, yonder. No shovel, no pick, no pan. What exactly are you prospecting with? Your picket pin?"

Ralston swallowed to moisten his dry throat. "I didn't say I aimed to do any digging this trip. I'm just looking around to see if I can find some color."

The scourge of the Territory sighed and squatted to wipe the Bowie clean on the grass. "There was a time when I would have given you the benefit of the doubt, mister. But I've learned better, the hard way. I know you're lying through your teeth. And so do they."

"They?"

"Oh. Where are my manners? I forgot to introduce my pards. Take a gander behind you."

Cpl. Ralston did, and his heart pounded madly in his chest. Four full-blooded Apaches flanked him. Four heavily armed, somber-as-death-itself, swarthy Apaches whose features were as flinty as quartz.

Until that moment, the trooper had been under the impression that one Apache looked just about the same as every other. It had been hard for him to tell them apart, even the Apache scouts who worked for the Cavalry and rode out with every patrol.

This time it was different. Perhaps due to his

predicament, which had sharpened his senses to their utmost, he saw four individuals standing before him, not four faceless savages.

The one on the right was the youngest. He wore a blue shirt and brown vest, and his eyes blazed hatred.

Next there was a slender warrior partial to a gray shirt. Above the top of the cartridge-belt strapped around his waist jutted a large black knife-hilt.

The third warrior had an air about him. His eyes were like those of an eagle, his expression that of a man who exercised supreme self-control.

Last of all was a square-shouldered bear of a warrior with fiery eyes and a nasty scar in the shape of a lightning bolt on his brow. This one sneered and stood hunched forward, resembling a grizzly about to pounce.

"That young one there is Ponce," the man across the stream said. "He's a mite riled that you killed his cousin. Next to him is Cuchillo Negro, or Black Knife as the whites like to call him. Then there's Delgadito. I reckon you've heard of him."

Overcome by unbridled terror, all Ralston could do was nod.

"As for that friendly cuss on the end, he's called Fiero. It shouldn't be hard to figure out why."

The corporal edged back into the middle of the stream. He had never felt so vulnerable in all his born days, and he swore his knees quaked as he said, "You've got to help me, Taggart. You can't stand by and let these butchers do what they want."

"It's out of my hands, soldier boy. I might be the leader of the band, but that doesn't give me the right to boss them around as I see fit. Apaches do as they please, when they please."

The one called Fiero moved toward the bank but stopped at a word from Delgadito, who glanced at the young warrior, Ponce. Ponce then stalked forward, a war club at his side.

"Oh, God!" Ralston cried, goose bumps breaking out all over his body. He fought down an urge to scream and retreated a few strides. "Tell them they can have my horse and mule, my supplies and guns and everything! All they have to do is let me live."

The renegade chuckled. "I think you're missing the point, pilgrim. They're going to take all your stuff anyway. After Ponce, there, bashes in your skull, of course. Then Fiero will likely skin you. He likes to make pouches out of white hides ever since he killed a trooper who had made a tobacco pouch out of the breast of an Apache woman." He paused. "After that, Delgadito and Cuchillo Negro will probably cut you into little pieces and scatter the parts around for the wild critters to eat. All I'll wind up with is the head, but that will be enough."

Cpl. Jim Ralston wanted to ask what Taggart meant by that remark, but his vocal cords were paralyzed. In fact, his entire frame had frozen of its own accord, and all he could do was stand there and tremble like a terrified mouse as the young avenger with the war club sprang high into the air and swooped down toward him just as he had swooped down on the White Apache in his dream. The last sight he saw was that of the heavy war club streaking toward his forehead. It grew larger and larger until, for a fleeting fraction of an instant, the war club seemed to fill the sky from end to end.

And then the world exploded.

Chapter Two

Fort Bowie sat on a hill in the Chiricahua Mountains on the eastern approach to Apache Pass. It had been built to insure that travelers using the Tucson-Mesilla road could do so in safety, and to safeguard a crucial spring, the only source of water for many miles around.

Careerwise, it was the bottom of the Army barrel, the post of last resort. Troopers from Maine to California dreaded being sent to Bowie, and when assigned, generally despised every miserable minute. The heat, the isolation, the hard work, they all made life a living hell. And as if that weren't enough, there was the constant threat of attack by renegades. Soldiers riding out on routine patrol never knew if they would live to see the high ramparts again.

So the troopers hated Fort Bowie. And their commanding officer was no exception. Colonel Thomas Reynolds stood outside the headquarters building and gazed with clear distaste at the dusty parade ground. In all his years of military service, he had never loathed any assignment so much as he did being sent to Bowie.

Reynolds had only himself to blame. He had blundered at his previous post and allowed a patrol to be needlessly wiped out by Sioux. Less than a month later new orders had arrived, dispatching him to Arizona Territory. Coincidence? Some would say so. Reynolds knew better. The Army frowned on incompetence. Those who didn't measure up to standard were thrown to the wolves.

But as the old saying went, there was a silver lining to every cloud. In this case, Reynolds had a chance to redeem himself if he could last his tour at Bowie without making any more boneheaded blunders—and if he could keep the Apaches in line.

So far, the colonel had not made any mistakes. But he was finding it harder by the day to keep a lid on the festering cauldron of the Chiricahua Reservation. Thanks to renegades like Delgadito and the White Apache, the potential for a mass uprising was greater than at any time since the death of Cochise.

Reynolds pulled his hat brim low against the sun and headed across the compound. He thought of all that had been done to avert war, and what needed to be done if the fragile peace was to hold.

Washington had done its typical inane bit to help. Shortly after the Chiricahua Reservation had been formed, word came down that henceforth Fort Bowie would be known as *Camp* Bowie. The political logic had been instructive. Since the post was located smack in the middle of the Chiricahua reserve, Washington had felt the tribe might resent its presence. But instead of dismantling the post and moving it outside the reservation, the higher-ups decided to simply rename it.

Who did they think they were fooling? Reynolds often mused. Washington could call it a camp if they wanted, but everyone at the post, and everyone in Arizona, still called it a fort. So, too, did the Apaches, who were a lot smarter than the politicians gave them credit for being.

Col. Reynolds came to the small building that housed the office of the Chief of Scouts. Without bothering to knock, he threw the door wide and walked in.

Caught in the act of raising a silver flask to his lips was Capt. Vincent Parmalee. Thin as a rail, with a sallow complexion from too much time spent indoors, Parmalee had made no secret of the fact he resented being picked to supervise "a bunch of filthy, ignorant heathens," as he called them. Nor was it a secret that he drowned his resentment in a bottle.

"I trust you're drinking water, Captain," Reynolds said stiffly. On several occasions he had warned Parmalee about being under the influence while on duty. Just as he had warned a score of others guilty of the same offense.

Alcoholism was rampant among the soldiers there, a consequence of the brutal conditions under which they lived. It was the only way many of them got through the day, and Reynolds knew that trying to stamp it out would be like trying to stamp out a raging forest fire. The best he could do was sweep it under the rug and only punish blatant offenders.

Parmalee stiffened as if snake bit and lowered

the flask into an open drawer. "Sir!" he exclaimed. Rising, he snapped to attention. "Of course it is, Colonel."

Frowning, Reynolds walked around the desk, picked up the flask, and held it under his nose. "Since when is spring water one hundred proof?" He held out his arm and upended the contents. "I've been lenient with you, Captain, because I sympathize with your plight. Let me catch you one more time, however, and you'll spend a few days in the guardhouse."

Captain Parmalee grit his teeth to keep from spitting out the string of curses he wanted to utter. He thought it unfair and cruel for his superior to begrudge him a few nips. But he wasn't about to risk having an official reprimand placed on his record. He already had too many. one or two more and he might be tossed out of the Army on his ear, and he only needed to tough it out for another eight years and he could retire with a small pension. Enough to keep him in whiskey the rest of his life.

"I'll get straight to the point," Reynolds said, placing the flask on the desk. "What's the latest on the renegades?"

"There's nothing new to report, sir," Parmalee said. "The scouts are doing their best but they have no idea where White Apache and Delgadito have hid out." He wasn't one to offer excuses for the savages serving under him, but at the same time he didn't care to have their poor performance reflect on his, so he added, "You have to bear in mind the size of the reservation, sir. It would take the entire Fifth Army a full year just to check every nook and cranny in the Dragoons, let alone the Chiricahua Mountains."

"Don't lecture me on the difficulties," Reynolds

replied. "I'm fully aware that the Apaches know these mountains as they do the backs of their hands. If your scouts haven't found the renegades, it's because they don't want to find them."

Parmalee opened his mouth to argue but thought better of the idea. The colonel was only saying what they both knew to be true.

"This impasse is intolerable," Reynolds continued. "If the scouts you have won't do their job, then dismiss the shirkers and sign up a new bunch."

"It's not that simple, sir," Parmalee said. "If we give the scouts the boot without a damn good reason, they're liable to hold a grudge. And once word spreads, there won't be a buck anywhere willing to work for us."

"Then what—" Colonel Reynolds began, but stopped when shouts broke out in the direction of the main gate. Boots pounded, and the piercing wail of a bugle rent the air. "Damn!" he said, speeding from the office with the captain on his heels.

The entire fort was in an uproar. Troopers were rushing toward the gate. Others were scaling ladders to the parapets. Still others were just emerging from their barracks, pulling on clothes as they ran or loading carbines on the fly.

From out of the midst of the confusion jogged a burly noncom. Sergeant Joe McKinn halted, saluted, and declared, "A sentry in guard tower two claims he saw several Apaches within spitting distance of the post, sir."

"Was that cause to call out the whole garrison?" Reynolds demanded, not a little peeved. He had lost count of the number of times the alarm had been sounded only to turn out to be false.

McKinn didn't bat an eye. "They left us a present, sir. Another one of *those*."

"Damn. Lead the way."

The sergeant did so with exquisite precision. He plowed through the milling troopers like a man-of-war through a turbulent sea, bellowing orders as he ran, rendering drilled order out of confused chaos. At the base of a ladder he stepped aside to permit his superiors to go ahead of him, and craned his head back to see the sentry. "Private Gibbs! Any more sign of Apaches?"

"Not a trace, Sarge."

McKinn was glad. He had already lost one commanding officer in his career and he had no intention of losing another. He noted with satisfaction that most of the troopers were at their positions, weapons at the ready. Any Apache foolhardy enough to fire a shot from close up would be shot to ribbons in the blink of an eye.

The two officers gained the senty tower, which was unlike most of its kind. But for that matter, so was the entire post.

Fort Bowie had been built in an arid area almost devoid of trees. So instead of having an outer palisade constructed of high wooden poles, as did the majority of Western posts, Bowie boasted walls of stone so thick no bullet could penetrate, and against which arrows and lances shattered on impact.

The sentry tower was similarly made. Guards kept watch on the surrounding countryside through small, square windows. It was to one of these windows that Colonel Reynolds stepped at the bidding of McKinn. "I don't see anything," he commented, scouring the ground below.

"Look a little farther out, sir. Just across the road," Sergeant McKinn advised. Having been the second one to see it, he could well understand why the commander put a hand on the wall and shut his eyes for a few moments.

"Bring it in, Sergeant," Colonel Reynolds directed. And then, out of petty spite over the failure of the scouts to locate the renegades, he added, "Go along, Captain. Cover him."

"Me, sir?" Parmalee said in surprise. It was well known that he rarely left the fort, and he liked to think that he had a good excuse. For one thing, his presence was seldom required in the field. His job consisted of sitting behind his desk and issuing orders to the Apaches who volunteered to serve as scouts against their own kind. Which suited him just fine. The thought of going up against a band of renegades terrified him half to death. In his office he was safe, or as safe as any soldier stationed in Arizona could be. "Shouldn't Private Gibbs go?"

Reynolds turned. "I want you to," he said sternly. "So hop to it."

Parmalee broke out in a cold sweat the moment his hands touched the ladder. At the gate, he drew his revolver and cocked it. He thought he noticed a twinkle in the noncom's eyes, a twinkle put there at his expense, but the sergeant was too canny to be obvious. "Open up," Parmalee barked at the four privates awaiting word.

For some reason the sun seemed hotter outside the walls than it had inside, but Parmalee chalked the feeling up to his imagination. He glued himself to the noncom's heels, his eyes darting in every direction.

The ground near the fort had been cleared of most vegetation and anything else hostiles could hide behind. But across the road the chaparral was thick enough to conceal an army. Mesquite and shindaggers predominated, plants that tore mercilessly into unwary horses and men.

Yet Apaches, as Capt. Paramlee knew, navigated mesquite forests with ease. He was sure that unseen eyes were on him as he crossed the dusty road to a low bank. So intent was he on spotting hidden warriors that he forgot all about the memento left by the renegades until he stood right in front of it. His stomach churned at the sight, and he thought he would be sick.

The severed human head of a white man had been impaled on a sharp stake. His eyes had been gouged out, his tongue hacked off. His mouth hung wide open, locked in his death scream.

"Sweet Jesus," Sergeant McKinn breathed. "It's Jim!"

Parmalee looked again and recognized the distorted features of Cpl. Ralston, a likeable cuss whose only failing was his cocky attitude. They had talked a few times over drinks, and it had been Paramlee's opinion that the young trooper failed to give the Apaches their due as fighters. "Given half a chance," the corporal had bragged, "I can hold my own anywhere, any time. Apaches don't scare me as much as they do the rest of you."

Now, staring down at the grisly handiwork of the renegades, Parmalee shook his head and said under his breath, "They should have."

Sergeant McKinn, about to wrest the stake free, looked up. "What was that, sir?"

"Nothing. Proceed."

McKinn choked back the bitter bile that rose in his throat, gripped the stake in both brawny hands, and yanked. The stake was looser than he had figured, and it shot up, the head bumping into his face. He inhaled the foul odor of sweat and something much worse.

Holding the hideous object at arm's length, McKinn hurried toward the gate. He was worried, but not about Apaches. Of more concern was whether anyone had seen him talking to Jim Ralston shortly before the corporal left the fort to go after the White Apache. He wouldn't want the colonel to suspect that he had been a party to Ralston's hunt, if only indirectly.

McKinn kept close tabs on the men under him. It was his duty to see that they were in a constant state of battle-readiness, to insure that morale and performance were at high levels. So he pried, he snooped, he spied on troopers if need be, all to insure that the cogs of the military machine ran as smoothly as they were supposed to.

It had been plain that Corporal Ralston had been up to something. The man had taken a furlough but let it be known he was staying in Arizona instead of going back East to visit his kin. That alone had aroused McKinn's suspicions. Then, when he learned Ralston had bought camping supplies and finagled the loan of a mule, he had taken it on himself to confront his subordinate.

Ralston had admitted he was going after Clay Taggart. Right then and there McKinn should have marched him over to the colonel's office and reported it, but McKinn had turned his back and let Ralston ride off. He still had the forty dollars Ralston had given him, that and the now empty promise of another three-hundred once Ralston received the bounty.

Col. Reynolds waited at the gate. He avoided

staring at the head again, and asked, "Any idea who it is this time?" Sgt. McKinn told him.

The commanding officer sighed, feeling suddenly older than his years and very, very tired. "This can't go on," he said bleakly. "The bastard is rubbing our noses in our own incompetence. Once word spreads, even the tame Indians will be laughing at us behind our backs. More young hotheads are bound to join the renegades, thinking they can do so with impunity."

"What would you suggest we do, sir?" Capt. Parmalee said, not really caring one way or the other just so long as it didn't involve his leaving the security of the fort. "We've increased patrols. We've sent our best scouts deep into the mountains time and again. All with no result."

Sgt. McKinn added his two cents worth, inspired by the three-hundred dollars he would never see. "It's too bad the Chiricahuas aren't as fond of money as we are, sir. If they were, we might be able to pay a turncoat to lead us to the White Apache's lair."

Col. Reynolds glanced sharply at the noncom. A strange expression came over him and he smiled broadly. "Sergeant, I do believe that you're a genius."

"Me, sir?"

"Find Capt. Forester and Lt. Peterson. I want them in my office within half an hour. You too, Parmalee."

Parmalee didn't like being included, but objecting was out of the question. "You sound excited, sir. Mind filling me in?"

The commander swiveled on a boot heel. "In due time, Captain. All you need to know for now is that at long last I've hit on a way of putting an end to the White Apache once and for all."

Blood Treachery

* * *

At that very moment, the man the Army most wanted to eliminate or capture was several miles distant, bearing to the northwest at a tireless dog-trot. His breechcloth and long black hair swayed as he ran. The burning sun warmed his bronzed back and limbs, but not to the point of giving him heatstroke, as it might have done once.

There were times when Clay Taggart marveled at the changes he had undergone. Before hooking up with Delgadito, he had never gone anywhere unless it was on horseback. And he never, ever ventured into the wilderness unless he had a water skin or a canteen along.

Now look at him, Clay mused. He was more Apache than white. Like those whose ways he had adopted, he could run half a day without tiring. A single swallow of water could last him for many hours. One meal every twenty-four hours was all he needed. And he could live off the land better than any white man in the whole Territory. His own mother, if she were still alive, wouldn't recognize him if he were to walk right up to her.

He was an Apache, by choice. Lickoyee-shis-inday, they called him. White Man Of The Woods. The only white-eye ever to be so honored. And Clay was honored.

There had been a time, back when Clay made his living as a rancher, that he'd regarded all Apaches as vermin, fit only to be wiped out to the last man, woman, and child. His attitude had been typical of most whites who lived in the Territory. And in a way, even now, he couldn't blame them.

For far too many years the citizens of Arizona had lived with the ever-present threat of Apache raids. Scores of innocent settlers had been ruthlessly butchered. Travelers had been waylaid as regularly as clockwork and slaughtered in horrible fashion. Women and children had been taken captive, never to be seen again. Small wonder the whites hated Apaches, all Apaches. Small wonder the whites wanted the Chiricahuas and every other tribe exterminated.

Sentiments Clay Taggart had strongly shared. Then came the day he had been framed by his wealthy neighbor, Miles Gillett, so Gillett could get his hands on Clay's land. Clay had been forced to flee, had been chased by a posse into the Dragoon Mountains. There they had caught him, strung him up, and left him for dead.

How strangely fate worked, Clay mused. He would have gone to meet his Maker that day had Delgadito not elected to cut him down so he could arrange a truce between the Army and the renegades. A truce that never came to pass.

As a result of circumstances no man could have predicted or prevented, Clay Taggart found himself a member of the most notorious Apache band in the Southwest. He was wanted by the Army and civilian law, and a huge bounty had been placed on his head, dead or alive.

Thanks to Miles Gillett, those who had once called Clay their pard had turned against him. His own kind were out for his blood. One mistake, and his corpse might end up on public display in Tucson, where the curious and the timid would come take a peek for a measly twenty-five cents. When the novelty wore off and folks no longer cared, the undertaker would likely as not toss his body out on the desert to be devoured by coyotes.

But Clay wasn't about to let that happen. Not

yet. Not while he had unfinished business to settle with Miles Gillett. One day, soon, he would launch a raid on Gillett's spread and pay the bastard back for the scar on his neck—and for the loss of his ranch and the woman he loved.

Suddenly Clay's reverie was shattered by the feeling that he was no longer alone. Instantly he halted and crouched, unslinging the Winchester as he did so. A study of both rims of the gully along which he was making his way revealed no hidden enemies.

He reminded himself that he must be extra vigilant. Being so close to the fort increased the odds of being spotted by soldiers. Should any recognize him, they'd be on him like rabid wolves on a panther, eager to bring him down no matter what the cost.

Clay saw no one. He reminded himself that Cuchillo Negro and Ponce were out there somewhere. They had insisted on tagging along on his trek to Fort Bowie to leave the keepsake. Then the three of them had split up in case the soldiers gave chase.

As usual, though, the troopers had not shown any such desire. He'd watched them for a while, seen them recover the head of the corporal and then go on about their daily routine as if nothing out of the ordinary had taken place.

Before Clay Taggart became the White Apache, he had been proud of the Army presence in Arizona, proud of the job the Fifth Cavalry was doing to keep the Apaches in line. Now that the shoe was on the other foot, as it were, White Apache wished they would all pack up and leave. Most were inept greenhorns, cannon fodder for glory-seeking politicians in Washington, sent to protect the frontier but in the process being duped into serving the ends of a wicked schemer like Miles Gillett.

It was Gillett, Clay had heard, who put up half the blood money for the reward on his head. Gillett who had saturated the area with wanted posters printed at his own expense. To Clay's way of thinking, his enemy was growing desperate to see him dead. He liked to think that Gillett lay in bed at night caked with sweat, unable to sleep for worry over where he would strike next.

Gillett's worry would mount on hearing of the head. It would show Gillett that no one could stop him, that he could go where he wanted when he wanted, with impunity. It would remind Gillett that one day soon he would show up in the middle of the night to claim his vengeance.

White Apache smiled at the image, then shook his head to derail the train of thought. He had to stay alert. It was another ten miles to the spot where he would reunite with Cuchillo Negro and Ponce. He had better be on his way.

Rising, he took but a few steps when somewhere up ahead a rifle cracked. Almost at the selfsame instant, an invisible hammer slammed into the side of his head.

Chapter Three

It happened so fast that Taggart was on his side on the ground with blood seeping from his temple before he quite realized someone had shot at him. Dazed, White Apache rolled onto his back and fought a rising tide of darkness that tried to engulf him. Giving in to the veil would doom him, because whoever had ambushed him would move in close to finish the job.

Forcing his arms and legs to move, White Apache pushed up into a crouch and closer to the left wall of the gully so he would be harder to hit. No other shots rang out, which indicated the bushwhacker had lost sight of him when he fell. It also meant the man was somewhere above the gully, secreted in the heavy brush bordering it.

Clay's senses reached out and probed the manzanita, as would a true Apache's. His posture mimicked that of a coiled warrior. Even the set of his mind was like that of a genuine

Chiricahua, devoted to one thought and only one: killing whoever had tried to kill him.

Clay Taggart truly lived up to his new name as he glided forward parallel to the left-hand rim. His moccasins made no noise when he placed them down. Soundless as a ghost, the hunted had now become the hunter. He had his thumb on the rifle hammer, his forefinger curved lightly around the trigger.

Suddenly White Apache heard the faintest of noises from the manzanita on the right side of the gully. Sturdy legs pumping, he went up the gradual incline in a rush, streaked over the lip, and dashed in among the shrub-like trees, which only grew to a height of five or six feet. Stopping behind a bush, White Apache did as Delgadito had taught him: he bent his body to imitate the shape of the bush. Anyone seeing his outline would mistake him for the plant's shadow.

From under narrowed eyelids, White Apache sought evidence of the ambusher. He assumed it to be a white man and was supremely confident he would spot the culprit before too long. Time went by, however, and White Apache spied no one, nor did he hear the whisper of footsteps. Whoever lurked out there was highly skilled. Maybe, he reasoned, it was one of the Apache scouts working for the Army.

Five minutes became ten. Ten became twelve. White Apache straightened and moved off, using every available bit of cover, blending into the background as expertly as would a real Chiricahua. Despite that, the ambusher caught sight of him.

White Apache was just about to dart from one manzanita to another when the bark of the one he was standing behind erupted in a spray of slivers that stung his cheek and nearly took out an eye. He dropped, relying on the gunshot to pinpoint the position of the one who wanted to kill him. It came from dense growth about twenty-five yards away.

Going to ground, White Apache scrutinized the wall of vegetation from top to bottom. Thanks to the training of the Apaches, he could ferret out a mouse at that distance, but try as he might, he couldn't find the rifleman.

It was baffling. White Apache considered himself the equal of any man in Arizona, white or red. Yet whoever wanted to rub him out was proving to be more than a match for him.

Crawling slowly, White Apache angled to the right in a wide loop that brought him to the rear of the stand where the killer was hidden. Parting high stems of grass, he had an unobstructed view, but still he saw no one.

Someone saw him.

Again a rifle banged, twice this time, and at each shot the dirt under White Apache's chin flew into the air, some getting into his mouth. He rolled to the left and kept on rolling until he was well camouflaged. Then, snaking along on his side, he moved a dozen yards to the west.

By this time White Apache's temple pulsed with pounding pain. He touched the wound and discovered the blood flow had stopped. By a sheer fluke he had been spared. Another quarter of an inch to the right, however, and the bushwhacker would have put a window in his skull.

White Apache moved behind a small boulder. It occurred to him that his unseen adversary might be playing him for a fool. The man could be trying to pin him down until a patrol arrived. As good as White Apache was, eluding over thirty mounted men while on foot would tax him to his limits.

Deciding that he would rather live to fight another day than to stay and possibly be overwhelmed, White Apache crept off to the northwest. When he had put enough ground behind him, he broke into a trot, ignoring the anguish that racked his head. The wound was swelling, a bad sign. As every frontiersman worthy of the name knew, more victims of gunshot wounds died from infections that set in after the fact than from the actual shots. He had to dress his as soon as possible.

To the north, a day's journey, lay a ribbon of a stream known only to the Apaches. White Apache bent his steps toward it and kept on the lookout for certain plants used by Chiricahua women to treat gunshots. The next second, without warning, White Apache caught sight of a figure in the underbrush in front of him. He promptly halted and brought the Winchester to his shoulder.

The figure was big but sped along with surprising speed, the flow of his movements betraying Indian lineage. As if the warrior sensed he was being watched, he abruptly stopped and spun. White Apache glimpsed features set in a mask of hatred, features he felt he should recognize but didn't. He fixed a hasty bead, then fired. Simultaneously, the figure dropped and snapped off two shots of his own, which were too high.

Diving flat, White Apache wriggled to a pipe-organ cactus. Another shot rang out and a section of the plant inches from his face blew apart. He scrambled onward, under a paloverde over ten feet high. Here, for the time being, he was safe.

After working the lever of his rifle to feed a new round into the chamber, White Apache slid around the paloverde into dry weeds. Here he exercised greater caution, since the stems were prone to rustle and rattle at the least little pressure.

His hunch about the bushwhacker being an Indian had proven correct, but he didn't know what to make of the warrior's behavior. Why try to kill him, then run off when he was hurt and at a disadvantage? Yet that was exactly what the man must have done, heading north from the gully minutes before he did, perhaps bound for the same stream.

It was a puzzle worthy of attention, later. For the moment White Apache had to devote himself to staying alive. He tested the sluggish breeze with his ears and his nose but neither revealed the warrior's location. Picking up a stone, he hefted it a few times, then pitched it as far as he could to one side. It clattered as it fell into the brush, spooking a pair of doves that took wing side by side. But it didn't do as he had hoped and lure the warrior into the open.

The pain in his head was growing worse. White Apache decided to take the fight to his foe and made straight for the spot where he had last seen the figure. He came on tracks, which were small given the size of their maker, leading off to the west. Once again the ambusher had fled.

Or was it even the same man? White Apache wondered. Maybe he had stumbled on a different warrior and mistaken him for the dry-gulcher. But if that was the case, why had the man's features lit with hatred on seeing him? Had it been a Pima or a Maricopa, traditional enemies of the Apaches?

There were plenty of questions and too few answers. White Apache stood and resumed his interrupted trek. He had to steel himself against the rising agony in his head, which was making it hard for him to think clearly. All he needed was some nice, cool water, he told himself. Once he reached the stream and dressed the wound, everything would be fine. It had to be.

He refused to die until Miles Gillett had paid for making an outcast of him.

From a patch of mesquite more than 100 yards off, a pair of beady dark eyes, simmering with raw spite, watched Lickoyee-shis-inday depart.

The eyes were set under thick beetling brows in a huge moon of a face belonging to Palacio, leader of the Chiricahuas. A rarity among Apaches, Palacio had the distinction of being the only fat warrior in the tribe. Yet when he moved, as he did now in trotting briskly to the southeast, his body showed a supple grace and hinted at latent strength that belied his bulk.

In the white man's world, Palacio would be considered a dandy. A yellow headband kept his black hair in place. He wore a bright rcd shirt and leggings decorated with blue and red beads. His moccasins were beaded, as was the sheath of his long hunting knife. Palacio dressed as he did because unlike the majority of his people he had a constant hankering for the finer things life had to offer. Good food, and lots of it. Colorful clothes such as the whites and *Nakai-yes* wore. Fine horses and guns. These were what mattered, in Palacio's estimation.

He had not always been that way. As a little boy, he had been just like his childhood friends. Many a day had been spent prowling the mountains dressed in a leather breechcloth, many a night huddled next to a campfire listening to the tales told by the elders of the tribe. Then

Blood Treachery

Mexicans seeking copper came to Chiricahua country. The *Nakai-yes*, they were called. And these Mexicans brought with them all manner of new possessions.

Palacio had been dazzled witless by the wealth of these smiling strangers. His father, a revered chief, had taken him time and again to visit Santa Rita del Cobre. He had seen *Nakai-yes* wearing pistols that shone like the sun and carrying rifles that killed men at distances unheard of before. He had eaten meals so rich and sweet and sometimes deliriously hot that afterward he had lain on the ground like a contented camp dog and savored the sensation.

Those were days Palacio recollected fondly. His father had been friendly to the *Nakai-yes*, and Palacio had followed in his footsteps when he assumed the mantle of leadership.

Much later the Americans came, and Palacio had been one of the few who advocated greeting them with open arms. But the people had listened to those who counseled war, and as a result the Chiricahuas were now confined to a reservation. Many remembered his earlier guidance, though, and his esteem had risen steadily to where Palacio was now the single most influential warrior in the whole tribe. His people did nothing without first consulting him.

There were exceptions. Delgadito had seen fit to break away from the main body and start his own band. Palacio had warned him that doing so was unwise and predicted that so small a band would be easy prey for soldiers from both sides of the border, not to mention the marauding packs of scalp hunters hired by the State of Sonora in Mexico to rid them of Apaches.

Once again Palacio had been proven right.

Delgadito's band had nearly been wiped out. He often regretted that Delgadito had not been among those slain, but such was life. He'd been content with having Delgadito's influence among their people shattered, and he had expected the few survivors to come slinking back into the village with their tails between their legs to admit they had been wrong to resist the whites.

Palacio had dreamed of that day, had dreamed of making Delgadito squirm for defying him. But then along came the so-called White Apache, and to Palacio's annoyance the small band of renegades made a series of successful raids that had stirred up the hotheads in the tribe into thinking that the time must be ripe for rising up against the Americans and driving them from Chiricahua land.

Not long ago Palacio had visited the renegades at one of their many sanctuaries in the mountains. Delgadito had set up the meeting to ask that his band be allowed to slip into the village now and then to visit relatives and friends. The renegades missed them, he had claimed. But Palacio knew better. The real reason Delgadito wanted to return was to persuade others to join his little band, and thereby weaken Palacio's hold on the tribe.

It had given the chief immense joy to refuse— tactfully of course. He had pointed out that the Army and the reservation police were everywhere, and keen to get their hands on the renegades. Should Delgadito's band be captured in the village, it would not sit well with the Americans, who might see fit to make reservation life harder than it already was. The Chiricahuas might be punished for Delgadito's deeds.

Reluctantly, Delgadito had agreed. They had gone their separate ways, and until that very morning Palacio had not set eyes on any of the renegades. Then he had spotted Clay Taggart.

It was safe to say that where Palacio despised Delgadito, he positively hated Lickoyee-shis-inday. It was Taggart who had saved Delgadito from the scalp hunters, Taggart who had gone on to lead a successful raid into Mexico and against several ranchers, Taggart who was now the most feared man on the frontier. Because of his reputation, many younger warriors were seriously thinking about joining the renegades.

The White Apache was a genuine threat to Palacio's leadership. Accordingly, Palacio would give anything to have the white-eye eliminated. How could he pass up the chance?

There Palacio had been, on his way northward to meet a pair of smugglers who brought him special items from time to time in exchange for gold nuggets, when he had seen White Apache enter a gully. It had been easy for Palacio to shadow him and wait for the right moment to take his life. Unfortunately, once again the white-eye's astounding luck protected him. Palacio, who could put out the eye of a squirrel at fifty yards, had merely nicked Clay Taggart.

It surprised Palacio that the White Apache had been able to track him northward from the gully. Despite his size, he was as adept as any of his people at leaving few tracks and disguising those he did make. He thought he had given the American the slip, and yet had he not turned at just the right moment to check his back trail, Lickoyee-shis-inday would have put a bullet into him.

Palacio was beginning to understand why White Apache was so widely dreaded. The man had an amazing knack for death and destruction. Not many moons ago, he had witnessed a formal fight between the white-eye and one of the most skilled knife fighters in the tribe and been stunned when White Apache won.

All of which confirmed Palacio's resolve to have the man disposed of. The only question was how to go about it. He wasn't about to try again himself. And none of the Chiricahuas were going to jeopardize their lives without ample cause.

Palacio jogged on under the hot sun. His meeting with the smugglers would have to take place another day. The White Apache had been heading northward too, and Palacio didn't care to run the risk of encountering the man again. Better by far to return to the village and have one of his two wives tend to his growling belly. Several helpings of the spicy bean dish so favored by the *Nakai-yes* would do wonders for his disposition. That, and five or six gourds of *tizwin*.

A leader had to keep his priorities straight or he was no leader at all.

It was shortly before sunset when Palacio heard the drum of hoofs and jingle of cavalry accoutrements. He set down the heady *tizwin* he had been drinking and nodded at his younger wife, who dutifully moved to the wickiup entrance.

"Four *soldados*," she reported. "White Hair leads them. Another is the *capitan* who killed Chivari. And Klo-sen trails behind."

This was most unexpected. White Hair was the Chiricahua name for Colonel Reynolds, the commander of Fort Bowie. The captain she spoke of was Gerald Forester, one of the few officers who had taken the time to learn some of the Apache tongue. And Klo-sen was an Army scout, a Mescalero but still Apache. For them to pay him a visit without first letting him know they were coming was most unusual.

"I will greet them outside," Palacio said, heaving erect. "Bring my pipe and tobacco pouch."

Lumbering outdoors, Palacio sank into a large chair he had obtained at the trading post. All around him was other evidence of his wealth. His wickiup was the only one in the village that sported canvas sides instead of being made from brush and grass. Nearby were three metal pails rather than earthen jugs. A metal pot containing cooking utensils sat by the entrance. And leaning against the side of the lodge was a new shovel.

The riders were twenty yards off. Men and animals were caked with dust, except for the Mescalero who somehow managed to look as if he had just come from his own lodge.

Palacio swelled out his chest and leaned back, his pudgy hands folded in his ample lap. It pleased him immensely to note that many of his people were on hand to witness the event. Here was the chief white-eye from the gigantic stone lodge paying him, Palacio, a visit. It would confirm the story he had been spreading that his council was widely esteemed by the whites, and that the white-eyes looked to him first when dealing with the Chiricahuas.

Clearing his throat, Palacio called out in near perfect English, "Greetings, Colonel. You honor my wickiup with your presence." He had made it a point to learn the tongue of the Americans, just as he had learned the tongue of the Mexicans before them. It was a gift of the *gans,* this ability to learn new tongues easily. The last Chiricahua to have the gift was Cochise, who had risen to be a legend among his people in his own time. Could Palacio do any less?

Col. Reynolds raised a hand in salute and reined up. The ride from Fort Bowie had been long and hot, and he had made matters worse by pushing the horses to insure he would arrive well before dark. Removing his hat, he plucked a monogrammed handkerchief from a pocket and wiped his face as best he was able to make himself presentable.

Sgt. McKinn was the first to dismount. He handed the reins of his horse to Klo-sen and hurried to hold the commander's horse.

Looking on, Capt. Vincent Paramalee smirked. In his eyes, McKinn was only sucking up to the colonel, a detestable act Parmalee would never commit. He licked his dry lips, thought of the flask secreted in his saddlebags, and wished with all his might that he could take a swig.

Capt. Gerald Forester swung down and let his reins drop to the ground. He made no attempt to improve his appearance, nor did his thirst show. Forester was a veteran of the Indians Wars, first in the Dakotas and for the past four years in Arizona. He could live off the land, spoke fluent Apache, and had patrolled the Territory from east to west, north to south. To put it succinctly, he was the most experienced officer in the Fifth Cavalry. It was a fact of which Col. Reynolds was well aware, and why he had brought Forester along. Of all his subordinates, Reynolds relied on Forester's judgment the most.

Palacio also knew the captain's reputation, and didn't like him. It was Forester, after all, who had tracked down and slain the renegade Chivari in personal combat over three winters ago. But Palacio's dislike stemmed more from the impression he had that Forester didn't think very highly of him than from the death of Chivari, who had always been a minor thorn in Palacio's side.

Klo-sen was the only one who stayed on his horse, a rifle slanted across his thighs. While he shared kinship to the Chiricahuas in that they were all Apaches, there had been a time long ago when Mescaleros and Chiricahuas fought against one another. He no more trusted them than he would Comanches.

"Hello again, Palacio," Colonel Reynolds said, advancing and offering his hand. "I'm glad you're here. I was afraid we'd travel all this way and miss you."

The Chiricahua chief shook. Palacio never had fully understood the silly white custom of touching hands, but he did it anyway to make them happy. "My heart is glad to see you again, my friend," he said solemnly. "Raven Wing is bringing my pipe. We will smoke, then talk over what brings you to my people." He emphasized the last few words.

Reynolds would much rather have gotten straight to the point, but he had visited the chief before and knew that failure to smoke might be taken as an insult. So he sat cross-legged with his subordinates and Palacio in a circle in front of the canvas wickiup and passed the lit pipe around. Palacio then raised the pipe to the heavens, shifted, and handed it Raven Beak.

"Now then, White Hair," Palacio said. "To what do I owe the pleasure of your visit?"

"Desperation," Col. Reynolds said. "I want to stop the White Apache once and for all."

"We share the same dream," Palacio said, his countenance clouding. "But we have tried many times and he is still alive."

"I have a new idea," Reynolds said. "I want to make one of your people very, very rich."

"Rich?"

"Yes. Do you think any of them would like to own eight new horses, forty new blankets, six new knives, an ax, and all the tobacco they can carry?"

The vision of so much wealth made Palacio's head spin. "Who would not?"

"Excellent. All those things will be given to the warrior who tells me where White Apache and Delgadito are hiding. And as a bonus, if the information leads to the deaths of the renegades, I'll throw in fifty dollars worth of credit at the trading post."

Palacio had to bite his lip to keep from howling for sheer joy. "Never fear, White Hair. The renegades are as good as dead."

Chapter Four

It was strange to have one's head feel as if it were an overripe melon.

Clay Taggart, the White Apache, staggered on through the darkness feeling just that way. His head pounded with every heartbeat. It had swelled horribly during the long hours he had been on the trail, and merely placing a finger on his temple provoked spasms so intense he could barely stand. If he were to trip and strike his head, he was sure he would never get up again.

All these factors made the decision to press on through the night the only logical one to make. White Apache needed to reach water as quickly as possible. Any delay, even a night's rest, might weaken him to the point where he would be unable to go on.

About midnight, White Apache had begun to feel oddly sluggish, and a distinct mineral taste filled his mouth. He had no idea what to make of it, but it did not bode well. Now the time was close to four in the morning and in another hour the eastern horizon would streak with pale harbingers of dawn. And still he had not reached the stream.

White Apache paused and studied the landscape to get his bearings. Even at the plodding pace he had maintained for the past six hours, he should have struck the stream by now. Either he had strayed off course or the stream had gone dry, which many did in Arizona during the hotter months of the year. But this one was supposed to run year-round.

It should be there.

He tried to lick his lips but his tongue was as swollen as his head. Slinging the Winchester over a shoulder, he cradled his chin in his hands, holding his head steady so he could think a little more clearly.

The landmarks, such as they were, weren't familiar. To the northwest dark peaks reared. To the northeast grew heavy timber. All around him lay dry land dotted with boulders.

There should be grass, Clay remembered. If he was close to the stream he would come on a quarter-mile strip of grass grazed by deer and antelope.

Goading his legs into motion, White Apache tramped northward, using the North Star to steer his course. It was yet another of the many tricks Delgadito had taught him, lessons that had already saved his hide more than once.

Reminisces of the renegade leader occupied him for a while. He thought of all they had been through, of the times Delgadito had pulled his bacon out of the fire, of the enemies they had faced and beaten. He considered Delgadito a pard in every sense of the word, although of late he had grown to suspect that Delgadito was using him in some manner to regain his lost standing in the tribe.

So what if he was? That was Clay's attitude. He owed Delgadito a debt he could never repay, which made it only fair for him to help the warrior become a leader again.

One thing was for sure. No matter how many successful raids Clay led, no matter how many whites or *Nakai-yes* he slew, or how much plunder he took, the Chiricahuas would never accept him as a leader because of his heritage. In the entire history of the tribe only full-blooded Chiricahuas had held such posts.

That was all right, too, in Clay's book. He had no desire to become a war chief. He had no urge to lead. His sole motivation for living was sweet and simple: revenge.

The next moment White Apache stepped on a stone that shot from under his foot and caused his leg to swing out in front of him. He tried to regain his footing, but in his condition it was like asking a drunk to walk a straight line. Down he went, hard, onto his back.

The pounding became thunder. The number of stars in the firmament doubled. He heard a low groan and realized the sound came from his throat. Racked by pain, he nearly blacked out.

For the longest while Clay lay there, his eyes closed, waiting for the torment to subside so he could go on. The wind stirred his hair and whistled among the boulders. He dozed off, briefly.

The patter of stealthy footfalls brought White Apache around. Ears pricked, he listened as the sound came closer and closer. Cracking his eyes, he spied a ghostly shape crouched about fifteen feet away.

Painter! Clay's mind screeched. Some called them panthers, some mountain lions, others cougars. However they were called, they infested the Southwest and were most numerous in the border country. Although normally they fought shy of humans, there had been occasions when bolder cats had pounced on people.

Girding himself, White Apache sat up and placed a hand on his pistol. At close range, at night, it was the better gun to use. He would be able to get off more shots, faster.

Normally, anyway. Tonight White Apache could barely lift the six-shooter and level the barrel. He saw the lion slink closer, crouched as if to spring, attracted, no doubt, by the stale scent of blood.

It was a gigantic animal. He had heard tales of panthers seven feet long from nose tip to tail's end, but this one was bigger, seven and a half feet if it was an inch. Now the cat growled, rumbling deep in its chest, its serpentine tail whipping like a berserk sidewinder.

To White Apache's dismay, he found that he was unable to hold the revolver steady. His hand shook as if from a conniption. And when he attempted to take aim, he couldn't keep the sight fixed on the panther.

"Damn," Clay said aloud.

Hissing, the mountain lion backed up a few steps.

"Don't like the sound of my voice, do you?" Clay said. "Well, here's something you'll like even less." So saying, he banged off a shot in the predator's general direction.

One moment the panther was there, the next it was gone. Blinking, Clay looked and looked but saw no trace of the beast. He recollected being told once that lions liked to circle around behind their prey so he shifted to glance over a shoulder. The movement triggered a blast of anguish between his ears. A black veil, blacker than the night itself, seemed to sweep toward him from out of the recesses of his own mind and enclosed him in its inky grasp.

White Apache struggled to stay awake, to stay alert. The mountain lion was liable to jump him at any second. But, try as he might, he slipped deeper and deeper into the indigo well. The last thing he felt was his cheek hitting the earth.

There is nothing quite like waking up to find yourself alive when you have every right to believe you should be dead.

White Apache squinted at the blazing sun, which hung low in the eastern sky, and gratefully inhaled the hot air. He slowly rose onto his elbows. The Colt was beside him, the panther nowhere to be seen.

The drumming inside his skull, though, persisted, as bad as ever. Propping his hands under him, he rose, picking up the pistol as he did so. No sooner did he straighten than a wave of dizziness washed over him, threatening to flatten him again. He held himself still until the vertigo passed, then shuffled northward.

Clay was so thirsty he would have dunked his face into a mud puddle to suck the moisture from the mud. He could barely open his mouth, and when he did so, his lips felt as if they were cracking in half.

Delgadito had taught him which cactus plants contained water, but there were none in that area.

The few clumps of vegetation he could see would provide no relief at all.

The best White Apache could do was slip a pebble in his mouth to suck on. But when he tried, his swollen tongue prevented him from inserting the pebble past his puffy lips. In annoyance he cast the pebble down. The movement of his arm jarred his head and the pain became almost unbearable. He stumbled, about to pass out again, but by the sheer strength of his willpower he was able to plod on, weak and weary and closer to death than he had ever been.

White Apache was only vaguely conscious of things around him. He knew the sun was climbing, knew the air was as hot as the scorching inferno of hell, knew when he nearly stepped on a gila monster and had to sidestep or be bitten, knew when, sometime about noon, his legs began to tingle and go numb.

This was the end, White Apache reflected. He had survived being hanged, survived being shot at, survived knife fights and clashes with the cavalry and *federales*, only to die because of an infected wound, lost in the middle of nowhere with no one to mourn his passing, not so much as a single living soul who would shed a single tear or remember him fondly once he was gone.

Dying alone and unmourned had to be one of the most horrible fates to befall a person. He thought of his folks, the only two people who had ever cared for him with their whole hearts.

Lilly certainly hadn't. The woman he had loved more than life itself had betrayed him, had forsaken him for Miles Gillett, had even helped Gillett capture him and done nothing when Gillett's hands had taken a bull whip to him and beaten him within an inch of his life.

Now Clay would never get to pay her back. Nor would he ever have the satisfaction of cutting her wicked, treacherous husband into little pieces, or of slowly strangling the bastard to death with his bare hands. Sometimes life could be so damned unfair.

That was the last thought the White Apache had before his legs gave out completely and his head smashed onto the hard earth. For an instant the pain flared and he hurt as he had never hurt before from head to toe.

Then there was nothing.

The face seemed to shimmer and dance above him like a mirage. White Apache attempted to focus, but his thoughts spun as if caught in a whirlpool, mimicking the image. Suddenly the features sharpened. The face became clear, or he believed it did, and he saw above him the lovely features and dark hair of his beloved.

"Lilly!" Clay breathed.

Someone spoke, but it wasn't Lilly's voice. The words were alien, a tongue he didn't know.

"Lilly, is that you?"

The whirlpool slowed to a crawl, then stopped. The shimmer faded, and the face became crystal clear. It was the face of a woman, but not Lilly Gillett. The woman's short hair was darker than Lilly's, as was the hue of her skin. She was an Indian.

White Apache went to rise on his elbows but the woman spoke sharply and held him down by the shoulders. Then a shadow fell over them.

In his delirium, White Apache assumed that the woman was pinning him in place so her man could finish him off. His logic ran thus: Was he not dressed like an Apache? Did he not look like an

Apache warrior in all respects? And wasn't it also true that every tribe in Arizona had a longstanding grudge against the Apaches over years of Apache raids? Therefore it seemed obvious to him that a roving band had found him lying there helpless and were about to rub him out.

The insight roused White Apache into defending himself. Mustering what little strength remained in his limbs, he lashed out, flinging the woman from him so he could sit up. His hand fell to the Colt, which the woman had foolishly left in its holster, and he twisted to confront the source of the shadow.

It was a boy, no more than ten or eleven, holding a water skin. He had frozen in shock in the act of opening it.

White Apache paused, confused. He looked for warriors but there were none, just a pair of small bundles lying a few yards away.

The woman had risen to her knees and was regarding him frankly, with no hint of fear in her pretty eyes. She put her warm palm on his chest and said in heavily accented English: "Please. Lie down. We help."

To hear English issuing from her rosy lips was enough to convince White Apache that he was imagining the whole incident. The wound and the sunstroke had taken their toll. His blood had become so poisoned that now he was hallucinating. "You're not real," he blurted thickly, hardly able to form the words. "This is a dream."

The woman beckoned the boy. When he just stood there, too scared to move, she spoke sternly in her own tongue and he handed the water skin over. She removed the stopper.

White Apache felt her press the smooth bag to

his lips, felt cool, delicious water trickle into his mouth, around his tongue and down his throat. It was the best water he had ever drunk, without exception. He swallowed, and thought his throat had ruptured. Unexpectedly gagging, he doubled over and came close to retching.

The woman squeezed his arm in reassurance. "Drink slow," she said in her sweetly lilting voice. "Make much sick if don't."

"Who—?" White Apache tried to ask, rasping the question between clenched teeth.

"Later talk. Now try drink."

Gradually the heaves went away. White Apache sat back up and the woman tried again, pouring with infinite care. He was able to swallow this time, and bit by bit the awful ache in his throat disappeared. He could move his tongue a little, even though it felt as if it were still swollen as thick as his wrist.

The woman was patient with him. Again and again she raised the water skin when he nodded, lowered it after a few sips.

By all rights White Apache should have been more interested in the water than in her, but oddly enough he couldn't take his mind, or his eyes, off his deliverer. She was short, no more than five and a half feet tall, but nicely shaped, with a full bosom, small hands, and even white teeth. She wore a loose-fitting top and a wrap-around skirt that clung to her in all the right places, accentuating her curves. Her body smelled of mint.

It had been a long time since Clay Taggart had lain with a woman. Too long. At night he often tossed and turned, dreaming of Lilly, of the rapturous silken glory of her sleek naked body snuggled next to his. Frequently of late, in the mornings he would awaken aroused and frustrated.

Clay wanted a woman of his own, but whenever the notion struck him he discarded it as downright foolish. He was an outlaw, an outcast without a home, wanted by white and red men alike, a price on his head high enough to interest every bounty hunter who lived. Taking a woman into his life would doom her to certain death.

Then there was the matter of Lilly Gillett. Although she had betrayed his trust and perverted their love, Clay still cherished her in his heart of hearts. She had been his first true love, and he figured on treasuring the memory of their time together for as long as he lived.

It was strange, Clay often mused, that a man could love a woman so passionately and hate her so intensely at the same time. How was that possible? Love and hate were opposites. They should cancel one another out. Yet, in some bizarre way, he felt both emotions for Lilly. It came from being addlepated, he reckoned.

The woman shook the water skin, frowned, and capped it. "Little left," she said. "Must save. Very sorry."

"Don't be," Clay croaked. "You saved my life. Who are you? What are you doing in these parts?"

"I am *Ma-ris-ta*. My son, *Col-let-to*. We be Pimas."

"Marista," Clay repeated her name. He had never met a Pima before, but knew of them.

A number of tribes lived in dangerously close proximity to Apache territory. One of the largest were the Pimas, farmers who grew beans, squash, and pumpkins. They lived in round, flat-topped dwellings built with grass and earth, and they were as peaceful as could be. Never once, to Clay's knowledge, had they attacked whites or Mexicans.

Even so, the Pimas were fierce in defense of their land and loved ones, as many Apache, Mohave, and Yuma raiders had found out to their dismay. The Chiricahuas regarded the Pimas as good fighters but looked down their noses at them on general principle; to the Apache way of thinking, anyone who tilled the soil for a living was beneath contempt.

Clay studied the woman and the boy. He wanted to ask a lot more questions but his mouth and throat hurt too much. Pointing to the north, he asked, "Do you know of a stream close by?"

"No," Marista said. "Country new. We lost. Little water." She tapped the water skin.

It dawned on Clay that the mother and son had sacrificed most of what little they had to save him. "Come with me," he suggested. "We'll find more together."

Marista bit her lower lip, her brow knit. The glance she bestowed on Colleto told why.

"I would never harm you," Clay declared. "I'm in your debt, and a Taggart never forgets an obligation."

There was hardly any hesitation on her part. "We come. I help you."

Before Clay could object, the Pima woman had a sturdy arm looped under his shoulder and was hoisting him off the ground. He was going to tell her not to bother, to assure her that he could manage by himself, but his legs put the lie to his claim by buckling. She strained, as the corded muscles of her neck testified, and held him upright.

"Go slow," Marista said, catching his eye. "Your name be?"

"Clay Taggart," he disclosed, and was on the verge of adding that he was also known as Lickoyee-shis-inday when he changed his mind. There wasn't a person in Arizona, white or red, who hadn't heard of the White Apache by now. And since a hefty reward was being offered for his head, dead or alive, he decided it was prudent to keep quiet.

"You dress like Apache," the woman noted. "You part Apache?"

"No," Clay said, and gestured for her to start walking. "Let's head on out. I'm a mite paper-backed at the moment, and I don't rightly know how much longer I can hold out."

Colletto fell in step behind them as Clay and Marista hiked northward. Neither the boy nor his mother carried weapons, which surprised Clay greatly. What could they be thinking, traipsing across the Chiricahua reservation unarmed the way they were doing? Could it be that they had no idea where they were? He set his questions aside for the time being and pushed himself as hard as he dared.

A snail could have gone faster. Or such was Clay's opinion after fifteen minutes had gone by. His legs felt as if they weighed tons. He was so weak that he couldn't lift his feet more than a few inches with each step.

An hour elapsed. Clay had to shake himself a few times to stay on his toes, and each time provoked new stirrings of acute agony. Once the woman halted and gestured for her son to bring the water skin to him but Clay shook his head and said firmly, "No. We'll save it for later in case we need it."

"You need now," Marista noted.

"No. Keep going."

Reluctantly, the Pima obeyed.

Clay shut the misery from his mind and stumbled along at her side. Up close, he could see tiny wrinkles at the corners of her eyes and mouth and noted that her skirt and top were worn and faded. Her sandals were close to falling apart; one had a cracked strap and flapped when she walked. Clearly she had fallen on very hard times. "Where's your husband? Did something happen to him?" he asked at one point.

"Too hot talk now," she said stiffly.

Clay posed no more questions for a while. As the afternoon waxed, the heat climbed. When it was at its worst, he indicated some mesquite off to one side and suggested, "Let's rest in the shade a spell."

Mother and son sat a few feet from him, her arm around the boy's shoulders. She had a large pouch slung over her shoulder, the only possession she owned other than the water skin.

"Do you have any food?" Clay inquired.

"We did." Marista opened the flap and held the pouch at arm's length so he could see it was empty. "Ate all last sleep."

"If I was fit, I'd rustle you up some grub in two shakes of a calf's tail," Clay said. "As things stand, we'll have to hold out until evening. If we can find the damn stream, there's bound to be plenty of game nearby." He patted the Winchester. "One shot, and we'll gorge on venison until it comes out our ears."

"Out our ears?" Marista said quizzically, placing a hand on one of hers.

Clay chuckled, then winced. "That's what they call a figure of speech. Words which don't make a whole hell of a lot of sense, but folks use them all the time anyway."

"I not understand."

"Doesn't matter. It's not important."

They sat in silence for twenty minutes. Clay's eyelids drooped and his chin bobbed several times but he refused to fall asleep, to appear weak in front of the woman. He found himself admiring her on the sly and being impressed by her bearing and composure.

At length they pressed on. The boy assumed the lead, the water skin slung over his shoulder.

More and more mesquite appeared. Through it wound a game trail bearing deer tracks not more than a day old. Clay became encouraged and kept craning his neck to see what lay ahead. He was the first to spot a tract of waving grass.

As they emerged from the mesquite, the boy jumped up and down and flapped his arms while jabbering excitedly in the Pima tongue. The stream glistened like a sparkling emerald necklace a hundred yards off, flanked by trees.

Clay lurched into a hobbling run, heedless of the consequences, and Marista kept pace. They were both nearly spent when they halted under the limbs of a cottonwood. Colletto, who had dashed on ahead, stood stone still at the water's edge. He had good cause.

From out of a high clump of bushes had stepped two grungy men in grimy buckskins, both armed with rifles. The taller of the pair chortled and exclaimed, "Why, lookee here, Zeb. We're goin' to have us some fun!"

Chapter Five

"*Lickoyee-shis-inday* should have been here by now."

Cuchillo Negro, he whose name meant Black Knife, heard the statement of his young friend but chose to make no comment. The young were always too impatient, and too prone to remark on the obvious when no remark was needed. He knew White Apache was late, but he would not waste breath complaining. It was not the Chiricahua way.

Ponce jumped onto a boulder to scan the canyon below. "We would see him if he were coming. Something must have happened to him."

"What would you have us do?" Cuchillo Negro asked. Not because he needed advice, since he already knew what their next step would be. He asked to test the younger warrior, to gauge whether Ponce had what it took to one day be a warrior of high standing in the tribe.

61

"We could try to find him," Ponce said, "but it would take us a long time, and in a short while the sun will go down." He swiveled to the northwest. "We would not be able to rejoin Delgadito and Fiero tomorrow morning as we said we would. They will wonder what has happened to us."

"What would White Apache or Delgadito do in such a case?" Cuchillo Negro asked. Using the example set by seasoned warriors to instruct the young was a time-honored Apache custom. How well he remembered his own upbringing, when his father and uncles had taken him under their wing and imparted important lessons that had saved his life many times over.

Ponce, though, had no father, no uncles. The young warrior had lost most of his relatives that terrible day the scalphunters had attacked without warning, slaughtering almost all those who had chosen to follow Delgadito. Only a handful of warriors had escaped, and Delgadito himself would have died had White Apache not whisked him from under the noses of the butchers.

White Apache. Now there was a mystery Cuchillo Negro had yet to unravel. When Delgadito saved the white-eye from being hanged, it had been Delgadito's intent to have the man called Taggart set up a meeting between the cavalry and the renegades. Delgadito's band had grown tired of always being on the run. They'd wanted to return to the reservation, to be among their own people again. Then along came the scalphunters, and changed everything.

Delgadito lost all his influence. He was bad medicine, the reservation Chiricahuas claimed. But never one to give up, Delgadito had seen a way to exploit the white-eye, to use Taggart to regain his lost prestige. And now?

Blood Treachery

Cuchillo Negro heard Ponce speak and turned.

"I think we should split up. One of us should go after White Apache while the other goes on to let Delgadito know what has happened."

The stripling had chosen wisely. Cuchillo Negro was pleased. "You go on. I will track down White Apache." Cuchillo Negro rose and stepped off the flat rock on which he had been perched.

"This very moment?" Ponce asked.

"You would have us wait until morning?"

Ponce made no reply. He knew he had spoken thoughtlessly. To explain would compound his mistake. Hitching at his cartridge belt, he spun and ran off up the mountain with the agility of a bighorn.

Cuchillo Negro lingered until the youth was out of sight before he made off to the southeast. By pushing himself, he would reach the spot where the three of them had separated shortly after dark. Tracking at night was difficult but it could be done, so he would keep going and hope *Lickoyee-shis-inday* was all right.

The Chiricahuas needed him, more than the man knew or would ever suspect.

Palacio sat toward the rear of his wickiup, resplendent in his finest garb, a new red headband framing his oval face and the warm smile he wore to make his five guests feel at ease. He raked them with a probing stare one more time and asked, "Are there any questions?"

Crusty old Nantanh looked up. "This is bad, this thing you want us to do. Chiricahuas do not help enemies kill Chiricahuas."

Chico grunted. "And since when do Chiricahuas care about how many horses they own? Or how many knives? We live for two things, and two

63

things only." He paused. "To kill without being killed and to steal without being caught."

Palacio had foreseen their argument and he was ready. "The welfare of our people matters, or it should to every Chiricahua worthy of the name. And I say to you that unless the renegades are stopped, hard times will befall our people. Is that what you want?"

"Of course not," Juan Pedro said, "but since the beginning of time, Chiricahua has not turned on Chiricahua. Delgadito might have chosen the wrong path, but he is still one of us, still of our blood, still worthy of our loyalty."

Palacio was unruffled. This, too, he had anticipated. For all their love of being independent, when braced by enemies, Apaches of all kinds banded together to preserve their own. "Does this hold true for *Lickoyee-shis-inday* also?"

"White Apache has sided with Delgadito," Nantanh said.

"But does that make him *Shis-Inday?* Does that entitle him to be treated as we would treat one another? Does that mean we should call him our brother?"

"Delgadito does," Nantanh persisted.

Palacio's smile broadened to cover the resentment simmering inside him. The old warrior might be well past his prime but his mind was as sharp as ever and in councils he was always quick to point out flaws in plans and battle strategies. Convincing him would be a challenge.

"Delgadito is entitled," Palacio said suavely. "From what I hear, this White Apache saved his life. But the White Apache did not save me, or any of you. Why, then, should we let him be the cause of the ruin of our people?" Five heads swung toward him.

Blood Treachery

"What do you mean, the ruin?" Gian-nah-tah said. "What do you know that we do not?"

Palacio played his part perfectly. Leaning forward to give the idea he was confiding a great secret, he said in a low voice only they could hear, "The *Americanos* have run out of patience. They want this White Apache, and they are willing to do whatever is necessary to get him. My good friend, White Hair, the chief of the soldiers at the stone lodge called Bowie, has told me of their plans so that we can take steps to protect ourselves."

"What plans?" Nantanh asked suspiciously.

"The white-eyes think our people must be sheltering the White Apache. They do not believe me when I tell them we want nothing to do with him. So they intend to send in soldiers, more soldiers than there are blades of grass in the hills, to round us up and move us to San Carlos. They will strip us of our lands and make us farm as do the Pimas and Maricopas."

Old Nantanh was red in the face. "I would like to see them try! Our land was promised to us for as long as the sun and moon exist. Their great chief gave his promise to Cochise. I was there. I heard."

"As did many of us," Palacio said. "But you know how the white-eyes can be. Sometimes they speak with two tongues. Sometimes their great chief says one thing and lesser chiefs say another. In this, though, I think they all speak as one. Unless we do something, our people will suffer."

Indecision etched five faces, and Palacio took advantage.

"White Hair is trying to help us by giving us a chance to help them. If we let them know where to find the White Apache, I have his promise that our people will not be moved to San Carlos." Palacio sat back, smugly confident they would give in. The story about being moved to San Carlos was untrue, a lie he had made to lend weight to his arguments. He knew that for some time there had been rumors the Army intended to relocate the tribe, which the Chiricahuas would do anything to prevent.

Nantanh snorted. "A promise! It is a threat. Unless we give in, we will be punished." He shook a bony fist in the air. "If Cochise were still alive the white-eyes would not treat us as they do!"

"No one wishes Cochise were still with us more than I do," Palacio claimed. The reality was that he had been overjoyed when the venerable chief passed on. Cochise had never liked him, had relegated him to a minor role in the peace talks and shunned him whenever possible.

Chico spoke next. "I have no objection to helping the soldiers find the White Apache but I will not betray Delgadito. He is my friend."

"Mine too," Juan Pedro said.

Palacio saw his grand scheme unraveling before his eyes. "How many times must I tell you? It is White Apache the *Americanos* want. White Hair gave me his word that he will try to take Delgadito alive."

"The word of a white-eye," Nantanh said in disgust. "Now there is something we can depend on." Most of the others smiled.

The old warrior's insult was like the thrust of a double-edged knife. It cut the whites, but it also cut Palacio for suggesting the Chiricahuas should do as the *Americanos* wanted. Palacio took the remark in stride, but he made a mental note to pay Nantanh back one day. He was not one to forgive an insult, no matter how slight.

"It seems we cannot reach agreement on this matter," Palacio said, "so maybe it is best if we spread the word among our people and let each warrior decide for himself whether he wants to aid White Hair or not."

"Anyone who does will never be welcome in my lodge," Nantanh said.

"I could never trust anyone who turned against one of our own," Chico said.

The meeting broke up, the leaders going their separate ways. Palacio had every reason to be disappointed by the end result, but he wasn't. He'd noticed that the youngest of those present, Giannah-tah, had not spoken in Delgadito's defense. Indeed, when the subject of the bounty came up, Palacio had seen a flicker of interest in the other's eyes.

Someone would take White Hair up on the offer, Palacio was sure. And when that happened, he stood to gain in three respects. First, the problem of what to do about White Apache would be solved once and for all. Second, he would finally be rid of Delgadito, who had been a thorn in his side for as long as he could remember. And third, he stood to gain in horses, blankets, and knives, because he had told the others that the whites-eyes were only offering half the number they actually were. The rest, naturally, would go to him.

Palacio grinned contentedly and motioned for one of his wives to bring him more *tizwin*. He deserved to celebrate a little. It wasn't every day that he deceived so many people at one time and ended up richer as a result. So what if some of those people were his very own? Stealing without being caught, that was the Apache way.

He couldn't help it if he was better at it than most.

On seeing the pair of cat-eyed Daniel Boones materialize out of the brush, Clay Taggart automatically lowered his right hand toward his Colt. He stopped when the one called Zeb, a lanky character whose lower lip had once been split by a knife or tomahawk, swung the muzzle of a big buffalo gun toward him and the hammer clicked back.

"I wouldn't, if I were you, Injun. This here Sharps will blow a hole in you the size of a pancake."

The tall man laughed. "Are you plumb loco, you jackass? Most of these rotten heathens don't speak our tongue, and even if this one does, odds are he wouldn't know a pancake if it was to bite him on the ass."

Marista walked up to her son and put an arm on Colletto's shoulders. "I speak white tongue," she boldly announced. "Who you be? What you want?"

Clay figured they were prospectors. Despite the risk and a ban by the Army on mining on the Chiricahua Reservation, scores of gold-hungry fools snuck onto Apache land every month. Most were caught and escorted off again. Some simply vanished.

Zeb ambled forward, his black whiskers creased by yellow teeth. "Imagine this! A squaw who savvies English. Why, next you know, Pike, they'll be wearin' frilly dresses and going to tea every afternoon."

Pike guffawed and advanced, leading a string

of horses, four of which were pack animals burdened with more supplies than a pair of prospectors rightfully needed, all covered over with canvas. "Ain't that a fact." He tied the lead animal to the cottonwood and turned. "As to who we are, squaw, and what we do, you might say that we're a travelin' tradin' post."

They were smugglers, Clay realized, hardcases who made their living selling ill-gotten goods on both sides of the border. Men without scruples, men who would as soon kill a man as look at him if there was profit to be made. More than ever he wanted to make a play for his Colt. But he wasn't about to commit suicide, and in his condition he wouldn't stand a prayer.

"You're a Pima, ain't you?" Zeb asked Marista. "You and the brat, both?"

"We are."

"And what about you?" Zeb said, moving closer to Clay and pressing the Sharps against his belly. "You sure as hell don't look like any Pima I ever saw."

"If I didn't know better, I'd swear he was an Apache," Pike said as he walked over behind Clay and claimed the Winchester and six-shooter.

"Can't be," Zeb said while scrutinizing Clay closely. "No self-respectin' Apache would let himself be caught flat-footed the way this one done." Pursing his lips, he paused. "There's something about this hombre, Pike."

"What?"

"I don't rightly know. But it sticks in my craw that I ought to know who he is. Reckon we've met him somewhere?"

Pike stood elbow to elbow with his companion. "The face ain't familiar, pard. But damn me if I don't think you're right." He slung Clay's rifle over his own shoulder. "Now ain't this mighty strange."

Averting his gaze, Clay hoped they wouldn't notice the color of his eyes. It would be a dead giveaway of his identity, and once they knew who they had in their clutches, they were the types to gun him down where he stood and then tote his carcass to the fort to collect their blood money.

Zeb glanced at Clay's temple. "Looks as if he got himself shot not long ago. Nasty wound. Take a gander at all that pus oozin' out. I reckon he ain't long for this world if he don't get some doctorin'."

"So what do we do with them?"

The pair backed up a few feet. Pike gave the Pima woman the sort of look that left no doubt as to his intentions. Zeb scratched his bushy beard, pondering.

"Well, the woman should fetch a tidy sum from the Comanches. They'll take anything in a dress. As for the brat, we'll take him to Sonora and let the scalphunters have him, cheap. They'll be able to pass off his hair as genuine Apache."

"And this buck here?"

Zeb shrugged. "I can't rightly make up my mind. It makes sense to fill him full of lead, but I have this feelin' we should hold off a spell. And since we're not going anywhere until Palacio shows up, we might as well tie him up until we decide."

The mention of the Chiricahua chief perked Clay's interest. Now he knew why Palacio had been heading north. It made him wonder what sort of business the wily leader had with the two smugglers, but he didn't dwell on the question long.

Pike had gone to one of the pack animals

and was rummaging under the canvas. When he stepped back, he held a coiled rope. "Cover the buck for me, pard."

Clay tensed, his arms close to his sides. He wasn't about to let them hogtie him, hurt head or no. Once he was helpless, they were liable to beat him half to death for the hell of it. And there was no telling what they would do to the woman. They had taken his guns but not his knife, a mistake that would cost them when they came within reach.

Marista had steered Colletto closer to the stream. Her shoulders were slumped in meek surrender, her face bowed low. She had taken the water skin from her son and held it in front of her chest.

Zeb wagged the Sharps. "Don't give us no grief, Injun, or so help me, I'll blow one of your legs off at the knee." He switched to passable Chiricahua and repeated the warning, concluding with, "Do you understand me?"

By then Pike was near enough, a few steps to the rear of his partner. "Step aside and let me at him."

As Zeb started to comply, Clay exploded into action. Springing, he streaked the Bowie clear of its sheath and drove the gleaming blade at Zeb's gut. The smuggler, taken off guard, shifted and tried to train the Sharps on Clay's chest. The Bowie and the barrel clanged together. Whether by accident or by design, the rifle went off with a tremendous boom. The slug missed Clay by a finger's width, striking the cottonwood instead.

Zeb, throwing himself backward, collided with Pike.

Clay raised the knife to strike at the smuggler's neck, but before he could follow through, another bout of dizziness drew him up short. His limbs turned to mush.

"Move!" Pike roared, giving his partner a shove. "Let me finish this mangy varmint off here and now!"

Caught flat-footed, Clay could do no more than stand there helplessly as the smuggler took a deliberate bead on his forehead. He saw Pike's wicked grin of triumph, saw the smuggler's forefinger closing on the trigger.

Suddenly Pike threw back his head and screamed like a she-cat giving birth. The rifle fell from nerveless fingers as he stumbled a few feet, clawing at his back with both hands. He bent double, revealing the reason.

Marista had drawn a dagger from under her blouse and stabbed him squarely between the shoulder blades. Pike clutched at the hilt, but it was out of reach. As she wrenched it out, Zeb leaped to his friend's aid, clamped an arm around Pike's wrist, and scurried toward the vegetation.

Clay would have gone after them had his legs not turned traitor once more. He saw the Pima woman start to give chase, but she stopped when she glimpsed him fall. In the nick of time, she caught him. He planted both feet and rose, mumbling, "I'm fine. You can let go."

The brush had swallowed the smugglers. Clay could hear the crash and crackle of limbs receding rapidly. He was mildly surprised Zeb hadn't stood his ground and made a fight of it, but then, smugglers weren't famous for having a lot of courage; they were the human equivalent of rats and behaved accordingly.

Clay turned toward the horses, which had shied when the Sharps banged but had not run off. "We've got to light a shuck for other parts," he declared, "before they see fit to come back."

Marista gazed uncertainly at the animals. "You want us ride?"

"Yes." Clay could feel what little strength he had left ebbing swiftly. They had to leave before he collapsed, or they might never get out of there with there hides intact. Gripping her arm, he pulled her toward the string. "We have to skedaddle."

The Pima balked, a hint of fear in her face.

Mystified, Clay halted. "What the blazes is the matter?" he demanded, more gruffly than he meant to. It was outright ridiculous, her being afraid now when the whole day she had not shown the least bit of fright. He looked at the boy and discovered Colletto was equally rattled.

The horses were the answer. Clay recollected hearing somewhere that the Pimas and Maricopas had never mastered the horse, and even regarded the animals with a degree of superstitious awe. "Hell," he groused. "We don't have time for this nonsense."

Seizing Marista more firmly, Clay pulled her to the lead sorrel. Her eyes widened and she drew away. "You must," he said, slipping both arms around her waist. Bunching his shoulders, he spun, seeking to heave her onto the saddle. Before being shot he could have done so with ease. Now, he only swung her halfway up, and it took so much out of him that he nearly keeled over. In pure reflex, Marista grabbed hold of the saddle horn and held on.

Clay shoved her foot into the stirrup and pushed her the rest of the way. She appeared absolutely petrified and made no move to grip the reins, so he handed them to her. The boy offered no resistance as Clay hauled him over and placed him in front of the woman.

Pike had shoved Clay's Winchester into the boot on the second animal and placed Clay's Colt on the saddle. After picking up Pike's fallen rifle, Clay reclaimed both of his own guns, then forked leather and headed eastward along the stream. His head needed tending worse than ever but it would have to wait. He remembered that Zeb still had the single-shot Sharps, and he seemed to recall that Pike wore a revolver. At any moment the smugglers might open fire.

The trio fled at a gallop, the White Apache swaying, on the verge of collapse, the mother and son clinging to one another and their mount in abject terror.

Behind them, the brush parted and a gritty, wrathful face peered out "You vermin!" Zeb called out. "You haven't seen the last of us! Count on it!"

Chapter Six

Col. Reynolds was out of his bed and shaving when reveille sounded. The first note of the bugle brought a smile, for it meant the day was officially underway and he could get done all the things he wanted to do before taps and lights out.

For the first time in months Reynolds felt confident that he would soon deliver the White Apache's head to his superiors on a silver platter, as it were. Palacio had pledged the cooperation of the Chiricahuas, and in all their prior dealings the chief had always kept his word.

Reynolds hummed as he shaved. Putting an end to the white renegade would be quite a feather in his cap. It might even get him reassigned to a better post back East, maybe to a nice desk job in Washington. *Anywhere* else would be nice.

A scratching noise made the colonel glance down. A large scorpion was scuttling across the floor toward his naked feet, its upcurved tail raised to strike, its stinger moving back and forth as if seeking prey to puncture.

Col. Renolds let out a yelp and leaped backward. His legs connected with the wash basin and he tumbled in. Unfortunately, it contained no water, and he slammed his spine onto the rim. The pain was awful. Without thinking, he leaped back out again, and froze.

Something had crawled onto his right foot.

The colonel looked and swore he could feel the blood drain from his face. The grotesque tan creature was balanced on his instep, that dreadful stinger hovering close to his skin. He imitated a tree, his heart pounding wildly. His body broke out in a cold sweat from hairline to ankles.

The scorpion twisted, its pincers swinging from side to side.

Reynolds had seldom been so scared. He opened his mouth to call for help but decided not to. The shout might provoke the many legged horror into striking.

As if in answer to his prayers, there came a loud knock at the front door to his quarters. "Colonel? This is Sergeant McKinn. Are you all right in there? I thought I heard a crash."

The officer remembered telling the noncom to be at his quarters at six, and with his customary diligence, McKinn had arrived early. Forgetting himself, Reynolds went to answer, then choked off the words in his throat.

"Colonel? Are you here?" the sergeant hollered. "I'm coming in, sir."

Reynolds heard the door open and vowed to put the noncom up for promotion at the earliest opportunity. Footsteps came closer. A shadow moved across the floor of his bedroom, and a moment later the noncom's stocky form filled the doorway.

"Sir?" McKinn said, puzzled until he glanced down. "Sweet Jesus! Don't move." He snatched a towel from the rack and advanced slowly. "I'll try and knock it off you."

The scorpion raised its pincers higher and backed up against the commander's leg. Reynold's gulped, and shook his head. The sergeant was so intent on the scorpion that he didn't see. Again Reynolds tried, afraid the scorpion would accidentally sting him in self-defense.

McKinn noticed this time and stopped. "What do you want me to do, sir? Stand here and wait for it to crawl off?"

Mustering his courage, Col. Reynolds whispered, "Yes."

"I have a better idea, sir. Don't you worry."

Reynolds could hardly believe his eyes when the sergeant whirled and raced out. He listened for some clue as to the noncom's plan. A name was shouted, but he didn't hear it clearly. The seconds ticked by, each an eternity unto itself. His perspiration dried, making him so cold he had to resist an urge to shiver. The scorpion, meanwhile, had hunkered down as if content to stay there forever.

Just when Col. Reynolds was about ready to scream from impatience and frayed nerves, Sgt. McKinn returned—with one other. Into the bathroom glided Klo-sen, the Apache scout, the quiet Mescalero who had few equals at tracking. Without hesitation he walked on around behind Reynolds.

Sgt. McKinn stayed near the doorway. "It'll just be a few moments now, sir. He's an old hand at this."

At what? Reynolds wondered. And almost jumped out of his skin when a copper hand holding a long knife appeared beside his right leg, next to his knee. He watched in riveted fascination as the slender blade slowly descended. A moment of panic seized him as he imagined the savage stabbing the scorpion while it sat on his foot.

"He's about ready, sir," McKinn said.

The knife dipped so low that it nearly scraped the scorpion's tail. The scorpion was facing the doorway and hadn't moved in quite some time.

Klo-sen leaned forward so that his head was next to the commander's leg. With delicate skill he eased the blade between Reynolds's ankle and the scorpion. Then, with a deft flip, he sent the scorpion sailing.

Sgt. McKinn was ready. As the scorpion slid across the floor toward him, he raised his boot on high and stamped. The crunch was loud in the confined bathroom. "There you go, sir," he said, lifting his boot to show the mangled mass underneath.

Col. Reynolds had to swallow a few times before he could respond. "You have my gratitude, Sergeant. You and Klo-sen."

The Apache had sheathed his knife. He walked to the door, then glanced back. "Maybe you see more, White Hair," he said in clipped English.

"I beg your pardon?" Reynolds said.

Klo-sen pointed at the mess on the floor. "Female. Make home here. Maybe many little ones around." Nodding curtly, he departed.

"Wonderful," Col. Reynolds said to himself.

"Anything else I can do for you, sir?" Sgt. McKinn asked.

"Not at the moment." The noncom saluted and left.

Blood Treachery

Reynolds quickly finished shaving, glancing at the floor every few seconds. After donning his uniform, he doublechecked his boots by upending them and slapping the soles, slid them on, and hustled out into the already warm sunshine. The troops were in formation, about to be put through their morning drill by McKinn.

The commander crossed to the officer's mess and was pleased to find all the junior officers in attendance, as he had requested. Taking his seat at the head of the table, he swept them all with a probing stare and said, "Good morning, gentlemen. By now I expect that all of you have heard the latest scuttlebutt. For those of you who might be skeptical, it's true. I've solicited the aid of the chief of the Chiricahuas in an effort to bring the White Apache and Delgadito to bay."

"Can you trust Palacio, sir?" Capt. Forester interrupted.

"I wouldn't trust that fat barbarian to water my horse," Reynolds said. "But he's not helping us because he's a pillar of red society. He's motivated by greed, pure and simple." Reynolds waited to see if anyone else would question his judgment but none had the veteran's temerity. "I don't know when Palacio will contact us. It might be today, it might be two weeks from now. But whenever it is, I intend to be ready to respond at a moment's notice."

Lt. James Peterson, the junior officer at the post, raised his hand. He was fresh out of the Academy, where he had had the dubious distinction of being ranked last in his graduating class. "Sir, I'd like to volunteer to lead the patrol that goes after this White Apache character when the times comes. Give me twenty-five good men and we can whip the renegades without working up a sweat."

Several of the older officers smiled. Capt. Forester glanced at the lieutenant, then rolled his eyes at the ceiling.

Col. Reynolds sighed. Far too many green officers had lost their lives on the frontier simply because they were too headstrong for their own good and as ignorant as a rock. "I appreciate your enthusiasm," he said tactfully, "but I've already picked the officer who will go after Taggart. In a situation like this, with the lives of so many innocents at stake if the renegades aren't stopped, I have to go with the most experienced man I have, and that would be Capt. Forester."

The lieutenant frowned but held his peace.

"Forester," Reynolds went on, "I want you to get together with Sgt. McKinn. Handpick the forty best soldiers at the fort. Organize them into a separate unit, answerable only to me. My Flying Detachment, as I like to call it."

"Yes, sir."

"The men you choose will be relieved from all normal duties until further notice. I want them fully equipped and whipped into shape within four days."

"Only four, sir?"

"You heard me. When Palacio contacts us, I want the Flying Detachment ready to fly to wherever the renegades are supposed to be holed up. By cutting down our response time, we increase the odds of success."

Forester nodded. "Consider it done."

Col. Reynolds glanced at Capt. Vincent Parmalee, who was close to dozing off. "One more thing," he added. "The Flying Detachment won't be going into battle alone. All seven Apache scouts and the officer in charge of them are to assist you. He will, of course, be under your direct command while in the field."

The orders jolted Capt. Parmalee half out of his seat. "Me, sir?" he bleated.

"You *are* the Chief of Scouts," Reynolds said.

"I know, sir," Parmalee said. He squirmed and licked his lips. "But I rarely go out with them. The Apaches work better under a minimum of supervision—"

"Spare me, Captain," Reynolds snapped. "So far the scouts have proven useless at finding the renegades. Maybe they'll perform better when you're out there with them to spur them on."

"But sir—"

The commander gestured for silence. "I'll brook no argument, Parmalee. You're going along, and that's final." He paused. "Look at the bright side. It might do you some good."

"Sir?" the captain said bleakly.

"You've been looking a little peaked of late. That's what comes of always being indoors and never getting enough exercise. Getting out in the sun and fresh air will do wonders for your constitution."

"If you say so, sir."

"I do." Reynolds was about to instruct the cook to serve breakfast when he thought of one final item. "Oh. Capt. Parmalee. From this day on, Klo-sen is to be the Assistant Chief of Scouts. He is being promoted to the rank of corporal. You will attend to the necessary paperwork and inform him at your earliest convenience."

Parmalee flushed crimson. "Sir, with all due respect, I don't need an assistant. It will undermine my authority."

"The Apaches might think differently. I believe

they'll welcome having one of their own act as go-between," Col. Reynolds said, and clapped his hands to signal the discussion at an end. "Now let's eat, shall we, men?" He smiled broadly. "I don't know about the rest of you, but I have the feeling our luck has finally turned and the White Apache is as good as ours."

Clay Taggart became aware of a damp, cool sensation on his brow. He stayed still with his eyes closed, trying to recollect what had happened to him. He remembered the shooting scrape with the smugglers, remembered fleeing eastward at a gallop for several miles and then feeling so dizzy and weak that he had been unable to stay in the saddle.

A soft hand touched his cheek. Close by, flames crackled. Water gurgled, indicating the stream was not far off. Clay opened his eyes.

A small fire had been built in a grassy glade almost at the water's edge. Colletto was busy skinning a rabbit, using his mother's dagger. Marista was on her knees beside him, a pan filled with water at her side. She removed a folded white cloth from his forehead, dipped it in the pan, and wrung out the excess. As she did so, she noticed he was awake. "At last," she said. "How you feel?"

"Better," Clay said. And it was true. The pounding in his head was mostly gone, and other than a dull ache where the bullet had glanced off his temple, there was no pain. "How long have I been out?"

The Pima woman jabbed her thumb skyward, where a myriad of stars twinkled like fireflies. "Two sleeps."

"That long?" Clay started to sit up but she placed a hand on his chest.

"You rest. Eat. Drink. Still very weak."

She had a point, Clay mused. He did feel woozy. His blood seemed to be pumping at a snail's pace, while his arms felt as heavy as two buffaloes. "What about Zeb and Pike? Has there been any sign of the smugglers?"

"No."

Clay let himself relax. Apparently the pair had elected not to follow, or they would have caught up by now. After he recovered, he would go find Delgadito and the others and persuade the Apaches to help track the smugglers down. The sons of bitches were going to pay, once they answered a few questions about their connection to Palacio.

"Son make stew," Marista informed him. "You maybe hungry now?"

"Are you kidding? I could swallow a horse, whole," Clay told her.

She gently placed the moist cloth over his brow again. "This and pan take off horse. Hope you not mind."

"Why would I?"

"Yours now, yes?"

Clay gazed at the string tethered across the clearing. Since he had seen fit to make off with the animals, the horses and everything on them were his plunder. "I don't mind at all," he responded, then mentioned without thinking, "What's mine is yours. Use whatever you need."

Marista visibly tensed. "Why you so kind?"

"Why shouldn't I be?" Clay retorted. "You've saved my life several times over. The least I can do is repay your kindness as best I can."

She stared at him a bit, then moved off to help prepare a stew, leaving Clay to his thoughts. He bent his neck to find the Colt in its holster and the Winchester at his elbow. It was a good sign; she trusted him enough not to have taken his weapons. Twisting, he saw the saddles and supplies piled neatly a dozen feet away. Given the Pima fear of horses, it showed great courage on her part to have stripped them down. He told her as much when she came over bearing a cup of hot broth.

"Had to do," Marista said.

Clay held the cup and talked her into dragging a saddle over for him to lean on. He sipped slowly. It had been so long since he had eaten last that the broth seared his throat like molten lava. His stomach did flip-flops for a while, but eventually he polished off the cup and was ready for more.

Marista hesitated before rising. "Must ask question," she said, rather timidly but forcefully. "Sorry, but must."

"Ask anything you want," Clay said. She shared a glance with the boy, whose worried look led Clay to suspect what was coming.

Plainly nervous, Marista said, "Your hair like Apache. Your clothes like Apache. Your skin dark like Apache. But you be white man."

Clay waited.

"We hear stories. Hear of white man turn on own people. Ride with Apaches, kill like Apaches. Kill whites, kill Mexicans, kill everyone. White Apache, he be called." Marista's gaze bored into him. "That be you, Clay Taggart?"

There was no sense in denying the truth, so Clay nodded. "I'm your huckleberry. But don't let it upset you none. I wouldn't harm a hair on your pretty head, yours or the boy's. I hope you'll take me at my word when I tell you that I'm not the cold-blooded fiend they make me out to be."

Clay wished he was able to read her mind so he'd know how she was reacting to the news. He couldn't blame her if she were to up and leave, and he certainly wouldn't try to stop her. But he didn't want her to go. He'd grown fond of her company. Quite fond. So he was all the more elated when she said the one thing that showed maybe, just maybe, his interest in her was returned.

"You think my head pretty?"

"One of the prettiest," Clay declared. "Fact is, I wouldn't be at all surprised if a fine filly such as yourself has a husband stashed away somewhere. Although why he'd let you wander Apache country by yourself is beyond me."

A cloud darkened Marista's features and she looked into the night. Hoping to prod the truth from her, Clay added, "If you want, I'll be more than happy to escort the two of you back to your village after I mend."

"Never go back. Ever."

"What? Why?" Clay inquired, at a loss to comprehend. The Pimas were a close-knit people who stuck together through thick and thin. She was bound to have kin somewhere willing to put the boy and her up for a spell.

"Can not go back," Marista emphasized bitterly.

"But what about your husband? Where is he? Is he alive?" Clay probed. She had to have had a husband at one time. The idea of a Pima woman having a child out of wedlock was unthinkable, since the Pimas were as noted for their chastity as the Apaches.

The woman let out a long breath, her shoulders drooping. "Husband not want," she said, scarcely above a whisper.

"Not want?" Clay said, unsure whether he had

heard correctly. "Is the man plumb loco? How can he not want a beautiful woman like you?"

"My husband Culozul."

The way she said it, Clay got the idea she thought it would explain everything. But the revelation only confused him more. Culozul was the name of a prominent Pima chief who had been written up in the Tucson newspaper a while back when he visited Washington D.C. The paper had gone on and on about how impressed the chief had been by all he saw, stressing again and again how superior the white culture was to the red.

The reporter had done his best to portray the chief in a comical light, telling how he gawked at street lights and steam engines and such, and how Culozul always scratched himself in public.

Clay had read the article. He remembered laughing when it was revealed that the chief had scandalized himself at a formal banquet by tearing into the food with his hands and teeth instead of using silverware. But back in those days he had laughed at anything that poked fun at Indians.

In a twisted manner, Culozul was famous. Now here was this beautiful woman claiming to be his wife. Clay scratched his head and said, "I've heard of him. Seems to me you must be wrong. He'll be right pleased to get you back safe and sound."

Marista bunched her fist and made a motion as if flinging an object to the ground. "Him cast me out. Never see again or I be killed."

Clay figured she was spinning a yarn. The Pimas would never tolerate murder. It was against tribal custom. There was only one exception that he knew of: they allowed women caught in the act of adultery to be stoned to death. Or shunned as outcasts. At the thought, he stiffened. "Culozul caught you with another man and had you kicked out of the village?"

The woman turned on him, anger and pain fighting for dominance. "I never sleep other man!" she said passionately. "Never do!" Her eyes moistened and she blinked, fighting back tears of frustration. "Culozul say I do. Not true. Him lie."

Clay knew he had already pried more deeply than he had any right to do, but he couldn't help himself. "Why would he do a thing like that?"

Her answer crackled with loathing. "Him want other woman. Younger woman."

Clay glanced at the boy, whose expression was cast in granite. "Your son ran off with you when you were thrown out?" he hazarded a guess.

"Colletto hates Culozul. Him want kill his father."

Enough had been disclosed. Clay asked no more questions. He stared into the fire, thinking of the terrible ordeal the woman had gone through, an ordeal in some respects similar to his own. Like him, she had been betrayed by the one she loved the most. Like him, she had been unjustly accused. Like him, she had been made an outcast.

More than ever, Clay admired her grit. She had headed off into the wilderness to fend for herself and the boy, never knowing from one day to the next how she would make ends meet or whether she would be alive to greet the next dawn. Damned if she didn't remind him of himself.

"You want we go now?"

The query startled Clay. "What gives you that idea? Hell, no, I don't want you to leave," he stated. "Fact is, I'm grateful for the company. If you want, you're welcome to tag along with me a spell. But I've got to warn you up front. Staying with me might not be too smart. I've got a price on my head. Every time I turn around, someone is trying to plant me six feet under."

As if to accent the point, in the darkness behind them a gun hammer clicked and the familiar voice of Zeb declared, "Do tell. Raise those hands of yours high, White Apache, or you die where you sit."

Chapter Seven

Delgadito had always liked the wind. It cooled him on hot days, brought news of rain long before clouds gathered, and carried the scent of enemies and game to his sensitive nostrils to alert him. The wind was his friend.

This night, late, his friend carried to his keen ears the faint rattle of a pebble. Instantly Delgadito was up and in a crouch, his rifle clutched at his waist. "Someone comes," he whispered.

Fiero was off the ground in a flash, shaking his head to dispel lingering tendrils of sleep. It bothered him that the other warrior's senses had proven more acute. He took immense pride in the fact many Chiricahuas considered him one of the best warriors in the tribe, and he did not like to be shown up. Fiero lived only to fight, to excel at war, to kill white-eyes and *Nakai-yes* until the rest were driven from Apache land.

The shelf on which the pair had made camp was situated high on a ridge overlooking a barren canyon. On one side lay a steep drop, hundreds of feet, while on the other was a gravel slope no living creature could climb without making noise.

The wind brought them no new sounds, so Delgadito crept to the rim and peered down the slope. At the limits of his vision a form moved, gliding toward them. He motioned at Fiero, who cat-footed off to the left and eased onto his stomach.

Delgadito did likewise. He had a fair idea who was down there but he was not about to take anything for granted. He moved to a point that afforded a clear view of the gravel strip and tucked his rifle to his shoulder.

Only a short while passed before the night air rang to the high-pitched bark-bark-bark of an agitated chipmunk, just such a sound as a chipmunk might make if disturbed in its burrow by a roving predator.

From Delgadito's lips issued an answer, as perfect as the original, so much so that a real chipmunk would have been fooled. A shape glided from the boulders and up the incline. Delgadito looked but saw no others and right away he knew that something was wrong. "You come alone, Ponce," he said as he stood.

The young warrior had been running for hours. He was tired and thirsty and his legs were sore but he was not about to let the two older men know. "Cuchillo Negro sent me on ahead," he reported.

Fiero loomed out of the night. "Why? What has happened?"

"*Lickoyee-shis-inday* never joined us as he was

supposed to. Cuchillo Negro went in search of him and sent me ahead to let you know."

"I told White Apache not to go," Delgadito said harshly. "Leaving heads for the white-eyes to find is foolish. It serves no real purpose."

"I like the idea," Fiero declared. "It shows the white-eyes that we are not afraid, that they will pay for taking our land and making our people live like dogs."

"All it does is stir them up to come look for us," Delgadito said. "I would rather they cower in their stone lodges so we can do as we please without interference."

Ponce had heard the merits debated many times and he made bold to comment, "White Apache says it strikes fear into their hearts. And who should know better than him since he was a white-eye before he became one of us?"

Delgadito had to clamp his mouth shut to keep from making a remark he might regret. He was the one who had given Clay Taggart the Apache name of *Lickoyee-shis-inday*, but he had not meant for anyone to take him seriously. It had been shortly after he saved the white-eye from the lynch party, when Taggart had been a stumbling simpleton who couldn't last three days in the wild without help.

How could anyone have foreseen what would occur? Delgadito reflected. Taggart, saving his life. Taggart, learning Chiricahua ways so readily it amazed even Delgadito. Taggart, becoming a respected member of the band, the man whose counsel the others sought when important decisions were to be made. Taggart, who had replaced Delgadito as leader. It was enough to make him want to scream with fury.

But whenever Delgadito felt his resentment

build, he reminded himself that White Apache had saved his life several times over, that if not for Clay Taggart his war against the whites would have ended in disaster many moons ago.

Delgadito had to possess himself with patience. Thanks to White Apache, the band had raided far and wide with sterling success, and tales of their prowess were a common topic around campfires at the reservation. Soon, now, the band would grow in size as young warriors flocked to join them. And when the band was big enough to suit him, he would find a means of taking up the reins of leadership once more. All he needed was patience.

"We waste time standing here," Fiero said. "I am ready to go this moment."

"And I," Ponce said, although he would rather sleep the rest of the night through.

"Then we will go," Delgadito said.

Like three tawny panthers they bounded over the rim and were soon shrouded in darkness.

Lightning reflexes sometimes work of their own accord. So although Clay Taggart heard a gun cocked and the smuggler warn him not to move, he automically reached for his Colt and started to whirl.

A hard object jolted against the back of Clay's head. He went rigid, unwilling to risk being bashed on the noggin just when he was beginning to recover from his wound.

"I'd make wolf meat of you this minute, Taggart, but I'm not about to lug your smelly carcass all the way to the nearest fort to collect the reward," Zeb said, stepping around to where he could cover the three of them with that big Sharps of his. "The heat tends to ripen a corpse real quick hereabouts."

"So you know who I am," Clay said, intending to keep the man distracted while he racked his brain for a means of turning the tables.

"It hit me while I was mendin' my pard," Zeb said. "Those blue eyes of yours are a dead giveaway." He snickered. "Then I heard you spillin' your guts to the squaw here and knew for sure I'd hit the mother lode."

"Where's your friend?"

"He's hurtin' real bad so I left him lyin' out in the brush a piece." Zeb pivoted and hollered at the top of his lungs. "Pike! Haul your ass in here. I've got 'em!"

Clay was desperate to do something. But what? If he made a grab for a weapon, he'd be shot before he could bring it into play. The Pimas would be no help. Marista had frozen, her hands on her knees. The boy appeared flabbergasted, hunkered there with the rabbit hide draped over one leg.

Zeb took another step. "Did you really think we wouldn't come after you, renegade? It took us a while, what with Pike feelin' so poorly, but we weren't about to let you make off with all our goods. I'm surprised you didn't keep on a goin'."

"We didn't have much choice," Clay said lamely. In the distance a twig snapped. It wouldn't be long before they had him disarmed and hogtied. He was a goner unless he made a move. But the smuggler was watching him like the proverbial hawk.

"Pike has been lookin' forward to seein' the three of you again, bastard," Zeb said. "Especially the squaw. Her dagger done put a nasty hole in him. Put an ear to it, and you can hear his lungs workin'."

To the surprise of both men, Marista spoke. "Him hurt bad? Very sorry."

"You are?" Zeb replied.

"Sorry not kill him," the woman said sweetly, and grinned, a mocking, taunting grin calculated to rile any man.

It riled the smuggler. Cursing lustily, Zeb moved toward her and raised the Sharps to smash her with the stock. He was so mad that all he could think of was wiping that smirk off her face. Her face was all he concentrated on, when he should have been watching elsewhere.

Clay saw Marista's hands drop to the pan and divined her purpose even as her fingers closed on the rim.

Zeb was almost upon her when she swept her arms upward and heaved the water full in his face. The smuggler recoiled and lowered the Sharps, his curses a strident litany of hate. For a second or two his vision was blurred, and he blinked to clear it.

Those two seconds were all Clay Taggart needed. Like most Arizona ranchers, he was uncommonly handy with a six-shooter, thanks in part to his pa, who had taught him to shoot as soon as he was old enough to hold a pistol. For years a six-gun had been one of the many tools he had used on his ranch, a tool little different from his hammer or hoe in that it had a specific use, namely to kill rattlers and protect him from marauding war parties.

Clay had practiced often. On several occasions he had entered the annual Tucson marksmanship contest and finished in the top five. He could unlimber his hardware so fast his hand was a blur and empty the cylinder in less time than it took to tell about it.

Blood Treachery

To a seasoned gun hand, two seconds was an eternity.

Clay cleared leather as the water struck Zeb. His draw was a shade slow because he was seated and at an awkward angle, but it was still plenty quick, so quick that he banged off two swift shots before Zeb realized he had drawn.

The smuggler twisted to level the Sharps, but the impact of the slugs punched him backward and jerked him half around. The rifle fell from arms suddenly grown limp. He looked down at it, then at the twin holes oozing blood in his chest. "Well, I'll be damned!" he said weakly. His legs gave way and he fell to his knees.

Clay, with an effort, rose to his own. The shots would forewarn Pike, who might try to pick them off. They had to get away from the fire, from the light. Suddenly Marista was at his side, assisting him, and he managed to stand.

Zeb was still alive, his arms convulsing, his mouth twitching. He glared at them, at Clay, and spat, "Finish it!"

Obliging, Clay cored the man's brain. Then, with the boy following, he hurried into the darkness. He felt stronger than he had in days but still not quite strong enough to get very far on his own, and he was grateful for Marista's help.

Colletto abruptly called out and pointed.

The other smuggler materialized out of the night, walking stiffly toward them, his legs thudding the ground heavily as if each step was a monumental exertion.

Clay halted, shifted, and was all set to shoot when he noticed that Pike's hands were empty. The man had the most peculiar expression, a blank sort of look with his eyes as wide as walnuts and his mouth gaping open. Clay tensed, wary of a trick, but Pike made no sudden moves. A few seconds later he found out why.

Pike crumpled as if all his bones had changed to mush. Slowly spinning to the earth, he thudded onto his stomach, revealing the black hilt of a long knife that jutted from between his shoulder blades.

"How—?" Marista said, and gasped.

From out of nowhere another man appeared, a full-blooded Apache who carried a rifle in the crook of an elbow and stood impassively next to the body. In a fluid move, he tore the knife out, wiped the blade clean on the dead smuggler's buckskin shirt, and straightened. *"Tu no vale nada,"* he addressed the corpse. Then, advancing, he raised a hand in salute and said in greeting, *"Lickoyee-shis-inday, nejeunee."*

"Nejeunee, Cuchillo Negro," White Apache responded, overjoyed to see his friend again. "My brother comes at just the right time."

"I have been searching for you long and hard," the warrior declared, stopping to stare at Zeb. "It makes my heart glad to see you are well."

"The others?"

"Shee-dah. Ponce went after them. They should be here before the moon rises again."

White Apache gestured. "Sit. Rest. Share our stew." He introduced the Pima woman and her boy, who had shied close together and were regarding Black Knife as they might their executioner.

"Is she yours?" Cuchillo Negro asked in the Chiricahua tongue.

Clay glanced at her. If he said no, the warrior might elect to take her for himself, which by Apache custom he had every right to do. There would be nothing Clay could do about it. But if he said yes, he was making a false claim, lying, in effect, to one of the few friends he had in the world. Switching to English, he told Marista, "He wants to know if you're my woman. Do you know what that means?"

Without missing a beat, she said, "Tell him I be your woman."

"I'd rather not lie," Clay said. "If you want to go your own way with the boy, feel free. I'll persuade my friend to let you be. I'll tell him I owe you a debt."

Marista faced him and threw her shoulders back. "I be your woman. If you want us."

Her emphasis on the last word wasn't lost on Clay. "Do you know what you're letting yourself in for? It won't be easy. None of us might live out the year."

She came over and gently placed a hand on his cheek. "You be kind man, Clay Taggart. I see it in eyes, feel it my heart. You strong man. Good man."

"Hell, I've been called a lot of things lately, but not that." Clay grinned wryly. "Most every soul in the Territory wants to see me strung up or staked out as buzzard bait."

Marista nodded at the wilderness encircling them. "Hard land. Hard for us live. Savvy, Clay Taggart? We have no one. You have no one. We belong with you."

Her simple eloquence brought a lump to Clay's throat. He hardly knew her, yet he cared for her a great deal, more than he had ever cared for any woman except Lilly. They shared a bond that came from deep within them. It was unexpected, it was strange, it was glorious. Before he realized what he was doing, he had bent and kissed her lightly on the mouth.

Marista smiled and touched her lips. Colletto gasped. Cuchillo Negro grinned and said, "I have my answer, White Apache. And I hope, my brother, that you know what you are doing."

"You are not the only one," Clay said, troubled by thoughts of the horrible fate that might befall the Pimas if they stuck with him. He didn't want to be responsible for their deaths, indirectly or otherwise. There had to be a place they could go to lie low where the woman and her son would be safe, or as safe as it was possible to be with every white in Arizona gunning for him.

Clay brought up the subject later, after polishing off three delicious helpings of stew. The food did wonders for his well being. He felt strong again, almost whole, almost his old self.

Cuchillo Negro listened attentively and replied, "I know Chiricahua country as well as any man. There is one place I can think of where your woman will not be found. It is called Eagle's Roost."

"Tell me about it," Clay urged eagerly.

"It is a cave deep in the mountains where few ever go, even Chiricahuas. The land is steep and there are many ravines. The only approach is up a winding trail. Horses cannot get close."

"Why do the Chiricahuas not go there? Is there no water? Is the hunting poor?"

"There is a spring in the cave. Game is scarce, but the real reason is that many believe Eagle's Roost is bad medicine. They think it is home to an evil mountain spirit."

Clay grunted. Since joining the renegades he had learned more than any white man alive about Apache beliefs and practices. He knew they believed in a supreme deity they called *Yusn*—the Giver of Life. They also believed in a host of lesser spirits, among them the powerful *Gans,* or mountain spirits.

The Apaches, by white standards, were highly superstitious. They feared witches, dreaded touching the dead, and were highly secretive about their burial customs. When an Apache died from disease, his wickiup and all his possessions were burned, and the spot was shunned forever after.

It was accepted by them that their everyday lives were under the direct influence of many evil spirits that had to be appeased or catastrophe would result. As a result, the Apaches had many rituals to ward off evil powers, illness and the like.

Eagle's Roost sounded like just the kind of hideout Clay needed, but there was one hitch. "What about you and the other warriors?" he asked. "Will all of you go to the cave with me?"

"I cannot speak for Delgadito and the rest, only for myself," Cuchillo Negro said. "While I do not like to tempt the Gans, I also do not want my white brother to think I am afraid. If you go, White Apache, I will go. But I warn you, brother to brother, not to. It is not wise to tempt the *Gans.* Something very bad will happen."

The earnest appeal almost, but not quite, convinced Clay. But he wasn't about to be scared off by a silly superstition. If Eagle's Roost was the safest place for the woman and boy to be, then that was where they would go.

Two hours shy of sundown the next day, Delgadito, Fiero, and Ponce arrived. They had pushed themselves, and it showed in their fatigued features.

Delgadito had insisted on the grueling pace. As

much as he despised White Apache, he was not about to let anything happen to the one man who could help him regain the position of leadership he coveted more than life itself. He would do all in his power to keep the white-eye alive—until he was chief again.

Clay was elated to see them. At last, events were going his way. The band was reunited. The swelling had gone completely away and the wound was mending nicely. He was fit to travel. And he now had a woman to call his own.

On seeing the trio approach the camp, Clay jumped to his feet and ran to greet them. In his excitement he clapped Delgadito on the shoulder and said happily, "Glad to see you again, pard. For a while there it was nip and tuck, and I didn't know if I'd ever be able to pay you back for all you've done for me."

"You will," Delgadito said in his thickly accented English. For months now he had been diligently trying to learn the white tongue, but try as he might he couldn't shed the accent.

They had made a deal, the two of them. Delgadito had agreed to teach Clay the Chiricahua tongue if Clay taught him English. Of the pair, Clay proved to be the better pupil, much to Delgadito's chagrin.

The newcomers were surprised to find the Pimas there. Fiero listened to Clay's explanation, then growled, "You make a mistake, *Lickoyee-shis-inday*. I know all of you think we need women to make our band whole again. But these two will slow us down, make us easy prey for the blue coats."

"You make the mistake," Clay shot back, since to give an inch to Fiero made him take a yard. "They will not slow us down because they will

Blood Treachery

not be with us. I am taking them to Eagle's Roost to stay."

It was as if a celestial puppeteer had yanked on the strings of three Chiricahua puppets. The heads of all three jerked up, and Delgadito said, "Eagle's Roost is bad medicine. Cuchillo Negro should have told you."

"He did," Clay said, "but I am going anyway, and he is going with me."

Delgadito glanced at Black Knife. "Has the sun roasted your brain? The mountain spirit will punish whoever dares step foot in that cave. Did you tell him the story?"

"What story?" Clay asked.

Cuchillo Negro had sat calmly sharpening his knife the whole time. Now he set the whetstone in his lap and said, "There is a reason Eagle's Roost is shunned by our people." He tested the blade on his thumb and smiled when it drew blood. "Many winters ago it was customary for many to use the cave since it is the only source of water for several sleeps around. Hunting parties passing through the area, raiders heading north to attack the whites, they would all spend a night or two there. Sometimes a warrior would take his family just to be alone with them for a few days."

"An Apache hotel," Clay quipped in English, but Delgadito failed to see the humor.

"One day a warrior named Toga-de-chuz and his woman went to Eagle's Roost. It was customary for whoever stayed in the cave to burn an offering when they first entered to appease the mountain spirit who lives there. But Toga-de-chuz spurned the *Gans*. He did not make an offering, and late that night his wife woke up to his screams and saw him being stabbed by his own knife."

Clay digested the tale, then said, "Stabbed how? By his own hand?"

"No. No one held the hilt. It floated in the air, stabbing again and again."

"How do you know this?"

"The woman saw it all. She was too terrified to help her man, and when he was dead, she cowered under her blanket until daylight, then fled. Since then Eagle's Roost has been bad medicine."

Skeptical, to say the least, Clay held his tongue. He would only offend his friends if he told them that he suspected the woman had killed her husband and blamed it on a nonexistent spirit. She had been shrewd in that regard. For a wife to kill her husband merited death.

"So what do you say, White Apache?" Delgadito asked in English. "Do you still intend to take the Pima there?"

"I do," Clay confirmed. "And I would be obliged if all of you would tag along. We can hide out there for a spell and plan our next raid."

Delgadito had half a mind to refuse. But he was committed to a course of action that required him to stay with the white-eye, like it or not, so he said, "We will come. But heed my words. The mountain spirit will be angry with us."

Clay Taggart smiled. He could live with that, he told himself.

Little did he know.

Chapter Eight

It was Dandy Jim who spotted the buzzards and pointed them out to Capt. Henry Derrick. The officer immediately halted the patrol and pulled out his field glasses.

Derrick had served in the Arizona Territory for slightly over a year. He was a competent, tough campaigner and a close personal friend of Capt. Gerald Forester. It was Forester who had taken Derrick under his wing when Derrick arrived at Fort Bowie and taught him all he needed to know to survive the relentless war against the Apaches.

One of the first rules of combat, as Forester had put it, was, "Jackasses rush in where cooler heads know to tread softly. Always check out the lay of the land before committing yourself and your men. Apaches love to lie in ambush."

Now Derrick did just that, studying the seven buzzards he could see wheeling high in the sky and the chaparral beneath them. He wouldn't put it past the renegades to kill some animal and leave it there so circling buzzards would lure the curious to their doom. Or perhaps the Apaches had spotted his patrol from a distance and set the trap up. Whatever the case, Derrick was not about to let himself be outfoxed. Turning to his two scouts, Dandy Jim and Dead Shot, both Cibicu Indians, he pointed and commanded, "Check it out and report back to me on the double."

Dandy Jim, who liked to wear an old frock coat, of all things, and a big white feather in his blue headband, said, "We go see plenty quick."

As the scouts galloped off, Derrick ordered Sgt. Bryce to have the troopers see to their carbines and pistols. If there was to be an engagement, the renegades would pay dearly. He kept his field glasses trained on the brush until Dead Shot appeared and waved.

At a trot Captain Derrick led the patrol to trees bordering a stream he had not even known was there. In a glade near the water they came on the bodies of two white men.

Both had been stripped naked but not mutilated. The buzzards had been at them, though, and their eyeballs had been gouged out, their noses pecked clean off, and their tongues ripped from their mouths.

"I recognize that small one, sir," Sergeant Bryce said. "His name is Zeb Plunkett. He's been in trouble with the law a few times. For the past ten years or so he's made his living as a smuggler, working the border country."

"Well, his smuggling days are over," Derrick commented. "Select a burial detail and see they are laid to rest."

"Yes, sir."

Blood Treachery

The two Cibicues had been prowling the area, eyes glued to the ground. After a while they hurried over and Dandy Jim, who knew more English, reported.

"Find tracks. Apaches do this." A gleam came into the scout's dark eyes. "One white man with them. He wear Apache moccasins."

Captain Derrick felt his pulse race. "How do you know it's a white man?"

Dandy Jim extended his right leg and held his foot so the toes pointed inward. "Indian walk like this." Pivoting, he pointed the toes outward. "White man always walk like this."

"Could it be the White Apache?"

"Maybe so," Dandy Jim said.

"Then we'll go after them as soon as the smugglers are planted," Derrick said, barely able to credit his good fortune. Every officer in Arizona was on the lookout for the notorious traitor; whoever brought Clay Taggart in would have his career made, as it were.

"One more thing," Dandy Jim said. "They have woman, boy with them."

"You don't say?"

"Pimas. Can tell by moccasins they wear."

The officer knew enough about the various tribes to remark, "Pimas running with Apaches? It was my understanding that they're mortal enemies."

"Sometimes Apaches steal Pima women," the Cibicu said, and leered suggestively.

Derrick had not heard of any recent Apache raids on Pima villages, but he tabled his doubts for the time being. *If* the scout was right, and *if* this was the White Apache's band, and *if* they did have a woman and boy along, it presented a golden opportunity which he was not about to pass up. "How far ahead of us are they?"

"Band leave here at first light. White Apache ride. Woman, boy on same animal. Rest on foot, leading other horses."

Twisting, the captain noted the position of the sun. Another lesson Forester had imparted was how to tell time by the sun and stars. Watches were prone to malfunction in the field, the veteran had pointed out.

Derrick judged the time to be close to ten o'clock. Out of habit he verified it by consulting his pocket watch. "That gives them no more than a four hour head start. If they're moving slowly, we can overtake them by nightfall."

The officer swung toward the burial detail. "Get a move on, Sergeant," he barked. "They're just a pair of smugglers, for crying out loud. Sprinkle some dirt on them, cover them with rocks, and be done with it."

In under five minutes the troopers were all mounted. At Derrick's signal, the patrol moved out, going at a brisk walk, the scouts well in the lead.

This was new country to Derrick. He had ranged over a good portion of the vast Chiricahua Reservation but seldom into the interior, into the heart of the mountain fastness where the renegades were rumored to have their strongholds.

It seemed only logical to Derrick and Forester and other seasoned officers to strike at the renegades where they were least likely to expect attack, but the higher-ups at headquarters had given explicit orders to the effect that no patrols were to penetrate into the heart of the reservation unless under specific directions to do so. Derrick, however, was not above disobeying the command in order to get his hands on the White Apache. If need be, he would dog the renegade to the gates of Hell. Headquarters would overlook the indiscretion if he brought in Taggart's bullet-ridden corpse.

For the next several hours Capt. Derrick pushed the horses hard, resting them five minutes out of every sixty. He had ample time to reflect on the man he was after, and to recall what little information he knew about his quarry.

Clay Taggart had been caught in the act of raping a neighbor's wife, had shot the cowpuncher who stumbled on them, then had fled deep into the Chiricahua Mountains. Everyone had about given him up for dead when reports filtered in of a band of Apaches being led by a white man. At first the Army had scoffed. But as more and more accounts were made known, it had been apparent that they were true. Finally the rancher whose wife had been raped, Miles Gillett, came forward to say that he had proof the culprit was Clay Taggart. Ever since, every person toting a badge or wearing a uniform had had his eyes peeled for the renegade. Whoever killed him would be famous.

The countryside through which the patrol traveled gradually changed from chaparral rife with manzanita to barren land, climbing steadily higher. Derrick was sure he would locate one of the renegade hideouts before the day was done, and he smiled in anticipation.

For three weeks the patrol had been making a routine sweep of the Chiricahua and Dragoons Mountains. For three weeks they had seen neither hide nor hair of a single, solitary renegade. And that was the way most patrols went. Ungodly long hours spent in the saddle under a blistering sun day after day after day, and for what?

But this time promised to be different. This time Capt. Derrick stood to become the envy of every officer in the Fifth Cavalry. In a year or so he'd make major, and from there the sky was the limit.

In the officer's excitement over being close to overtaking the White Apache, he failed to heed another piece of advice that Gerald Forester had once imparted.

"Watch your dust," the more experienced captain had said. "Thirty horses kick up a lot of it, especially at a full gallop. Apaches can see the cloud from miles off. So when you're closing in on some, be sure to go slow when you figure that you're close enough for them to spot you."

It had been sound advice, as Capt. Derrick would have realized had he been able to soar as high as the red hawk wheeling above his column and see the figures hidden behind boulders on a slope ahead.

Fiero, ever the most alert of the renegades, had seen the dust cloud first and pointed it out to the other warriors. He yipped a few times while waving his rifle, then cried, "It is a good day for white-eyes to die!"

Clay had studied the cloud a few moments, gauging distance and how fast the pursuers were moving. They had to be whites, since no self-respecting Apache would be so careless. He estimated the riders were three or four miles off and coming on at a gallop. Let them come! he mused. He would be ready.

Once, Clay Taggart would have balked at the notion of shooting soldiers who were only doing their duty. But that was before Gillett framed him, before Gillett manipulated the Army into doing what Gillett wanted done in the worst way. And since Clay had thrown in with the renegades, he had come to see things from the Apache point of view. He found himself siding with them against those who had forced the tribes to accept reservation life at gunpoint.

So on spying the dust, instead of feeling guilt at the idea of killing troopers, Clay Taggart felt outrage. Or, rather, the White Apache did. He thought and acted as a true Chiricahua, that part of him that was white buried by the part of him that had become Apache.

A talus slope dotted with boulders gave White Apache an inspiration. Veering to the right, he took a game trail up along the edge of the slope to the mountain above. The horse was unnerved by the narrow footing and the drop-off to one side. Several times White Apache had to jab his heels into its flanks to keep the animal climbing.

Marista, close behind, was also having trouble with the mare she rode, and not having been on a horse before she had no idea what to do. White Apache kept a close eye on her. When the mare suddenly stopped and refused to go on, he said, "We have to hurry. Use that pigsticker of yours and poke it in the rump. That ought to do the trick."

It did, but not in the way he had hoped. Marista pricked the horse lightly twice without result, so she jabbed it harder a third time. The animal's response caught her off guard. Without any warning whatsoever, the feisty mare bucked.

The Pima had one arm looped around her son, the reins held loosely in her left hand. She was nearly thrown by the violent motion, but by grabbing the saddle horn she hung on, her body swinging precariously to one side.

The mare landed with its legs straight, its back arched. The impact caused Marista to slip even more. She was poised above the talus slope, clinging for dear life. Another such jolt would send her plummeting.

White Apache reined up and slid off. Dashing to the mare, he grabbed the reins and held on tight. The animal tried to jerk back but he dug in his heels, buying time for Marista to scramble back into the saddle and get a good grip on the boy. Then, leading the mare, he held onto the end of the reins while mounting and pulled the animal along beside him to the top of the slope. There was scant cover save for a dry wash in which the horses were tied. They left the Pimas to keep watch.

White Apache led the warriors onto the slope. They fanned out, each seeking a sheltered nook. All five levered rounds into the chambers of their Winchesters.

Sprawled at the base of a boulder resembling a gigantic egg, White Apache braced his elbow on a smooth rock and scanned the terrain below, noting where there was cover for the soldiers and where there was not.

The dust cloud grew in size. Tiny stick figures appeared, becoming larger and larger as the range was narrowed.

White Apache adjusted the sights on his .44-40, setting them for one hundred yards. The 15-shot rifle had proven remarkably accurate at that range. Indeed, the Winchester Model 1873 was proving to be one of the most popular guns ever made, and there could be no greater testimony to its stopping power than the fact that every member of the band owned one. The rifles had been taken as part of the plunder from a wagon train.

Blood Treachery

The soldiers, White Apache knew, were armed with carbines, shorter versions of his rifle which were just as accurate but at a slightly shorter range.

At a swift clip the patrol approached. White Apache noticed a pair of Indian scouts at the head of the column. He couldn't tell which tribe they belonged to, but they definitely were not Apaches.

Presently the scouts drew rein and the young officer in charge raised his hand to halt the patrol. The officer conferred with them. Apparently a disagreement broke out, with the scouts shaking their heads and pointing repeatedly at the mountain. The officer overrode them. With an imperious gesture, he started them toward the talus slope and gave the order for the troopers to follow.

The scouts were uneasy, as well they should be. They held their rifles close to their chests so they could snap off shots at a moment's notice.

White Apache almost felt sorry for them. They suspected the patrol was riding into an ambush but the officer wanted to push on anyway. It served them right for turning against other Indians, for hiring out to track down those whose only crime was in wanting to go on living as their ancestors had lived for generations, long before the coming of the whites.

A scout with a feather in his headband was slightly out in front. He raked the talus slope from top to bottom and side to side, his lanky frame curled so that most of his body was screened by the head and neck of his bay.

White Apache fixed a bead on the Indian's head, then changed his mind and swiveled to take aim at the cocky young officer. He waited, letting the patrol get closer, not about to fire until he was sure he couldn't miss. The others would wait for his signal.

Suddenly the Indian wearing the feather yanked on his reins, jabbed a finger at the slope, and cried out in alarm.

The words were indistinct but the meaning was clear. The scout had caught sight of one of the Apaches or else seen sunlight glimmer off a rifle barrel. Immediately the officer rose in his stirrups and snapped a hand into the air to halt the cavalrymen.

At that exact moment White Apache fired. He had fixed his sights on the officer's chest and would have killed the man then and there had the officer not risen. As it was, the shot took the trooper low in the stomach and punched him off his mount.

All hell broke loose.

The renegades opened up with a vengeance, the warriors firing as rapidly as they could work the levers of their Winchesters. Simultaneously, the troopers charged, all except for a noncom and two others who rushed to the aid of the stricken officer. Spreading to either flank, the soldiers fired their carbines at random. The couldn't see the renegades, but they could see the puffs of gunsmoke that told them where the warriors were hidden.

Slugs whined off boulders, ricocheting wildly. White Apache pressed his face to the ground as a firestorm of lead chewed up the earth around him. Rising up again, he shot a soldier out of the saddle, then winged another in the shoulder.

The boom of guns was deafening. Added to the din was the lusty curses of the soldiers, the strident war whoops of the Apaches, and the frightened nickers of cavalry mounts.

In the midst of this bedlam, White Apache kept his head. He fired methodically, picking targets with care, never wasting lead. And since the troopers would be virtually helpless without their mounts, he shot as many horses as he did men.

The soldiers were fearless and determined and they outnumbered their foes by five to one, but they were out in the open, racing headlong into a withering rain of bullets that no living thing could withstand. Men and horses crumpled, some mortally stricken, some suffering minor wounds.

It was the noncom who rallied the survivors and got them out of there. Bellowing like a madman, he regrouped the shattered detachment and retreated to the south, the wounded being helped by their fellows.

Miraculously, neither of the scouts was hit. At the outbreak of gunfire they had slipped onto the sides of their animals, Comanche fashion, and fled while hanging by one arm and leg. Not until they were well out of range did they straighten and stop to await the soldiers.

White Apache rose as the last of the troopers sped off into the swirling dust. He sighted on the back of one of the men and was about to squeeze the trigger when he had an abrupt change of heart. For a fleeting moment some of Clay Taggart asserted itself, some of the white man who had been reared on a ranch and taught that only cowards shot others in the back.

Lowering the Winchester, White Apache stepped around the boulder. Fiero and Ponce, howling like wolves in the grip of bloodlust, were bounding down the talus slope. Delgadito and Cuchillo Negro had risen but did not join them.

Turning, White Apache headed for the ridge to check on the Pimas. At the crown he glanced back and saw the firebrand and the young warrior mutilating a soldier. Fiero had gutted the body and was gleefully waving the slimy intestines in the air.

Marista and Colletto were near the horses. She gave White Apache a long, searching look, then reached out to touch his left arm. "You be hit."

A slug had creased him, breaking the skin and drawing blood but doing no real damage. White Apache shrugged. "It's a scratch. Nothing to get concerned about." He faced the battleground. "Now you see why hooking up with me is downright dangerous. The soldiers want me dead in the worst way, and they won't rest until they bring me down."

"I not care. We stay with you."

White Apache felt her hand slip into his. She squeezed and he did the same. Then, as he was about to peck her on the cheek, he saw the boy glance sharply at the crest. Letting go, he discovered that Delgadito and Cuchillo Negro had arrived.

The former was delighted by the outcome. "This was a great victory! When the warriors in the village hear, they will flock to our cause." He screeched for joy. "The white-eyes never learn. Again and again we send them running with their tails between their legs, and still they try to stop us."

"This was a little skirmish, nothing more," White Apache disputed him. "Whipping one measly patrol doesn't mean a thing. They'll go back to their post to report, and before you know it we'll have patrols combing every square inch of this country."

114

"Let them," Delgadito said. "They will never find us."

Confidence was fine, but it was White Apache's opinion that his mentor had a little too much. A fine line existed between faith in one's ability and arrogance, and once that line was crossed the offender frequently paid a heavy price. "I don't know, pard," he said. "Those two scouts knew their business. It wouldn't surprise me if they show up again real soon."

"Cibicues," Delgadito said in disdain. "They are skilled, but not skilled enough. We will conceal our trail in case they come back."

"There is the matter of their guns," Cuchillo Negro reminded them.

Every last body was stripped of weapons and ammunition, which were loaded onto the pack horses. White Apache resumed their trek with Marista at his side while the four warriors lingered to wipe out their tracks.

There was a technique to it. Using a bush or a limb to brush away every last print wasn't enough. The brush marks themselves had to be covered with a fine layer of loose dirt so that the ground appeared perfectly natural. Rocks had to be strategically placed. Apaches were masters of the art, and within twenty minutes the Chiricahuas had caught up with the horses.

White Apache noticed the boy secretly eyeing him and figured Colletto was taking his measure. The youngster rarely spoke and acted awed by all that had occurred.

Having the sprout and the woman to look after gave Clay a lot to think about. Another lifetime ago he had longed to have a family, to marry Lilly and raise a passel of young ones, a brood to carry on the Taggart name. That dream had been dashed the day Lilly betrayed him, but every so often he would recall those days and wish his dream might still come to pass.

Toward evening, in the middle of some of the starkest, most rugged landscape Clay had ever seen, Delgadito jogged up next to his horse and pointed at an isolated spire to the northeast, a needle of rock thrusting skyward as if in defiance.

"Eagle's Roost, *Lickoyee-shis-inday*. We will be there before the night is half done."

"Fine by me," Clay responded. "The woman and boy are plumb wore out. The rest will do them good." Stretching, he commented, "I just hope this place is as safe as Cuchillo Negro claims. I don't want the cavalry to show up."

Delgadito turned somber. "It is not the cavalry you need to worry about. It is the *Gans*."

Chapter Nine

His name was Gian-nah-tah and he was in the prime of his life, a strapping, robust young man of twenty winters whose sole ambition was that of most young men his age. It had to do with a woman.

Gian-nah-tah had long coveted the daughter of Soldado, a radiant beauty whose name meant Corn Watcher. To him, she had the most lustrous hair and vibrant form of any woman in the tribe. At night he dreamed of her, tossing and turning in fervent desire. During the day he dreamed of her too, and often he could not resist sneaking close to her father's lodge so he could admire her without being seen.

Gian-nah-tah was in love, although he would never admit as much. For an Apache warrior to admit to such weakness was demeaning. He told no one, but almost everyone knew, including the father of the *ninya*, who one day encountered the young warrior by chance and said that which stunned Gian-nah-tah so much, his tongue seemed to go numb.

"You want my daughter."

Soldado waited for a reply, and when none was forthcoming, he went on. "It is no secret. Just as it is no secret she has other suitors, warriors who have proven themselves time and again. What do you have to offer her?"

Gian-nah-tah had nothing to say, for in truth he had the clothes on his back and the rifle in his hand and that was it. He had not yet taken a wife, so he still lived in the wickiup of his father.

"It is true Palacio is your uncle, and he thinks highly of you," Soldado continued, "but his praise will not put food in my daughter's belly or help make the hard work women must do any easier for her to bear."

"This is so," Gian-nah-tah finally blurted.

"I will be honest with you," Soldado said. "Corn Watcher prefers you over all her other suitors, and she longs for the day you will bring your horse to our lodge so she might lead it to water." His pause was much longer than it needed to be. "But you do not have a horse yet, do you?"

Gian-nah-tah was too crestfallen to answer.

"I have raised my daughter to make a good wife. She is healthy, strong, a virgin. She could have any man she wanted, but she wants you." Again the father paused. "If you want her, prove yourself worthy of the prize. If you do not, I will forbid her to go to you. You have four moons to show me her trust is justified."

The young warrior had watched the older one walk off in mixed elation and dismay. He was thrilled to learn that the woman he cherished cared for him, but he was shattered by the ultimatum. How was he to prove himself in so short a time? Stealing a few horses would not be enough. He needed to do something more spectacular, something that would show everyone he was worthy.

Then came the meeting Palacio called, and Gian-nah-tah was surprised to find himself invited along with four of the most influential men in the tribe. Only when he heard of the offer made by the white-eyes did he understand.

His uncle Palacio knew of his talk with Soldado. Palacio was trying to help him, giving him a chance to earn Soldado's respect and Corn Watcher's hand by allowing him to get a head start on other warriors who might be inclined to turn in the renegades for the bounty.

That very night Gian-nah-tah borrowed his father's stallion and left the village to begin his search. First he traveled to Sweet Grass, which was deserted, and from there to several other remote places known only to the Chiricahuas. At each and every one he met with disappointment.

A new day dawned. Gian-nah-tah rose early and made off toward Rabbit Ears. He could think of two or three other spots that deserved attention, and he would not rest until he had checked them all.

As the young warrior rode along with the warm wind blowing his long black hair, he happened to gaze to the northeast and spied in the far distance the spire known as Eagle's Roost. He remembered the cave there, which he had seen once as a small boy. Briefly he considered making a detour but he dismissed the idea. Eagle's Roost was the haunt of an evil mountain spirit. Everyone knew that. Not even the renegades would dare go there.

Or would they?

Torn by indecision, Gian-nah-tah pressed on toward Rabbit Ears. Perhaps he would go check Eagle's Roost another time. Perhaps not.

Marista's laughter dazzled Clay Taggart. He sat propped on his saddle near the spring in the spacious cave they now called home and watched as she skinned a rattlesnake Colletto had killed. There was no squeamishness on her part. She went about the task with cheerful precision, cutting and slicing so quickly that her hands flew.

"Tell me more about your people," Clay urged.

Marista had been explaining how her tribe diverted water from the Salt and Gila Rivers to irrigate the soil for farming. She had mentioned that as a very little girl she had often jumped naked into the ditches to splash and play on hot days, and Clay had replied that there was a sight he would like to see. Which sparked her mirth.

"Pimas have two clans," she revealed. "White Ant people and Red Ant people. I be White Ant."

"Where are your antennae?"

She looked up, puzzled. *"Neh?"*

Clay put his hands to his head and waved two fingers around and around. "Antennae," he said, grinning.

Marista chuckled heartily. Her cares and woes had been forgotten for the moment; she appeared ten years younger. "My father White Ant. His father White Ant. His father also White Ant."

"I get the idea," Clay said, and absently asked, "Couldn't your pa help you when your husband wanted to kick you out?" The sorrow it provoked made him regret his blunder and he hastily added, "Sorry. I reckon I have the brains of a mule."

"Father no can help," Marista said sadly.

Desperate to change the subject, Clay observed the Apaches huddled at the cave mouth and thought of their superstition regarding the *Gans*. "Tell me. Do your people believe in the Almighty? In God? Or in Yusn, as the Chiricahuas call him?"

She brightened. "Pimas believe two gods. Earthgiver and Elder Brother."

"Never heard that one before," Clay admitted. "How about evil spirits? The Apaches put a lot of store in them."

"Yes. There be Evil Spirit over all."

Clay stared into the pool and saw his likeness reflected. "Makes a man wonder," he said. "If so many different people believe in one, there must be one." He dipped a hand in the water and raised a mouthful to his lips.

"Delicious, yes? That right word?"

"It sure is," Clay said. "Which reminds me. Where did you learn to speak the white man's tongue?"

Marista stopped peeling the skin from the snake. She pronounced her next words slowly and distinctly. "From Doctor David Wooster of San Francisco. You know him?"

"Heard of him," Clay replied. Wooster had lived among the Pimas for quite some time, tending their sick and doing what little he could to raise their standard of living. The physician had grown warmly attached to the Pimas and was still spoken of highly by them even though several years had gone by since he left for California.

"He heal mother when she sick. Heal many Pimas. White Ant, Red Ant, all be same to him."

Clay wondered what motivated people like the good doctor. He didn't see how anyone could be so selfless and devoted to easing human misery, the world being the way it was. It had been his experience that most folks would as soon stab another in the back as look at them. He was a prime example. Lilly had turned on him, Gillett had tried to have him lynched, the Army was after him for taking revenge on the backstabbers who had strung him up. Simple decency and goodness were dying out, and soon the human race wouldn't have a shred of either. As for justice, there was none in the world unless it was the justice dispensed by the business end of a pistol or rifle.

Just then Delgadito called out, breaking Clay's train of thought. "*Lickoyee-shis-inday*. Come see."

Rising, Clay hastened over and crouched beside the warriors. They were staring at a lone figure moving across the wasteland far to the southwest, a figure so distant it was the size of an ant, a tiny speck moving along against the brown backdrop of parched countryside.

"One man on horseback," Delgadito said.

"A *Shis-Inday*," Fiero added.

Clay squinted but could not distinguish a single detail. "How can you be sure it is an Apache?" he asked.

"I am sure," the firebrand declared. "He is heading for Rabbit Ears, where we stayed two moons ago."

"Could it be an Army scout hunting for us?" Clay questioned.

Fiero leaned forward. "No, he does not wear a blue coat. Perhaps he is a hunter in search of antelope." He wagged his rifle in the figure's direction. "I will go see who it is, if you want."

Blood Treachery

"He might spot you," Clay said. "It is best if no one knows where we are, not even other Chiricahuas. So I say we should let him go his way in peace."

No one objected, which Clay took as a good sign. There had been a time when they argued every time he opened his mouth. Moving to the very brink of the ledge fronting the cave, he surveyed the area.

Eagle's Roost was aptly named. Two-thirds of the way up the stone spire was an old nest built by eagles a long time ago in a niche in the rock surface. It wasn't being used, so either the eagles had aged and died or been killed.

About a hundred feet below the nest, the spire flared to a wide base. Here the cave was situated. It measured some eighty feet across and forty feet from front to back, including the pool, which was six feet in diameter.

A narrow trail, barely the width of two moccasins, wound from the cave mouth to the canyon floor below, a distance of approximately three-hundred feet. Brush and a few trees grew in the canyon, and in one of those sparse stands the horses were secreted.

In Clay's opinion, it was the ideal hideout. Water was there for the taking, game could be had with effort, and the cave was so far off the beaten path that the odds of anyone stopping by any time soon were remote. For the time being they were safe. They did not have to keep looking over a shoulder every minute of every day. They could relax, really and truly relax.

Fiero let out with a long sigh. "I, for one, do not like all this sitting around. We are warriors, not women. We should be off raiding the Mexicans or one of the white-eyes who hanged White Apache."

"We will soon enough," Clay said. "Be patient."

Fiero grunted. Everyone knew that of all the Chiricahuas, he was the least patient. "If I cannot kill enemies, I will kill something for our supper pot." So saying, the burly warrior stepped to the trail and descended.

Clay opened his mouth to call him back but stopped when Cuchillo Negro placed a hand on his shoulder.

"Always remember, my friend, that Apaches are free to do as they want. You cannot hold Fiero here against his will. If he wants to hunt, he can."

"He might give our hiding place away," Clay complained. "Is it right that all of us suffer because he does not know how to be patient?"

Cuchillo Negro countered the query with one of his own. "Is it for us you are so worried, or for them?" He pointed at the Pimas.

Ponce had risen and was inspecting the cave floor and one wall. "Look at all this dust," he remarked. "No one has stayed here since the death of Toga-de-chuz."

"His bones should be here somewhere," Cuchillo Negro said.

"Unless the mountain spirit ground them to dust," Delgadito mentioned.

Peeved that Fiero had gone off, Clay was in no mood to talk about their silly superstition. He walked back to the spring and sat down close to Marista, who took one look at him and asked, "Something be wrong?"

"No. I'm fine," Clay said. No sooner did he speak than an inexplicable shiver ran down his spine. He faced the opening, thinking the wind had kicked up, but the air was sluggish. For a few brief moments he had the eerie feeling that unseen eyes were upon him. He scanned the dark walls and ceiling, feeling foolish doing so, but saw nothing out of the ordinary.

Nerves, Clay reckoned. A case of bad nerves was all it was, spawned by Fiero going off by his lonesome. One day soon the hothead was going to get them all into a heap of trouble. He just knew it.

Col. Reynolds was buried in paperwork at his desk when the orderly rapped on the office door and announced that Capt. Forester wanted to see him. "Show him in," the colonel said, setting down his quill pen.

Gerald Forester was in a huff, as the flinty cast of his features revealed. He marched up to the desk and stood at attention until told to stand at ease.

"What's the prognosis?" Colonel Reynolds inquired.

"The surgeon says that with a little luck, Derrick will pull through, sir. He'll be laid up for two months, possibly longer. And he'll never be the man he was before. But he'll be alive, which I suppose is some consolation."

"Why so cynical, Captain?"

Forester ran his fingers along his sweeping mustache and tweaked one end. "It's this whole White Apache business, sir. The man is a butcher. He deserves to be stood in front of a firing squad."

"I couldn't agree more."

"Then why won't you let me go after him?" Forester clenched his fists. "I know that country well, sir. Sgt. Bryce told me exactly where the ambush took place. The Flying Detachment can be there in two days if we limit ourselves to four hours of sleep each night. We might be able to catch Taggart, at long last."

"Might, Captain. Might," Reynolds said severely. "No, I'm afraid my decision is final. The Flying Detachment does not leave Fort Bowie until we hear from Palacio."

"But sir," Forester said, forgetting himself and gripping the edge of the desk, "with all due respect, I can't help thinking that you're making a grave mistake. You know as well as I do that Headquarters has made the capture or slaying of the White Apache a top priority. And we may never get a better chance. My men and I are ready. Say the word and I'll bring the son of a bitch back draped over a saddle."

Reynolds folded his hands in his lap and sat back. "I appreciate your zeal, Captain. However, I can't help wondering if it stems from our standing orders or your longstanding friendship with Captain Derrick." The Colonel sighed and gazed out the window. "As for missing an opportunity, I doubt that's the case. Clay Taggart has proven to be quite shrewd. He's not about to stick around the site of an ambush. And since it took Bryce four days to get here after the attack, by the time you reach the area almost a whole week will have gone by. Hell, man. Taggart could be in Canada by then."

Captain Forester straightened. He reluctantly had to admit that his superior had a valid point. He had allowed his friendship for Henry Derrick to sway his judgment. "You're right, of course, sir. I'm sorry I bothered you. May I be excused?"

Reynolds hesitated. He liked Forester more than most of his subordinates. The man was a topnotch soldier and one of the few genuinely dedicated officers he had ever met. Most, himself included, were more interested in merely putting in their twenty years and leaving the military with a modest pension to see them through their golden years. Forester couldn't be bothered with counting the days until his retirement. The man was actually devoted to his country, to serving in the best capacity he knew how.

"As my dear, departed grandmother used to say to me when I was knee high to a colt and always acting up, you must possess your soul in patience, Captain. The wheels have been set in motion. It's only a matter of time before one of the Chiricahuas learns where the renegades are hiding out. Then you'll get your wish."

"I can hardly wait, sir."

Fiero had not earned his name for nothing. He had a temperament that blazed as hot as the sun when he was angry or upset, and he was upset now. Hiding out in a cave wasn't his idea of how to wage war on the despicable white-eyes who had stolen Chiricahua land right out from under the tribe. It would take many raids, and many Americans would have to die before the chiefs of the whites would give thought to leaving the territory. White Apache had told him as much.

Thinking of *Lickoyee-shis-inday* only made Fiero more upset. Begrudgingly, he had grown to like White Apache, to regard him as a full-fledged member of the band. Then the man went and did something like this, bringing them to a cave inhabited by an evil mountain spirit just so the Pimas would be safe!

It was added proof that, just as Fiero had long maintained, women were a burden. They made strong men weak. They clouded the judgment of those caught in their spell. It was why Fiero would never take a wife. He was pledged to resist the white invaders until the day he died, if need be, and he would not let any female weaken his resolve.

Delgadito had been weak once, Fiero mused, and the result had been disastrous. It was Delgadito who had insisted on taking women and children into Mexico when the band splintered off from Palacio's followers. "We cannot leave behind those who depend on us for their welfare," Delgadito had claimed.

Noble sentiments, but impractical. The band had not been able to travel very fast with so many women and children to watch over. It had enabled the scalphunters to catch them when and where they were most vulnerable. Few would ever know how close the band came to being exterminated that day.

Fiero had not been there, but he had seen the aftermath. He had stood on the rim of the hollow in which the massacre had taken place, and he had felt as if his insides were being ripped apart.

The slaughter had been horrendous. Women had been shot to shreds as they fled with infants in their arms. Small children had been sliced wide open, their innards left hanging from their bloated bellies for the scavengers to feast on. And every last one had been scalped.

It mattered little to Fiero that later White Apache had led the band into Mexico and tracked down the scalphunters who were to blame. He had learned his lesson. Never again would he entangle himself with women and young ones. Yet here he was, doing just that because of White Apache.

Scowling, Fiero paused to take control of his

emotions. A warrior must never let his mind wander, he reminded himself, and raised his nose to the wind to test for the scent of game, or enemies. Turning, he saw Eagle's Roost far off, the mouth of the cave like a black spot on the stone spire. There was no sign of the others, which was to be expected. They had grown foolish but not that foolish.

A little farther on, Fiero came on fresh deer tracks left by a doe and a fawn that had passed that way earlier in the day. He trailed them, jogging tirelessly into the gathering twilight. A promise was a promise, and he had said that he would bring meat for the cooking pot.

Perhaps because Fiero was upset, or because of his promise, or because it was growing late and he wanted to return to the cave before it was too dark to track, he hurried on, giving no thought to his own tracks.

No thought at all.

The sun had not yet rimmed the eastern horizon when Gian-nah-tah swung onto his father's stallion and headed eastward from Rabbit Ears. The renegades had not been there. No one had in quite some time. His list of possible places to check was growing shorter by the day, and with each waning moon he stood in greater jeopardy of losing Corn Watcher.

Gian-nah-tah had not eaten in a day and a half. His stomach rumbled constantly but he paid it no heed. He would eat after he located the renegades, not before.

Leaving the twin peaks behind, Gian-nah-tah set off across a flat plain into a region of twisted gullies and steep canyons. He was riding with his chin low, depressed at the prospect of losing the woman he wanted to another warrior, when the strong scent of spilled blood made him snap up and look around.

Sixty feet away lay the carcass of a dead deer. The young warrior rode over, expecting to find a cougar kill. Instead, he discovered a butchered doe and fawn. The doe had been dropped by a single shot to the head. The fawn had had its throat slit when it refused to leave its mother. Only the doe had been skinned, and most of the choice meat was gone.

Gian-nah-tah sat on the stallion and tingled all over. Not because of the doe. He had slain scores of them himself. Nor because of the fawn, even though its death had been needless. No, he tingled because of the tracks in the dirt beside the deer.

The tracks of the warrior who had killed them.

The tracks of an Apache warrior.

Of a Chiricahua.

And they made off straight toward Eagle's Roost.

Chapter Ten

Palacio was astride his finest horse and dressed in his finest clothes. He had a new Bowie knife strapped to his ample middle, received in trade from the same two smugglers who had sold him the three rifles he kept hidden under a pile of blankets in his lodge.

Riding with the Chiricahua leader were his nephew, old Nantanh, Juan Pedro, and Chico. Palacio had brought the last three along so they could see for themselves the esteem in which the white-eyes held him. And to be sure he was treated with the respect that was his due, he had sent a messenger on ahead to inform White Hair that they were coming.

Palacio smiled in delight when one of the *soldados* high on the stone lodge saw him and bellowed for all to hear.

"It's the chief! Open the gate!"

For the benefit of the others, Palacio translated.

131

He took the liberty of embellishing a little by adding the word "great" before chief, and then said, "See? It is because the white-eyes hold me in such high regard that I can do much good for our people."

"Since when is it good for Chiricahua to betray Chiricahua?" Nantanh asked with a pointed glare at Gian-nah-tah.

"Would you rather live at San Carlos?" Palacio retorted, beginning to regret that he had invited the venerable warrior. The old fool had groused the whole trip, sniping at Palacio for allowing such treachery. "That is where we will end up if the White Apache and the misguided men with him are not stopped."

Juan Pedro grunted agreement. "San Carlos is for those who want to live like dogs. Chiricahuas do not go around on all fours."

Nantanh was not cowed. "I, too, hate the idea of being forced to live with tribes who have been our enemies longer than any man can remember. But the white-eyes are no better, despite what Palacio claims. They use us to their own ends. Just as they use us now to do that which they have not been able to do in all the moons Delgadito has waged war against them."

Palacio was glad when the huge gate creaked inward. It shut the old fool up so he could lead them on in, his head high. To his surprise, White Hair had arranged a reception.

Twenty troopers in clean uniforms stood in a long line, polished rifles at their sides. At the head of the line was White Hair himself, holding a gleaming long-knife. At his command, the soldiers presented arms, and all activity in the fort ceased as all eyes swung toward the visitors.

Giddy at this tribute to his importance, Palacio

beamed at the row of soldiers as his horse pranced past them. To a man, they gazed straight ahead, as motionless as a row of trees.

Unknown to Palacio, the reception had been Capt. Gerald Forester's idea, not Col. Reynold's. On being called into the commander's office the day before to receive word of the impending visit, Forester had remarked, "Maybe you should roll out the honor guard. The fat bastard loves it when he's treated like royalty. It makes him easier to deal with."

Now, watching Palacio act like some sort of foreign potentate from the front porch of the main building, Capt. Forester nudged Sgt. McKinn and said out of the corner of his mouth, "I swear, if that head of his swells any bigger, it'll go floating off like a balloon." The noncom, who hated Apaches with a passion, snickered.

Neither was aware that Col. Reynolds overheard the comment but overlooked it. Stepping around in front of the honor guard, Reynolds performed a left moulinet with his saber, then a right moulinet, then slid the saber into its scabbard and offered a salute. He could not but notice the look Palacio gave the other warriors, and he realized that Forester had the man's character pegged.

"Greeting, friend," Reynolds stated. "Climb down. I have everything set up so we can get right to business." He indicated the side of the building, where blankets and stools had been set out for the council.

Palacio slid off his horse, smoothed his frilly blue shirt, and extended his hand in the white manner. "I am happy to see you again, White Hair. But you did not need to do all this for me."

The false humility was thick enough to be cut with a knife. Reynolds took it in stride and shook. For a man whose body resembled whale blubber, the chief was immensely strong. "I have looked forward to this day with relish. At long last the White Apache will be brought to account for his many crimes."

"Once you learn where he is."

Something in the Chiricahua's tone bothered Reynolds. "You did find out? That is the reason you came?"

"Oh, most assuredly," Palacio said, his grin as slick as that of a saloon cardsharp. "And, as we agreed, the information will be yours in exchange for the bounty you offered." He made a show of surveying the compound. "As I recall, there was mention of eight horses, forty blankets, six knives, an axe, and tobacco. Yet I do not see them."

Reynolds was anxious to send the Flying Detachment on its way. Any delay could prove costly; Taggart might elect to go somewhere else. But short of throttling the information out of Palacio, there was nothing he could do but play along and hope the devious savage didn't keep him waiting all damn day.

"A quick visit to the stable and the sutler's and you'll have all the bounty I promised you," Reynolds said.

Palacio lumbered toward the blankets. "Not too quick, I trust? I am thirsty after my long ride. And I have been thinking the whole time of my last visit, my friend, and those scrambled eggs you shared with me."

Col. Reynolds turned to his adjutant. "You heard the man. Have a pitcher of water brought. And tell the cook I want heaping portions of scrambled eggs out here in ten minutes."

"Do not forget some sweet cakes," Palacio said. He licked his thick lips. "I do so love those wonderful sweet cakes you have for your morning meal."

There were times, Col. Reynolds reflected, when he swore it would be easier dealing with Delgadito.

Clay Taggart had the nightmare on the seventh night the band stayed at Eagle's Roost. In it he was fleeing on foot from a large number of troopers who peppered the air with hot lead. He had his rifle and he fired as he ran, but to his amazement the bullets bounced off the soldiers. They gained rapidly. Just when he thought they would run him down, he spied a cave. Darting into its dark depths, he fired at the horses of his pursuers, dropping five or six before the soldiers scattered to take cover. He congratulated himself on his narrow escape and took stock.

The cave was huge, so huge Clay couldn't see the ceiling or tell how far underground it extended. There was a spring, though, which meant he could hold out indefinitely. Kneeling to take a drink, he heard a scraping noise overhead and looked up to see a pair of blazing red eyes the size of saucers fixed on him.

Startled, Clay cried out and tried to bring the rifle up. Before he could, a vague black shape swept down and caught him its in grip. The thing was monstrous, with the shape and consistency of a wet blanket and the power of a bull buffalo. Clay was helpless in its iron grasp. Little by little the life was being crushed from his body while those awful red eyes glared into his and hot, fetid breath fanned his face.

Clay's ribs shattered, popping like fireworks one after the other. He opened his mouth to scream and the creature's own gaping maw yawned wide. Out of it shot a vile, slimy black tongue that rolled down Clay's throat, piercing his vitals. He struggled mightily, thrashing and kicking, but it was to no avail.

With a last, Herculean effort Clay tried to break free. He managed to straighten, and suddenly found himself seated on the smooth floor of the cave, his body caked with sweat. Something covered his mouth. He clutched at it and grabbed a slender wrist.

Soft lips brushed his ear. "You be all right, Clay. You have bad dream."

Slowly Clay came to his senses. His body gave a convulsive shake and he gently pried her hand away. Gulping in the cool night air, he whispered, "I'm obliged."

"You cry out in sleep. Why?"

Clay wondered the same thing. He glanced at the ceiling, then at the walls, which were plunged in inky darkness. No piercing red eyes glared back at him, but he had that strange sensation again of being watched by someone unseen. It was downright spooky. "Maybe something I ate didn't agree with me," he fibbed.

The warriors slept soundly over near the cave mouth. About six feet away Colletto snored lightly.

Clay mopped his brow with the back of his hand and laid back down. Marista snuggled beside him, resting her head on his shoulder.

"You be troubled?"

What should he tell her? Clay mused. That he was letting some stupid superstition scare him silly? Or was there more to it than that? Was it a premonition of some sort? His ma had been a big believer in ghosts and spirits and such, which his pa had branded as so much nonsense. Clay had been partial to his father's way of thinking, but now he wondered.

"Clay?"

"I don't know what the dickens is wrong with me," Clay confessed. "But it might be smart to think about moving on. There must be somewhere else we can go where you and the boy will be safe."

"Chiricahuas be happy. They not like cave." Marista paused. "I not like much."

Clay shifted to face her. Their noses were tip to tip, her breath caressed his face. "You too? Then there's no doubt about it. I might be dense at times but I know when to take a blamed hint. We'll leave tomorrow after I palaver with the others about the best place to go."

Marista smiled.

The shadows highlighted her natural beauty, rendering her more sensual and alluring than any woman Clay had ever seen. It took his breath away, this beauty of hers, and before he could help himself he kissed her. Not a light kiss, either, which he had been prone to give in front of her son and the warriors. He kissed her passionately, all the ardor he had suppressed welling up out of him. It was the single greatest kiss of his entire life, and it seemed to last forever.

Then, as all such exquisite moments do, it came to an end. Marista stiffened and drew back.

Clay saw that she was looking over his shoulder, and half fearing she had seen the horrible red eyes of his nightmare, he spun. A husky shape loomed a few steps away. Clay started to reach for his Colt.

"Lickoyee-shis-inday, come quickly."

It was Fiero. Clay rose, snatched up his Winchester, and padded beside the warrior to the rim of the cave. He was taken aback to find all the Chiricahuas were awake and staring intently into the night. "What is it?" he asked.

"Listen," Delgadito said.

Clay did, but for the longest while he heard nothing other than the lonesome sigh of the wind and the occasional rustle of trees on the canyon floor. He was beginning to think his brother Apaches were imagining things when he heard a faint metallic clink. A few second later there was a sustained rattle.

They were sounds Clay recognized. Back in his ranching days he had delivered beef to area forts numerous times. He knew the many little sounds large bodies of soldiers made as they went about their daily routine, sounds exactly like these he was hearing. "Soldiers," he said.

"Many soldiers," Cuchillo Negro amended. "They left their horses far up the canyon and came the rest of the way on foot. They seek to block the trail to keep us from escaping."

"Then we must leave immediately," Clay declared, "before they realize that we know they are there."

"And before they find our horses," Cuchillo Negro said.

Delgadito motioned at the huge pile of smuggled goods, which had been placed against the left-hand wall. "We will have to leave the plunder, Lickoyee-shis-inday. It cannot be helped."

"Keep watch. I will be right back."

Clay hurried to the Pimas. Marista had roused her son and the pair were huddled next to the spring. "Soldiers," he announced. "We have to skedaddle, pronto."

Marista paused just long enough to retrieve her water skin. She kept a firm grip on the boy and trailed Clay to the opening where the Apaches were streaking their faces and broad chests with dirt. Imitating them, Clay listened for more telltale noises from the canyon. It seemed awfully quiet down there now, too quiet for his liking.

Fiero stepped lightly to the narrow footpath. "I will go first," he volunteered. "Any white-eyes I see, I will slit their throats before they can cry out."

Clay worked the lever of his rifle. "If we should be separated," he whispered, "head due east. We will join up again at Council Rock."

As silently as a ghost, Fiero started down the ribbon of a path. He moved low to the ground, his body blending into the earth as if part of it. Delgadito waited a minute, then he followed.

Clay's turn was next. He took Marista's hand, she took Colletto's, and after bestowing a reassuring smile on both of them, he descended.

It had been easy to climb to the cave in broad daylight, when a person could see where to step. But in the murky gloom every stride was fraught with peril: a single misstep would result in tragedy. On either side there was a sheer drop of hundreds of feet, and at the bottom waited jagged boulders to dash the unwary to bits.

Clay avoided looking to right or left. Concentrating on the trail and nothing but the trail, he wound lower yard by precarious yard. Every now and then he did glance into the canyon but saw no sign of any troopers. He could only hope they were too busy getting into position to notice anything else. Twenty feet in front of him

Delgadito came to a bend and snaked around it surefootedly. He could no longer see Fiero, who had descended at a reckless rate.

There was an urgent tug on Clay's hand. Stopping, he twisted and was appalled to see that the boy had slipped and hung over the side. Marista's grip was all that kept Colletto from plummeting to his death.

Quickly Clay eased closer to her, leaned forward as far as he dared, and snagged the boy's wrist. Between the two of them they pulled Colletto high enough for him to regain his footing.

The boy's eyes were wide and his face pale, but to his credit he had not cried out when he fell nor uttered a sound while he dangled heartbeats from oblivion.

White Apache pressed Marista's shoulder, then moved on. Delgadito, unaware of the mishap, had more of a lead than before. White Apache looked over a shoulder and saw that Ponce had nearly overtaken them, while much farther back was Cuchillo Negro.

Resisting an urge to go faster than was prudent, White Apache slid one foot forward, then brought up the other leg, and repeated the process again and again. He tried to keep his mind on the matter at hand but his thoughts strayed.

Staying at Eagle's Roost had been a monumental blunder, and if he hadn't been so worried about the Pimas he would have seen the truth sooner. There was only the one way into and out of the cave, which offered no handy escape route in case of an emergency. And not being able to keep horses close by precluded a quick getaway.

Clay told himself that he should have listened to the Chiricahuas. As Delgadito had pointed out, there was no safe haven for them anywhere in Arizona. He had to accept that fact and deal with it.

Which brought up the issue that bothered Clay most of all: What should he do about Marista and Colletto? He yearned to keep them with him, but how could he do that if he couldn't find a spot where they could hide out without fear of being discovered by the Army or the law or bounty hunters? By staying with him, they would, in effect, be committing suicide. He couldn't let them do that.

Suddenly the breeze brought a low rustling noise that stopped as abruptly as it began. Clay stopped and strained but heard no more. He thought it might have been the sound of a struggle, perhaps Fiero dispatching a trooper. If so, other soldiers were bound to have also heard.

Hurrying on, White Apache came to the bend. As he edged around the curve, a sharp shout rent the night, punctuated by others, then a gun flashed and was answered in kind and suddenly the night pounded to the boom of manmade thunder.

Clay made no move to enter the fray. For one thing, he had no clear targets. For another, he was exposed and vulnerable, and more importantly so were the Pimas.

Then Ponce cut loose, firing at clusters of gun flashes on both sides of the canyon. Seconds later Cuchillo Negro joined in.

The soldiers could do the same, and did, loosing a staggered volley at the flame and smoke that belched from the rifles of the warriors. Many underestimated the range or shot wildly.

Slugs smacked into the path all around Clay, Marista, and Colletto or whizzed past their ears, so many that it seemed the sky rained lead. Clay had no choice but to return fire. He banged off several shots, turned, and urged, "Go back! Into the cave! It's our only chance!"

The woman complied, her son glued to her side. They reached Ponce, who back-pedaled up the incline and fired to cover them, but in doing so he drew more fire in their direction.

Afraid for their lives, Clay levered round after round, trying futilely to drive the soldiers to ground or at the very least make them slack off. There were just too many. He saw Delgadito hastening toward him and retreated. Of Fiero, there was no trace.

A shout rose above the thundering din, an officer, perhaps, who bellowed, "Keep firing, men! We've got them right where we want them!"

The man's meaning was plain. By forcing the band back into the cave, the cavalrymen would have the Chiricahuas trapped. The troopers could keep the band pinned down until the warriors weakened from lack of food or were all killed off.

Never in all Clay's life had he experienced such an unnerving ordeal. Bullets kept hitting the path or cleaving the air on either side. At any moment he dreaded one would hit Marista or Colletto and they would fall to their doom before he could catch them.

Clay had gone about halfway when a searing pain lanced his left arm. He looked down and saw a black furrow where the bullet had nicked him, blood trickling freely. Snapping the Winchester to his shoulder, he fired twice at gun flashes close to the base of the spire and thought he heard a shriek of pain. He worked the lever again and squeezed the trigger but this time a muted click told him the chamber was empty.

Reloading as he climbed, Clay saw Delgadito jerk to one side, totter, and lose his footing. He was certain the warrior would fall, but by flinging out a steely arm Delgadito caught hold of the edge of the footpath and saved himself temporarily. The warrior's other arm was pressed against his chest; he would not be able to hold on indefinitely.

"Hang on, pard!" Clay cried, and scurried to his friend's aid. The lead flew fast and furious. It was a miracle that neither of them was hit.

In moments Clay had yanked Delgadito onto the path. The warrior took but a second to tuck his wounded arm close to his chest, then they sped upward, Clay eager to rejoin the Pimas, Delgadito to avoid being shot again.

At last the cave materialized. Clay watched the Pimas slip into the shadows and gave a silent heartfelt thanks. If anything happened to her, he would never forgive himself for letting them become part of his life—a violent life certain to end in violent death. Cuchillo Negro and Ponce had flattened along the rim and were shooting methodically.

White Apache gained the entrance. He checked to verify Marista and her son were safely away from the rim, then went prone and added his Winchester to the unequal battle.

Grunting loudly, Delgadito crawled up over the edge and lay on his side, panting and grimacing. A large dark stain on his brown shirt marked where he had been hit. He tried to open his shirt to examine the wound but could not get his fingers to function.

Marista glided over, her water skin still at her

side. She glanced at Clay and said, "Should I?"

Not even hesitating, Clay answered, "Help him." It pleased him mightily that she had asked, for in doing so she gave added proof that she considered him to be her man and showed she would rely on his judgment where other men were concerned. At any other time he would have reveled in her devotion, but now he bent his cheek to the Winchester and was about to fire when the shooting below unexpectedly ended. The warriors promptly stopped firing.

Clay leaned back to collect his wits. It had all transpired so swiftly that only now could he fully appreciate the predicament they were in, which was summed up nicely by Ponce.

The youngest member of their band spat in disgust and bowed his chin to his chest. "I knew we should not have tempted the wrath of the *Gans*. Now we are dead men."

Chapter Eleven

Capt. Gerald Forester was fit to be tied.

Everything had gone smoothly until the Flying Detachment was almost in position, and then sheer bedlam had broken out. As a result, he had lost five good men, seasoned troopers cut down in the prime of their lives by the bullets of the renegades. Four of them, at any rate. The fifth man had been stabbed twice in the chest.

That in itself was disturbing, Forester reflected. It meant at least one of the Apaches had reached the valley floor before the firing broke out and must still be at large.

Now, with dawn mere minutes off and the situation stabilized, Forester had sent for those best suited to deal with whoever had slipped through his carefully laid net. Hearing a commotion, he looked up from the plate of cold beans he was wolfing and saw the answers to his problem approaching, all seven of them. Unfortunately, at their head tramped the biggest pain in the ass in the United States Army.

"You sent for me?" Capt. Vincent Parmalee said without ceremony.

"I sent for the scouts," Forester said.

"Who are under my command," Parmalee retorted. "Col. Reynolds was quite explicit on that point."

"As he was when he informed you that *I* would be in overall command."

Parmalee made no attempt to hide his spite. He resented being sent out with the Flying Detachment, resented being forced to follow the orders of a self-righteous stickler for rules and regulations like Forester, and resented being treated as if he were a worthless imbecile. "Where the scouts go, I go. So what can we do for you?"

Ignoring his fellow officer, Capt. Forester addressed Klo-sen. "Take all the scouts. Find the renegade who knifed Pvt. Confort. Bring me his head."

Parmalee sputtered, "Now see here!" But it was too late. Klo-sen had not waited for his approval but had turned and barked a single word that set all the scouts in motion. In no time they had vanished among the boulders and brush.

Captain Forester spooned more beans into his mouth. He had no use for Parmalee; the man was a waste of uniform. For the life of him he couldn't imagine why their superior had seen fit to send the sot along. In his estimation it was a pity the renegade hadn't knifed Parmalee instead of poor Pvt. Confort.

"I intend to file a protest with the colonel after we return to Fort Bowie," the Chief of Scouts snapped.

"You do that."

"Just because you were put in charge doesn't give you the right to ride roughshod over me. If for no other reason than common courtesy, you should clear all your orders to my scouts through me in advance. I don't like having you usurp my authority."

Forester set the plate down and stood. "If you're so damned upset about the scouts going off by themselves, there's a simple solution."

"There is?"

"Go with them," Forester suggested, knowing full well the man never would. Just as it was no secret that Parmalee drowned his troubles in a bottle, so was it no secret the man was an errant yellowbelly.

True to form, Parmalee sniffed and said, "I don't see where that's necessary. Besides, I'd never catch up to them." He walked off in a huff, saying over a shoulder, "I'll be working on my report to the colonel if you need me."

"I won't."

Outraged, Parmalee held his temper in check until he was safely behind a boulder the size of a buffalo. Then he vented his spleen in a series of blue oaths muttered nonstop. When that was done, he fumbled in his pocket for his silver flask, opened it, and greedily took several gulps. The alcohol burned his mouth and throat but he didn't care. To him it was the elixir of life, the balm of Gilead, the salvation of his frayed nerves.

Parmalee had been terrified when the battle erupted. Having been informed that they were close to the renegade stronghold, he had deliberately held his scouts to the rear of the column and then advanced at a snail's pace into the canyon. At the outbreak of gunfire, his scouts had dashed off to be in the thick of things, leaving him alone and defenseless, hiding behind a bush no bigger than a breadbasket. Several wild shots had nearly ended his life. One, in fact, had kicked dirt into his face, at which point he had come awfully close to soiling himself.

Shuddering at the memory, Parmalee took another sip, corked the flask, and slid it into his pants pocket. Squaring his shoulders, he started around the boulder, striding past a dry bush that rustled after he went by. Why it should rustle when there was no wind, he had no idea. It occurred to him to turn and look but he was too eager to get as far from the stone spire where the renegades were holed up to bother. At any moment another battle might break out, and he didn't care to be in the vicinity.

But just as Parmalee was about to walk out into the open, something clamped itself on his windpipe and he was drawn up short. Startled, he tried to cry out and reached up to find an iron forearm looped around his neck. It shocked him so badly that he froze, and the next instant felt an agonizing spasm in his abdomen, a spasm that rippled higher, deep into his chest, and choked off the breath in his throat.

The arm was withdrawn.

Parmalee felt a warm, sticky sensation creeping down over his stomach and thighs. He glanced down and his knees turned to water at the horrifying sight he beheld. His stomach had been sliced clean open, his uniform and flesh sheared as neatly as you please by a blade so sharp he had been disemboweled in the blink of an eye.

It couldn't be! Parmalee told himself even as rock hard hands seized him by the back of the shirt and flung him to the earth at the base of the boulder. A swarthy face bearing a scar in the shape of a lightning bolt on its brow appeared above him and dark, fiery eyes regarded him with blatant contempt. Softly spoken words fell on his ears, but he did not understand them.

"Pindah lickoyee das-ay-go, dee-dah tatsan."

Parmalee tried to answer but his vocal chords were paralyzed. The face disappeared and he felt hands stripping him of his revolver and personal effects. In a little while the face reappeared, studying the flask. He saw the savage take a swig, grimace, and toss the whiskey aside. Then the Apache was gone.

Shocked to his core, growing weaker by the moment, Capt. Vincent Parmalee gazed at the heavens with eyes moistened by tears. It wasn't fair. He hadn't wanted to be there. He had done his best to avoid combat. And look at what had happened! He had one last thought before the world turned inside out and a yawning black pit swallowed him up, one last thought that summed up his existence as succinctly as any epitaph:

Life made no damn sense.

Fiero slipped off soundlessly, conforming the shape and motion of his body to the terrain. He hadn't intended to kill again so soon, but he could not pass up the opportunity to rub out a little chief of the white-eyes. Thanks to White Apache, he knew how to tell the chiefs from the soldiers under them by the strange braids on the shoulders of their uniforms.

It amazed Fiero that the white-eye had not realized he was there. The man had practically stepped on top of him. But then, every Chiricahua knew that the whites had senses as keen as a two-day old infant.

Like all Apache warriors, Fiero had learned at an early age how to move without making noise, how to blend into the landscape so that he was virtually invisible. By the age of eight, he had been able to imitate a bush or a boulder so expertly that no one could tell he was there. His father had also taught him how to dig a shallow depression in which to hide and then cover himself lightly with loose dirt. Plus many other tricks that had saved his skin time and time again.

Now Fiero was bearing to the southeast. He planned to swing wide around the soldiers and see how close he could get to Eagle's Roost. There had to be something he could do to help the rest of the band, although he had no idea what it might be. He did not like to think of the fact that some of them might be dead.

In his mind's eye Fiero reviewed the battle. He recalled descending the footpath well ahead of the others only to find the area swarming with troopers. Flattening, he had tried to crawl through their lines undetected, but an unwitting idiot had stumbled on him and he had stabbed the man to keep him from shouting. Unfortunately, nearby soldiers had heard, and the next thing Fiero knew, the night was ablaze with gunfire. He had done what he could to keep the troopers away from the base of the footpath so that his companions could reach the bottom in safety, but the odds had been hopeless. He had been forced to give ground to save his own life and had hidden close at hand, watching the whites, until the little chief nearly stepped on him.

Blood Treachery

Pausing, Fiero looked back to gauge how far he was from the enemy line. The soldiers had formed a partial ring around the great stone spire, with most of them concentrated near the footpath. Others had taken possession of the horses left secreted in the trees and added them to the string of cavalry mounts, which were under guard.

Fiero saw that he was several hundred yards from where the horses were tethered. He also saw that which brought a savage smile to his lips. Several Army scouts were advancing swiftly in his direction. One had his face to the ground, reading sign. Whoever he was, the man was very good. He was right on Fiero's trail.

High on the spire, Clay Taggart paced like a caged animal, racking his brain for a way out of the fix the band was in. He moved a step nearer to the rim to peek down at the troopers and had to jump back when a slug bit off slivers of stone from the edge.

It had been that way since shortly before dawn. Evidently the soldiers wanted to keep anyone from firing down at them, so whenever one of the troopers saw so much as a flickering shadow, he fired. So far the shots had struck the mouth of the cave and whined harmlessly off.

Clay gnawed his lower lip and pondered. Marista and the boy were by the spring, fixing breakfast. There had been a parfleche of venison jerky among the effects belonging to the smugglers, as well as coffee and flour.

Delgadito lay close to the small crackling fire. His side had been bandaged with torn strips from his own shirt and he was resting comfortably enough. The bullet had gouged a deep furrow in his side, chipping part of a rib bone, cracking another, and exiting low on his back, making a hole the size of a human fist. His organs had been spared but he had lost a terrible amount of blood.

Cuchillo Negro and Ponce squatted just back from the rim, rifles across their thighs. Neither had spoken or even moved in quite a while.

Clay slapped his leg in irritation and said in the Chiricahua tongue, "There has to be way to beat the white-eyes. We cannot let them keep us penned in here. Our food will only last a few days."

"We have water," Ponce said.

"Which helps, but will not keep us alive for long after the food is gone," Clay stressed. Staring at the rear of the cave, he said, "Are all of you certain there is no other way down from here? Have you looked to see if there is a passage?"

Delgadito had been listening attentively. "We were told there is none so we have never searched." Rising onto an elbow, he gazed across the spring. "I will check."

"You rest, pard," Clay reverted to English. "I'll take a look-see."

The cave narrowed at the rear, forming a dark pocket partially blocked by the spring. Keeping his feet close to the wall, Clay moved around the pool. The ceiling became so low that he had to stoop. Despite the obvious—that there was no passageway—he groped every square inch of the rough wall. At length he sighed and returned to the main chamber. "There is only the footpath," he announced in Chiricahua, then, for Marista's benefit, added, "It looks as if those soldier boys have us over a barrel. Unless we can sprout wings and fly, our goose is cooked."

Blood Treachery

"Goose?" she repeated.

"We don't stand a snowball's chance in hell," Clay amended while stepping close to the entrance. He refused to accept that they were beaten. If there was one lesson his pa had impressed on him again and again and again, it was that the Taggert clan weren't a bunch of quitters.

Clay had lost track of the number of times he had figured to cash in his chips, only to have his fat pulled out of the fire at the last minute. Grit and clever wits had saved him before; maybe they could do so again.

Rising on tiptoe, Clay scanned the path. Dozens of rifles glistened in the sunlight at the bottom of the spire. Venturing out there invited swift execution. Yet there was no other way down. They were trapped! How long before he was willing to admit the truth to himself? he wondered.

Exasperated, Clay rubbed his chin and idly raised his head to look up at the sky. The ceiling of the cave, which was no more than ten feet above him, limited his view. Like a bolt out of the blue, an idea struck him, and he nearly made the fatal mistake of stepping to the very edge to study the spire above.

Cuchillo Negro had been watching intently. "You have an idea, White Apache?"

"Yes," Clay said. "Has anyone ever tried to climb around to the other side of Eagle's Roost?"

"No one who wanted to live," Cuchillo Negro said with a straight face.

"I am serious," Clay insisted. "We can wait for the sun to set, then work our way around and down. The white-eyes are all on this side of the spire. We can slip right out from under their noses."

"The stone is too smooth," Ponce interjected. "Not even mountain sheep could do it."

Clay moved to the right-hand corner and craned his neck for a glimpse of the outer surface. Thin cracks laced the stone, but he couldn't tell if they were wide enough to allow a person to gain purchase or strong enough to hold the weight of a full-grown man.

The crack of a shot from down in the canyon fell on Clay's ears at the selfsame instant a bullet buzzed past his ear and bit into the cave wall. The whine of the ricochet was like a piercing whistle. A fraction of a second later, Colletto yipped in pain.

Clay crouched, realizing that he had nearly had his fool head blown off. He scooted over to the Pimas, where Marista was examining a crease on the boy's shoulder. The spent slug had torn the skin but done no real damage.

Cuchillo Negro came over, his countenance sober. "I agree with you, Lickoyee-shis-inday, that we must act before the white-eyes think to use the cave to their advantage."

Clay was about to ask what the warrior meant when the answer hit him. All the soldiers had to do was fire sustained volleys into the cave until eventually the ricochets wiped out every last one of them.

"As for climbing down the other side," Cuchillo Negro went on, "for the boy it would be impossible. I think it would sap the strength of the woman, and she would fall long before she reached the bottom. Delgadito, in his condition, would not get halfway."

The warrior had given an accurate assessment of factors that Clay in his enthusiasm had failed to take into account. But he wasn't ready to abandon the plan. "One of us has to try. Since the idea was mine, I will be the one. *Shee-dah.*"

Marista faced him, her eyes pools of worry.

Deliberately not meeting her gaze, Clay said, "If I make it down, I'll find a way to lure most of the boys in blue off. When the times comes, you will know it. Be ready."

"You risk all," Cuchillo Negro said.

"I led us here."

Aware of the woman's eyes boring into him, Clay stepped to the pool and splashed water on his face and neck. He saw no reason to mention that he had long been skittish of heights, and as a sprout he had never dared climb high into trees for fear of falling. It had taken every ounce of self-control he had to climb the path to the cave. For the life of him he didn't see how he was going to climb down the spire, but he had to do it. There was no shirking his responsibility.

Soon breakfast was ready. The food took Clay's mind off the frightful feat he had set for himself. As he downed his third cup of piping hot black coffee, he was taken aback to hear his name being shouted outside.

Setting down the battered tin cup, Clay hurried over. So did the others. Leery of a ruse to draw him into the open, he halted a few feet from where the rock path merged into the cave.

"Clay Taggart!" the hail was repeated. "This is Capt. Gerald Forester, Fifth Cavalry Flying Detachment speaking. If you're up there, give a holler."

Cupping a hand to his mouth, Clay replied, "I'm here! What do you want?"

"Step out where I can see you."

Clay laughed long and loud. "What do you take me for, Captain? A damned greenhorn?"

"I give you my personal word of honor that none of my troopers will fire," the officer bellowed. Then, lowering his voice just a little, "Did you hear that, men? Anyone who fires faces a court martial when we get back to the post."

Intrigued, Clay inched forward until he could see a lone figure standing on the footpath. The officer spotted him and held out his hands to show they were empty.

"What do you want, Captain?"

"To save us both a lot of aggravation. You can't come down, we can't come up. But we can wait you out. So why not make it easy on yourself and surrender? I promise to see you safely to Fort Bowie to stand trial. Beyond that, it's out of my hands."

"Why all this concern for my welfare?" Clay asked.

"To be honest, mister, I'd rather string you up from the handiest tree. Or let my men use you for a pincushion. You're scum, a traitor to your own kind, and you deserve to be exterminated."

Forester pushed his hat back. "But I can't let my personal feelings dictate my actions. I'm a soldier. And I don't care to have my men and animals roast under this broiling sun any longer than they have to. So what do you say? Give it up. You're butchering days are over, one way or the other. You might as well make it easy on yourself and the bucks with you."

Clay had to smile at the officer's audacity. "I'm not about to surrender, not until I've settled accounts with Miles Gillett."

"The rancher? What the hell does he have to do with any of this?"

"Everything. He framed me. Made me an outlaw."

"It won't wash, Taggart. He sure as hell didn't make you join a band of renegade Apache."

Clay knew that to try and explain would be wasted effort. "Have it your way, Captain. I'm not giving up." A thought pricked him. "But I would like to let the woman and boy come down, if you'll pledge to release them. They had no part in any of the killings."

The officer stiffened. "There's a woman and child up there? Damn. I didn't know. Who are they?"

"A Pima and her son. What do you say?"

"Unlike some I could mention, I don't make war on females or kids. Send them down."

Nodding, Clay turned. Forester struck him as being honorable enough, as a man who could be trusted, within limits. Marista and Colletto would be safe. But he saw right away by the set of her jaw that she wasn't about to go. "It's for your own good," he urged.

"No."

"Think of your son. He has his whole life ahead of him. Why have him die when there is no need?"

"Son not want go. I not leave you. He not leave me." A hint of fear crept into her tone. "You want me go? Like Culozul?"

Although he knew he should tell her that he did, Clay couldn't bring himself to mouth the words. She had been betrayed once; he'd be damned if he was going to make her suffer the same agony again. "I do not," he said softly.

Heartfelt gratitude radiated from her features. Marista placed a hand on his wrist and said tenderly, "Thank you. I tell you before. You be good man."

Troubled and pleased at the same time, Clay

swiveled and regarded the waiting officer a few moments. "I wish they would come but they won't. They aim to see this through to the end."

Forester's shoulders slumped. "I'm sorry to hear that, Taggart. I truly am. Ask them one more time. Beg them if you have to."

"It wouldn't do any good."

The officer nodded. "So be it. But you have to understand my position. We have enough water to last us three days at the most, not taking into account the time it will take us to reach the nearest stream once we leave. I don't have any choice."

"What are you getting at?"

"Just this," Captain Forester said. Whirling, he shouted for all the troopers to hear, "Open fire!"

Chapter Twelve

For all of two seconds the White Apache stood riveted in shock at the officer's abrupt turn-around. Then, as dozens of carbines cracked in booming cadence and slugs filled the cave mouth or chipped at the ceiling and floor, he threw himself to the rear. A shot stung his arm, another his calf, but neither did more than draw trickles of blood.

The Chiricahuas and the Pimas also fell back, bending low to keep from being hit by the scores of rounds that ricocheted throughout the cave. Lead flew back and forth, up and down, at all angles.

Ponce suddenly held out a bleeding hand and shook it.

Cuchillo Negro hit the floor and rolled toward the spring.

Delgadito was moving as fast as he could, a

hand wedged against the bandage to staunch the renewed flow of blood.

"All the way to the rear!" Clay directed, first in English, then in the Chiricahua tongue. The band obeyed, the warriors allowing the woman and her boy to precede them.

Miniature geysers burst from the pool as bullet after bullet pockmarked its surface. Some of the water splashed onto White Apache's feet, nearly causing him to slip on the slick floor.

Then they reached the sanctuary of the pocket and huddled together, shoulder to shoulder, White Apache and the warriors on the outside, protecting the Pimas with their own bodies.

The firing went on and on. Hundreds, perhaps thousands of rounds were expended. Bits of stone rained from the ceiling and the walls. Small clouds of dust formed, hugging the floor like fog.

White Apache grew enraged at the officer's callous disregard for the welfare of Marista and Colletto. He couldn't help questioning whether Forester would have given the order to fire if the pair had been white and not Pimas. Maybe the captain was one of those who believed all Indians should be exterminated like lice, regardless of whether they were women, men, or children.

White Apache made a vow. If he lived, he would make it a point to track down Capt. Gerald Forester and repay the man for the cold-blooded deed done this day.

After what seemed like half an hour, the firing ceased. Clay motioned for the others to stay put and dashed to the rim. The soldiers were taking a breather, perhaps to let their guns cool, since overheated carbines had a tendency to jam. Or maybe they were conserving ammunition. He saw

Forester surveying the cave through field glasses and couldn't resist popping up just to let the man know they were still alive.

"Fire at will! Now! Quickly!"

The troopers had to scramble to load and shoot, giving White Apache more time than he needed to reach the pocket. The shooting went on twice as long. Cuchillo Negro was the only one hit, suffering a flesh wound.

At last quiet reined. White Apache moved to the front of the spring and drank. Crawling to the entrance, he spied on the Flying Detachment without revealing himself.

Down below, Capt. Forester was in a quandary. He was confident that the steady firing had killed or maimed most of the renegades since it was unthinkable that any living creature could have survived, but he couldn't bring himself to send any men up the footpath, not yet, if there was a chance that even one of the renegades lived. A single warrior could pick off anyone who tried to reach the cave.

Forester had to content himself with waiting. He moved among the troopers, complimenting them on a job well done. It was important to keep their morale high, to remind them that they were dealing with the worst cutthroats in Arizona Territory. Much to his relief, no one asked him about the woman and child. It tore him up inside knowing that he had weighed their lives in the balance and decided that eliminating the renegades took priority.

Unknown to the officer, a quarter of a mile away Fiero had heard the shooting and stopped in his tracks. He had outdistanced the scouts, who were poking about in a large cluster of boulders where he had left a few clear footprints pointing in the wrong direction to tantalize them. Sooner or later they would figure out the ruse. In the meantime, he would check on the others. On all fours he slipped into dense brush, then rose and sped toward the rear of the stone spire.

Up in the cave, White Apache rested his chin on his forearms and waited for Forester's next move. Cuchillo Negro joined him without speaking. For over two hours they lay in the sun, and just when White Apache thought that the worst was over, the captain ordered his men to resume firing.

Twice more that day the same tactic was repeated. After each onslaught White Apache crept to the entrance to watch. Finally his patience was rewarded.

It was half an hour before sunset when Capt. Forester decided the time had come. There had been no sign of life in the cave. None of the volleys had been answered. Acting on the assumption the renegades were riddled with bullets, he turned to Sgt. McKinn and ordered, "Send four men up. Have the rest ready to give covering fire, just in case."

White Apache quivered when the quartet began to climb the path. He looked at Cuchillo Negro and said, "Wait until they are too high to jump."

It was like shooting clay pigeons. The four soldiers had no chance at all. Two of them dropped, shot through the head, and the other two whirled to flee. They were each drilled between the shoulder blades. Too late, the Detachment opened fire.

Capt. Forester was furious, but there was nothing he could do. He had run out of ideas and daylight, and if he wasn't careful he would run out of ammo before too long.

For White Apache, sundown was the moment

he had waited for. He wiped the sweat from his limbs with a piece of cloth, swallowed a cup of water, and went to the corner of the cave without speaking. No words were needed. They all knew what was at stake, what he had to do, or else.

White Apache had made a sling for his Winchester out of strips of rawhide. He slung the rifle now, eased to the edge, and reached out, seeking a handhold. There was one, a horizontal fissure with sharp edges. Taking a firm grip, he gingerly extended his foot and located a spiny knob.

Don't look down! White Apache's mind shrieked as he took a deep breath and stepped out into space, clinging to the side of the spire like an oversized lizard. He pressed his body flush and felt goosebumps cover his skin. He had to close his eyes a few moments before he could muster the courage to go on.

Locking his left hand on the fissure, White Apache extended his right as far as it would go and felt for another handhold. He found none, and feared the band was doomed. As he brought the hand toward him, he brushed a crack barely wide enough for his fingertips. It was all he had to work with so he inserted his fingers and slid farther from the opening.

And so it went. Slow inch by slow inch, every muscle as rigid as piano wire, every nerve frayed to the breaking point, never knowing if the next breath might be his last, White Apache worked his way around the spire.

The darkness helped some; it hid the bottom. White Apache could glance down without having to worry about becoming dizzy. Once on the far side there was the temptation to go faster, which he resisted. Nor would he move a hand or foot unless the other hand and foot had firm support. Several times handholds and thin ledges crumpled to dust when he applied pressure, but he was braced and didn't lose his balance.

To the east a quarter moon arced into the heavens. It had climbed to the apex of its circuit when, much to White Apache's amazement, he lowered his left leg for what must have been the two hundredth time and his sole made contact with what felt like terra firma.

Elated, White Apache shifted the moccasin to the right and the left to verify he had found footing on the ground and not merely a wide ledge. Daring to lift his cheek from the spire, he saw a few bushes nearby.

As if the drain in a wash basin had been pulled, all the strength ebbed from White Apache and he sank to the ground, exhausted, his body slick with perspiration. Lowering his forehead to the dirt, he made no attempt to go on. There was no rush. He could spare a few minutes to recover from the nightmare.

Presently White Apache girded himself and stood. The air felt deliciously cool and he took several invigorating breaths. Then, unslinging the Winchester, he turned to the south and moved around the bottom of the spire.

White Apache was a credit to the warriors who had taught him. He made as little noise as would Delgadito or Fiero or any true Chiricahua. Stopping often to look and listen to insure he wouldn't blunder onto concealed troopers, he covered scores of yards and was approaching the southwest side of Eagle's Roost when a low cough glued him in place.

Patience was an Apache virtue honed to a degree few whites could match. White Apache had learned its value and worked hard to imitate the example of his red brothers. He practiced it now, remaining in a crouch for minutes on end, heedless of a cramp in his thigh that grew worse as time went by. Only when the cough was repeated and he pinpointed the position of the soldier did he flatten and move off in another direction.

It soon became apparent he had stumbled on the last man in a long line of troopers partially ringing the spire. White Apache swung wide, moving on his toes and fingers, resembling nothing so much as a gigantic gila monster as he scuttled from cover to cover.

After a while, convinced he had gone far enough, White Apache rose to his knees and debated the best course of action to take. He had promised Marista and the rest that he would draw the troopers away from the footpath. But how should he go about it?

Then a nicker wafted on the breeze, and White Apache smiled. The cavalrymen were many miles from the nearest post. The last thing they would want would be for their mounts to run off. It would mean a long forced march with no food and little water. They would keep that from happening at all costs.

White Apache stalked toward the horses. Soon he heard the sounds typical of a large group of horses, and low voices. Lowering his belly to the ground, he wriggled toward a cluster of brush. The next moment one of the bushes uncoiled, flattened, and came toward him.

White Apache had the Winchester in front of him. All he had to do was point and fire. He started to, when a whisper no louder than the murmuring breeze revealed it wasn't an enemy.

"Lickoyee-shis-inday! I thought you were still in the cave."

"Fiero!" White Apache whispered, and clasped the warrior's wrist. "We feared you were dead."

Fiero was moved by the show of affection but he did not betray his feelings. It was unseemly for a warrior to display emotion so openly. White Apache did so often, which Fiero blamed on the man's flawed upbringing. The whites did not know how to do anything right. "Are the others with you?"

In a few words, White Apache explained.

Incredulous, Fiero craned his head and stared up at the stone spire, which seemed to touch the stars themselves. It astounded him that anyone would attempt to climb down from so lofty a height. He knew that he would never have attempted it, and his estimation of Lickoyee-shis-inday rose a notch.

"I have a plan," White Apache added. He shared his thoughts on the horses.

"We think alike," Fiero said. "That is why I am here."

"We will work together."

Side by side, the pair advanced. Once in the brush, they crept another twenty-five yards, to the lip of a shallow hollow, where they saw the string tethered under the watchful eyes of three soldiers, two of whom were talking beside some mesquite while the third made a circuit of the restless animals.

Using hand signs, White Apache conveyed his intent. Fiero slipped off without a word.

After waiting a few moments, White Apache angled toward the pair of unsuspecting troopers. He smelled the acrid odor of smoke. An orange dot flared in the night, revealing why; one of the soldiers was enjoying a cigarette.

Enough mesquite lined the hollow to permit White Apache to creep within ten feet of his quarry. Lying the Winchester at his side, he drew his Bowie knife.

The taller trooper was speaking quietly. "—told me the captain wasn't very upset about Parmalee. Which ain't surprising. The two of them never did get along very well."

"Forester was sure as hell upset at the scouts, though," said the other man. "He couldn't see how they lost the trail."

"If you ask me, the savages are all in cahoots, the renegades and the tame bucks alike," declared the tall one. "The only way to stop this bloodshed is to wipe every last Injun off the face of the earth."

White Apache noted that the short man had placed the stock of his carbine on the ground, that the tall man had his in the crook of an arm. Both wore revolvers but the flaps to their holster were closed. No matter what, he had to keep them from squeezing off a shot.

Like a mountain lion waiting for the moment when its prey would be most vulnerable, White Apache bided his time.

"I just hope we finish off the stinking renegades soon, Garth," the short man said.

"Me too, Brett. I never thought I'd say this, but I'm actually looking forward to being at Fort Bowie."

Brett pivoted and surveyed the hollow. "Say, where the hell did Winslow get to? He was over there a second ago."

Garth shifted to look, which put the backs of both men to White Apache. Instantly he rose and sprang, taking three lightning bounds. He speared the Bowie into Garth's ribs, felt the edge scrape bone, and heard the gasp Garth uttered as the point pierced his heart.

Wrenching the blade out, White Apache spun to dispatch the short one, but Brett was too quick for him and sidestepped the thrust. The trooper tried to bring his carbine to bear but his foot caught on a plant, and he fell. White Apache pounced as Brett frantically scrambled upright.

The soldier opened his mouth to shout for help. Automatically White Apache slammed a knee into Brett's groin so that the only sound that came out was a strangled whine. Flicking his arm, White Apache cut the man's shoulder, and Brett, desperately darting aside, lost his grip on the carbine.

White Apache could not give the man a moment's respite. He attacked, swinging waist height to keep Brett from unlimbering the Colt. The soldier dodged, twisted, feinted right and went left. White Apache missed him by a hair. Again Brett threw back his head to shout. This time White Apache snapped his right arm to his shoulder and let the Bowie fly.

The blade flashed like a meteor, impaling itself to the hilt in the man's jugular. Brett, shocked, halted and grabbed the hilt. Gurgling and spitting, he tore the knife free. A torrent of blood spewed in its wake.

White Apache raised a fist to batter the man senseless, but no further blows were needed. The trooper sagged, blubbering softly, his eyelids fluttering. White Apache snatched the Bowie and stood aside while the man sank onto his side and died within seconds in a spreading crimson pool.

White Apache wiped the Bowie clean on

Garth's shirt, retrieved the Winchester, and turned to the horses. From out of the darkness whisked Fiero, the new loop-style cartridge belt adorning his muscular midsection ample evidence that the other guard had been disposed of.

"Now we drive the horses off!"

"No."

"No?"

"Now we stampede them straight past Eagle's Roost," White Apache said, and Fiero grinned, understanding. Moving slowly forward so as not to spook the animals, they each picked a horse and cut it loose from the string.

White Apache freed the rest of the animals while Fiero sat ready to chase any inclined to run off. None did, although many were agitated by the scent of blood. White Apache rode to the west side of the hollow, directly across from Fiero and near the rear of the herd.

Suddenly White Apache spied a pair of figures approaching on the run from the direction of the spire. Waving his rifle to signal Fiero, he rose up off his bay, yipped shrilly, and banged three swift shots into the air. Fiero followed his lead. The result was exactly what they wanted.

The herd broke into motion. With one accord the dozens of horses fled on out of the hollow, pounding up and over the side, making for Eagle's Roost in a milling mass of drumming hoofs and flying manes and tails. Panicked whinnies rent the air.

White Apache jabbed his heels into the bay and stayed abreast of the herd. He saw the approaching figures dash eastward to get out of the way of the horses, heard rough shouts that were answered from the vicinity of the spire. Fiero's rifle boomed and one of the figures dropped. The other dived behind a bush and brought a six-shooter into play.

Whooping and hollering, White Apache spurred the herd to greater speed. As he had hoped, the animals were spreading out. They were also raising tremendous amounts of dust that choked the air. In no time he could hardly see more than fifteen feet with any clarity.

Gunfire blasted, courtesy of troopers firing wildly, the shots for the most part going high.

Through a break in the dust, White Apache spotted nine or ten soldiers running to meet the herd. The men were yelling and waving and jumping up and down, trying to stop the animals. He shouted louder and emptied the Winchester to keep the horses stampeding, and they did.

The dust grew thicker. A trooper materialized directly ahead, turning every which way as if uncertain which route offered safety. He spied White Apache and clawed at the pistol on his hip.

Without slowing, White Apache galloped past, swinging the rifle like a club. The impact lifted the man off his feet and left him sprawled senseless.

A gruff voice rose above the riot of noise.

"After them! Don't let the horses get away!"

Off to the right several soldiers were sprinting in pursuit of the herd. White Apache reined up so they wouldn't spot him and sought to get his bearings. By his reckoning he was west of the spire by no more than thirty or forty yards. Drawing his Colt, White Apache trotted toward it.

The bay unaccountably shied. White Apache looked down to find the battered body of a scout lying face down. The Indian had been trampled to death. He went a little farther and saw another trooper limping to the north.

A flurry of shots reminded White Apache that not all the troopers had gone after the herd. Moments later he came on three dead cavalrymen close to the base of the footpath. Closer still was Fiero, probing the dust cloud for more enemies.

White Apache drew rein at the very end of the path, then wheeled the bay. He was not going to budge until the rest of the band showed up, even if the entire Detachment returned.

Fiero, as usual, was aglow with the lust of battle. "Ho! It is a fine night to die!" he cried.

But no cavalrymen appeared. Gradually the dust began to settle. To the north there were curses and shouts that indicated the troopers were rounding up the horses.

White Apache anxiously watched the footpath, telling himself that it shouldn't be long, that the Pimas and the Chiricahuas would show up at any second. But another minute went by, then two, and they failed to appear. He gripped the bay's mane, about to slide off and go see what was taking them.

"Here they come!" Fiero declared.

Delgadito was in the lead, moving slowly because of his wound. Marista and the boy were next. Cuchillo Negro carried her water skin, while Ponce brought a leather pouch bulging with ammunition.

White Apache vaulted from the bay and gave it a resounding smack on the rump, sending it fleeing on the heels of the herd. Taking Marista's hand, he hastened to the southeast.

From out of the tendrils of dust a grimy trooper appeared and made the mistake of using his mouth instead of his carbine. "Hey! Over here!

The damn Apaches are getting away!" Cuchillo Negro shot the man dead.

The band raced nimbly across the canyon, Delgadito keeping up despite the shape he was in. From the shelter of high boulders they looked back and saw five or six forms moving about near the footpath.

"It will take them a while to organize," White Apache remarked. He jogged onward, knowing that several miles beyond lay country so rough that horses would be a hindrance rather than a help.

A cleft in the canyon wall brought them to a tableland, which they traversed at a pace that soon had Colletto tottering with fatigue. White Apache scooped the boy into his arms and ran on.

Within three hours they entered a maze of ravines and dry washes. White Apache halted under a rock overhang and set Colletto down. "We are safe now," he announced. "By the time the whites pick up our trail, we will be far away."

Delgadito sat down, examined his side, and grimaced. "We should never have gone to Eagle's Roost. We made the *Gans* mad."

"I will never doubt your beliefs again," White Apache said, and meant it.

Ponce voiced the question most of them had in mind. "What now, lickoyee-shis-inday? What do we do next?"

The White Apache glanced at Marista and her son, then at the warriors, and said in English to himself, "I wish to hell I knew." Changing to the Chiricahua tongue, he declared, "We will work that out later. But I can make all of you one promise."

"Which is?" Cuchillo Negro asked.

"As Fiero is so fond of saying, every day will be a good day to die."

DOUBLE EDITION
They left him for dead, he'll see them in hell!
Jake McMasters

Hangman's Knot. Taggart is strung up and left out to die by a posse headed by the richest man in the territory. Choking and kicking, he is seconds away from death when he is cut down by a ragtag band of Apaches, not much better off than himself. Before long, the white desperado and the desperate Apaches have formed an unholy alliance that will turn the Arizona desert red with blood.

And in the same action-packed volume....

Warpath. Twelve S.O.B.s left him swinging from a rope, as good as dead. But it isn't Taggart's time to die. Together with his desperate renegade warriors he will hunt the yellowbellies down. One by one, he'll make them wish they'd never drawn a breath. One by one he'll leave their guts and bones scorching under the brutal desert sun.

_4185-5 $4.99 US/$5.99 CAN

Dorchester Publishing Co., Inc.
65 Commerce Road
Stamford, CT 06902